The Mermaid and the Drunks

BEN RICHARDS

PHOENIX

A PHOENIX PAPERBACK

First published in Great Britain in 2003
by Weidenfeld & Nicolson
This paperback edition published in 2004
by Phoenix,
an imprint of Orion Books Ltd,
Orion House, 5 Upper St Martin's Lane,
London WC2H 9EA

Second impression 2004

A CIP catalogue record for this book
is available from the British Library.

ISBN 0 75381 775 6

Printed and bound in Great Britain by
Clays Ltd, St Ives plc

Alas, the more beautiful a country,
The greater the pain when enemies of beauty
Take possession of it.

Yevgeny Yevtushenko,
'A Dove in Santiago'

Acknowledgements

Sergio and Veronica Contreras, Alfredo Rodriguez, Gabriela Araya, Ruben Contreras, Carolina Escalona and her family, the Adriazola family, the players of Arsenal La Pintana, Michele Hutchison, Pete Ayrton.

I would particularly like to thank Rose Deakin, 'Pepe Tren' and Tilly for their generous hospitality in the Cajon del Maipo.

Extra-special thanks are also due to my agent Lesley Shaw.

The story of the disappearance of Pablo Errazuriz was partly suggested by a real case in Chile – the unresolved vanishing of Jorge Matute Johns from a Concepcion disco in 1999, which caused great national disquiet. The story and characters in my fictional case, however, bear no resemblance whatsoever to those of the Matute Johns case or to the investigation into his disappearance.

Also still unresolved are the whereabouts of most of the small group who fought with Salvador Allende in the battle for La Moneda on September 11th 1973. This book was often inspired by them and I hope it will serve in some small way to keep their memory alive. The details of the unequal battle and the subsequent inhumanity of the victors towards defenceless prisoners are largely drawn from the testimony of Dr Oscar Soto in his book *El Ultimo Dia de Salvador Allende*. Much of the information on Bernardo O'Higgins and the struggle for Chilean independence was taken from Robert Harvey's book *Liberators*. The book which Joe reads in Concepcion about the pre-war Balkans is *The Bridge over the Drina* by Ivo Andric. The book that Roberto is reading which prompts him to mention the 'competing cicadas' is *The Wind-Up Bird Chronicle* by Haruki Murakami.

This book is dedicated to Rossana.

Introduction

Was it the sound a bird made (Chi-le, Chi-le) or the name of a legendary gold-abundant valley, a name which the Spanish extended to the entire province, from the desert to the glaciers?

An archipelago of tribes lived in the thin strip of land between the mountains and the sea, long before the Niña, the Pinta and the Santa María set sail from Andalusia, before the great navigator Columbus mistook a cluster of islands for Japan, before Cortés and his small band of men rubbed their eyes at Montezuma's watery kingdom and wondered if it were all a dream.

In the north there were Changos and Diaguitas, while Picunches inhabited the fertile central valley between the Maípo and the Maule rivers. From the Itata to the Bío-Bío and beyond to the River Toltén lived the indomitable Mapuches. The strange rain-swept island of Chiloé was home to the Cuncos and on the scattered shrapnel of islands further south were the Chonos. There were Tehuelches and Alacalufes and Yaganes. And on the curling tip of the continent, at the very end of the world, were the Onas, a tribe who would, centuries later, be hunted down and exterminated – a price put on their head as if they were seal pelts.

Magellan came by sea until he found the straits that spat him from turbulent Atlantic into Pacific blue. Diego de Almagro crossed the mountains from the north in search of gold. Pedro de Valdivia travelled from the desert to the lakes and forests of the south where he discovered Mapuche warriors just as the wave discovers the harbour wall. Other dreams would replace the disappointed gold and silver cravings of the conquistadores – dreams of flags and printing presses; of nitrates and copper; of exile and return.

Above the ocean, a sea bird dips into the spray, a narwhal raises its tusk from the foam, every type of shellfish clings to the rocky shore. Just a stretch or shudder of the earth can make the sea suck in its breath and return as a Tsunami roaring towards land. People have seen their relatives wave goodbye from the tops of their houses as they are swept away and carried off by the returning sea. Safe from such calamity, higher and further to the

1

east, a great mountain bird hangs above snow and rock, clinging to the updraughts with barely a tilt of its heavy wings. Higher and further still – although it is bright and clear – the atmospheric plates collide, invisible waves swirl and clash, the sky begins to tremble.

PART ONE

Fasten Your Seatbelts

Turbulence! God how she hated it.

Five hundred miles from the coast of northern Brazil, 40,000 feet up in an Air France Boeing 777, Fresia Castillo had been shaken violently from her dream. It was a dream in which her father had told her that she should not be returning to Chile, that she should stay in Britain. This puzzled her because he would have been pleased by her journey. So why did he say it in the dream?

She gripped the sides of her seat, staring down the fuselage of a plane which was now jolting and shuddering, buffeted by the uncontrollable, malevolent air currents outside.

Please stop, she begged, her lips mouthing the words. *Please, please, I can't stand this.*

The *Fasten-your-seatbelt* sign flicked on overhead. It was much more than ordinary turbulence. A luggage locker flew open and a carton of Kent cigarettes spilled from a duty-free bag and skidded down the gangway. Somebody cried out. Towards the back of the plane a child began to wail. A flight attendant hurrying towards a seat slipped and supported herself on the head of one of the passengers. Fresia could not understand how the plane could survive this assault; it must surely break up, they would fragment, disintegrate, it was too much for the imagination to contemplate. All the petty paraphernalia of their voyage sucked into that freezing black void. And Fresia Castillo – twenty-nine years old, a lapis-lazuli dove on her throat, hair-scrunch on her wrist, bottle of Evian clasped tightly in her hand – Fresia Tamara Castillo Morganstein cartwheeling through the thin air into the Atlantic where she would be pounded into insignificance by the waves.

Somebody cried out as the plane plunged violently. Fresia bit her lip and murmured to herself. Suddenly she became aware that the person sitting next to her had taken hold of her free hand and was saying,

'Don't worry, it will all be OK. Planes don't crash because of turbulence.'

The voice belonged to a man in his early thirties. He had a Scottish accent. She had seen him on the short flight from London to Paris and then again when she was killing time in the duty-free shop at Charles de Gaulle Airport. How could she have guessed as they wandered aimlessly among cheeses and chocolates and tins of *foie gras* that they were both waiting for the same flight to Santiago de Chile? He had cropped hair, dark brown eyes with a mischievous glint in them, a small scar above his eyebrow. His trainers were slid under the seat in front of him. During the flight he had enjoyed his meal, demanding two little bottles of wine at a time, flirting with the flight attendants.

The plane shuddered violently again.

'The only way people die from turbulence is if they're not strapped in and they bounce up and hit their head on the ceiling. But you're safely strapped in. It's not very nice but we'll be through it soon . . . ahhh!'

Somebody at the back began to howl unashamedly. The man gulped several times. Fresia squeezed his hand sympathetically. They were quiet.

'You do speak English?' The jolting appeared to subside a little and he made another stoic attempt at distracting conversation. She nodded.

'But you're Argentinian? Chilean?'

'I was brought up in England. My family are Chilean.'

'Where from?'

'Where from in Chile or where from in England?'

'Both.'

'I was born in Concepción . . . oh shit this is horrible . . . I spent my childhood in Oxford. But I've lived in London for years.'

'I knew Chileans in Scotland,' he said. 'It's an explosive cultural combination.'

'As explosive as Chilean Scousers?' she asked.

He laughed. 'Nail down your handbags!'

The plane lurched again. He closed his eyes for a second and then grinned at her as if to say, Let's keep trying.

'What's your name?'

'Fresia.'

'Fresia,' he repeated with a pleased look on his face. 'Ah, now there's a name with some history!'

'My father . . .' she began but could not finish, swerved away from it. 'You know about Chilean history,' she half stated, half asked.

'Well, that's my job.'

'What's your job?'

'I'm a lecturer in a politics department. I teach the Latin American course but Chile is my speciality.'

'You don't look like a lecturer,' she said.

'Don't I? What does a lecturer look like? My pipe and cardigan are in the suitcase.'

Her father seated at his desk, his favourite cardigan with leather patches on the elbows hanging on the back of the chair, turning to smile at her as she brought a cup of tea into his study, the branches of the tree dark against the window, rain on the surface of the river outside.

'How long are you staying in Chile?' she asked.

'Six months or so,' he said and grinned suddenly as if this were a very pleasing thought. 'I'm on a year's sabbatical to write my book.'

'What's your book about?'

'Violence.'

Fresia raised her eyebrows.

'Political violence,' the man clarified.

'You'll have plenty of material then.'

The turbulence subsided and they did not speak much again. The man took a CD from his bag and put it on his Discman. Fresia glanced at the box before closing her eyes – *Maybe It's Right to Be Nervous Now* by Magazine. She tried not to remember somebody else who had liked that band, shut her eyes and fell asleep. She dreamed that she was sitting between her mother and father and the plane was falling out of the sky. They were holding a hand each and telling her how much they loved her. When she awoke later, there were tears on her cheek.

'You're lucky to be able to sleep,' said her neighbour. 'I can never sleep on planes.'

Fresia stretched and yawned and smiled at him as she tied her hair back. 'I can sleep anywhere,' she said.

'Lucky you. They're bringing breakfast. We'll be in Buenos Aires in an hour.'

He gestured at the little plane on the video screen, its red line trailing across the Atlantic Ocean, inching across the leg of South America towards the Argentine capital. Fresia wrinkled her nose at the smell of microwaved omelette.

When they disembarked in Buenos Aires, Fresia wandered around the transit lounge and then the duty-free area, looking in

7

shop windows at blue-and-white-striped football shirts, silver mate *bombillas*, little tango-dancing figurines. Elegant Argentine women in tight pink skirts and high heels stood like flamingos at the shop entrance, waiting to spray people with perfume. Fresia longed for a shower and proper sleep, the soft caress of clean clothes. She returned to the lounge and saw the young lecturer who had held her hand during the turbulence. He was smoking a cigarette and looking at his feet. She did not feel like conversation and could not stand the idea of cigarette smoke so she went to sit on the other side of the transit lounge.

The plane crossed the flat, seemingly endless Argentine *pampas* on the last stage of their long journey. Fresia listened to an old Café del Mar CD. She strained for her first glimpse of the mountains which divided the long strip of her birthplace from the rest of the continent.

She had made this journey before.

Her mother had gone into labour on a night in early spring, during the month that Chileans fly kites and celebrate their independence by drinking red wine, eating *empanadas* and twirling handkerchiefs to the national dance of the *cueca*. In that particular year of 1973, however, the insurrection of the wealthy against Salvador Allende's socialist government reached its peak and the kites of September were accompanied by a military coup. Fresia was born shortly after the firemen had doused the smoking rubble of the presidential palace and the new rulers had announced that her father – along with hundreds of others – should report to the nearest police station. There was a recording of the list being read out – it still struck terror into her heart. But by that time, her father was in the boot of a car being smuggled out of the country. Her mother left later, crossing the Andes by bus with her tiny son and newborn baby.

I was waiting in Mendoza. Your mother held you up to the window of the bus. That was the first time I saw you.

Five years ago she had returned for the first time but the visit had not been a success. Her aunts and uncles on the Morganstein side had raised their eyebrows in polite condescension when she had said that she was working as a photographer. They had sniggered at any mistakes she made in Spanish and made semi-veiled references to the fact that poor Rebecca had ruined her life by marrying a Marxist – even such a clever one. They were determined to let Fresia know that this was not the same unruly country that her parents had left; it was modern, efficient, no longer really part of Latin America.

8

Fresia had departed vowing never to return to a place whose society was sick with snobbery and inequality and whose only virtues as far as she could see were its extreme geography, summer climate and crazy abundance of seafood. Sometimes she thought about the shining mountains around Santiago after the rain had lifted away the smog. But then she remembered all the petty hypocrisies, the moralising clichés, banal aphorisms and outright class-hatred of her aunts.

'I'll never go back,' she had said to her father. 'I can't stand Chileans.'

He had laughed and ruffled her hair.

'Fortunately your mother's family is not very representative. You'll go back. Some day.'

And now here she was, and people were moving over to their side of the plane which offered the best view of the mountains. A know-all man was pointing out the highest peak of Aconcagua to a French girl and saying that he still thought that nothing beat the Alps. The young lecturer next to her sighed as he leaned across her to look out.

'I love this bit,' he said. 'No matter how tired I am.'

But Fresia had started to feel sick.

Maybe it's right to be nervous now . . .

The plane began its bouncy descent. She packed away her stuff as nausea clawed her stomach. Then she stared from the window and prayed that the kind but notoriously disorganised and absent-minded Uncle Guillermo would be waiting for her at the airport. Down, down they went, the altitude on the flight-information screen falling rapidly, and now she could see green fields rather than icy peaks. Further down and her ears popped as she caught sight of the airport, planes waiting on the tarmac, vans scuttling about. The landing gear was deployed, the final seconds of flight and then the bump and rapid deceleration. There were laughing dark-skinned men in blue overalls on the tarmac, the pretty tricolour with its lone-star was fluttering in the spring breeze.

A tornado of butterflies swirled in her stomach. She had arrived.

What's in a Name?

Early-morning rain had cleansed the air and now the Andes stood out sharply behind Santiago against a clear blue sky. On the balcony of a flat borrowed from a Chilean academic on sabbatical at the University of Texas, Dr Joseph MacMillan was working on his laptop. He stopped typing for a moment and stared out at the white peaks of the mountains to the east of the city.

The first Spanish expedition to Chile had been led by Diego de Almagro and had been a disaster. It had been followed some years later by a band of men led by Pedro de Valdivia who also travelled with his beautiful, illiterate lover Inés de Suarez. They were greedy men, brutal men, tough men from Extremadura, schemers and chancers. It was impossible not to feel some sympathy, however, for these violent adventurers, their hearts thumping with anticipation and fear beneath their armour, their blackened frostbitten toes dropping into the snow when they removed their boots.

And although they found little to compare with the riches of Peru, they journeyed through a country of astonishing variety and beauty, almost always in view of either the snow-capped mountains or the ocean. They crossed burning deserts, the temperate and fertile central valley, a bay surrounded by hills where a captain exclaimed, 'Oh this is like a valley of paradise' (thus giving a name to what would become a great port). They headed south and found huge lakes beneath volcanoes, rain-swept islands, the delicate red bells of the *copihue* flower, fuzzy-armed monkey-puzzle trees, great rivers winding away into the interior.

Almost halfway down the strip of land, this long thermometer which stretched from burning red to icy blue, the *conquistadores* had rested in a half-encircled spot at the fork of a river. And they had named their encampment Santiago del Nuevo Extremo in honour of their birthplace. The architect Pedro de Gamboa had planned out the main square of the Plaza de Armas, the streets and principal buildings of the nascent city above which Joe now sat.

In spite of the smog, in spite of the fact that the city was now a testimony to residential segregation and unimaginative planning, Santiago had *something*, a strong pulse; even its name on an airport departure board thrilled him. It was a capital city which dominated almost every aspect of national life – political, economic and cultural – this was the place where things happened and the place where things had happened. Joe might be walking down the street and suddenly find himself assailed by an almost wild elation at being here, a great surge of freedom and happiness incomparable with that produced by any other city.

Joe was about to return to his typing when he heard the loud buzz of the flat's intercom.

'Hey, Doctor Joe!'

It was Magdalena, Joe's best friend in Chile. He buzzed her in and stepped out into the hall to stand by the lifts, listening to the doors closing at ground level, the clunk, whirr and whine as it climbed to the tenth floor of the apartment block.

'Hey, *flaca*,' he grinned at her as the lift doors opened and they embraced each other.

'You should have told me your flight number, I would have come to the airport.'

'I was fine. I don't like meeting people when I'm jet-lagged.'

It was two days now since he had stood at the airport watching the girl he had met on the plane as they waited for their suitcases by the luggage carousel. He had thought about speaking to her again but decided not to – they were back with their respective histories and geographies now and he would never see her again. For an instant, this had filled him with a strange melancholy, especially when the girl leaned forward and pulled a red rucksack from the carousel. Then he had sighed and gone to order a taxi, his melancholy quickly giving way to the intense pleasure of returning to Santiago. He chatted to the taxi driver and counted off the red metro signs as they drove through the spring sunshine down the Alameda, Santiago's main artery.

'So, what's going on in Chile?' Joe asked Magdalena as she snooped about his flat.

'What's going on in Chilito? Well, they've found a virgin who weeps blood in La Pintana and all the lumpen are queuing up to see her. The Under 17 football team have qualified for the Olympics. A kid has gone missing in Chillán and nobody knows where he might be. And I'm starving.'

11

'That's strange.'

'Why? It's twelve-thirty. That's lunch-time in Chile.'

'No, finding a virgin in La Pintana.'

'Maybe that's why she's crying,' Magdalena said. 'She feels left out. Come on. Feed me.'

They took the lift down to the warm street below. Joe's flat was in the wealthy area of Providencia where men in suits ate lunch at café tables, the spring sun flashed on the plate glass of offices, and slender girls with shining hair strolled in light cotton dresses, causing office workers to divert their eyes and tongues momentarily from their ice-creams.

'Do you mind walking for a bit?' Joe asked, also watching one of the girls as she passed by.

'Sure. Just watch out for lamp-posts.'

They set off towards the centre of town, past the Plaza Italia, neon-lit at night, meeting place for goths and transsexuals and punks and the supporters of Colo Colo or Universidad de Chile football teams. They passed by the Catholic University and under the hill which the natives had called Huelén and which the Spanish – with their penchant for renaming things – had christened Santa Lucía. Across the road from the Santa Lucía hill bored traders sat in the artisan market, smoking and chatting beneath leather rucksacks, wind-chimes, joss-sticks, images of familiar icons beaten into copper – Salvador Allende, Marilyn Monroe, Victor Jara, John Lennon.

'Are we walking all the way?' Magdalena complained.

Joe hailed a taxi.

Sunlight streamed in through the high wrought iron of the fish market as Joe and Magdalena ignored the entreaties of the vendors and made their way to their favourite restaurant in the centre of the market where they ordered shellfish soup and a bottle of Rhín Carmen white wine.

'Make sure it's very cold,' Magdalena ordered the waiter, lighting a Belmont cigarette. Her lighter had a leather case with a little smurf-like figure climbing up one side. She exhaled smoke and studied Joe as if he were some alien that had just disembarked from the mother ship. Then she laughed.

'What's up?' Joe said.

'Nothing. I just always find it strange when you come back. Will you be going down to Villa Caupolicán soon?'

The legendary Mapuche warrior had given his name to many things: a street in every town, Santiago's municipal theatre, a brigade of Pinochet's secret police. His name also belonged to a shantytown in the municipality of La Pintana, an area famed principally for its high levels of crime. The military regime may have been committed to neo-liberal economics but it had been even more determined to remove poor people from parts of the city where land prices were high. And so, during the 1980s, a highly visible hand had directed the building of basic houses and flats in a semi-rural area to the south of the city where land was dirt cheap and social infrastructure zero. They had given the residents seventy-five-per-cent subsidies on the tiny properties and not bothered chasing them much for the rest, so that the houses were effectively a free gift from Pinochet. The General and his team of technocrats had rarely sought to make political capital out of this policy – all that mattered was that the rowdy and the criminal classes were out of the way, constituting a danger only when the more angry, impatient or drug-fuelled among them ventured back to the rich areas to mug the wealthy or burgle their houses.

The notoriety of La Pintana had fascinated Joe, and so Magdalena – who had run sex education classes there for a local research institute – introduced him to some of the community leaders from the area. They organised a football club – Caupolicán FC – which also served as a forum for the grievances of local residents. Joe had written a paper on the club as a new type of social organisation for the *Journal of Latin American Studies*, which had been very well received. He had also started to play for the team when he was in Chile.

'I spoke to Lalo yesterday,' Magdalena continued. 'They're doing quite well. He was really pleased you were here. Will you play for them?'

'I'll call him tomorrow.'

'I'm pleased you're here as well,' Magdalena added.

'I'm pleased to be here,' Joe said and felt a momentary elation which almost made him shudder. He stirred his shellfish soup which was filled with mussels, clams and *erizos* – the red iodine-charged sea urchins that he loved. He looked up at Magdalena and grinned.

After they had paid the bill and Joe had bought himself a fresh sea bass for supper, they walked back to the Plaza de Armas where they sat for a while to eat an ice-cream beneath one of the palm trees. Magdalena gave him a copy of the left-wing magazine for which she sometimes wrote. Her principal interest lay in detailing the whereabouts and occupations of ex-torturers – a hazardous pursuit that had earned her more than one death threat.

'Your fish is starting to smell,' she wrinkled her nose.

Joe felt the fat body of the fish through the wet paper and thought happily about how much a whole, large, wild sea bass would have cost in Britain.

'I'd better get it home,' he said.

They said goodbye to each other and Joe walked with his fish and magazine down the pedestrianised Paseo Ahumada filled with office workers, schoolkids in blue uniforms, street vendors, crippled beggars, blind accordion players, dollar touts, men selling copies of the rent laws and the municipal code. When he reached the busy Alameda he caught a bus to Providencia, accustomed now to the flat that had seemed so new and strange when he arrived.

Back home, Joe put the fish in the fridge, then checked his contact list and marked the important ones. He stared at the list for a moment and then turned the TV on and watched the news. A crowd queued outside an impoverished shack to see the blood-weeping statue of the Virgin; a weeping mother in Chillán pleaded for news about her son who had not come home after a night out with friends.

Rodrigo Petrovic – the flat's owner – had left a bottle of pisco with a welcome note. As night fell, Joe made himself a pisco and coke. He sometimes suffered from terrible panic attacks but tonight he was able to enjoy his solitude, the hum of the TV in the background as he padded into the white-tiled kitchen with bare feet to put the coke bottle back in the fridge, listening to the crack and hiss of the ice in his drink as he stared out at the lights of the city. He thought of when there were no buildings here, of how the dark terrain might have looked four hundred and fifty years ago when Pedro de Valdivia, Inés de Suarez, and a small band of *conquistadores* stood on the banks of the River Mapocho beneath the Santa Lucía hill. Since then, the city had grown like a drop of ink on blotting paper, lights flickering away to the south like faraway galaxies.

Joe finished his drink, switched the TV off and went through to the bedroom where he lay on the bed and closed his eyes. He thought about Research Assessment Exercises, about playing football, and about the girl he had met on the plane. Fresia. Her historical namesake was the wife of the warrior Caupolicán. Unfortunately for Pedro de Valdivia and his men, the Mapuches were one of the least submissive nations in the whole of Latin America and had no intention of quietly accepting slavery. Caupolicán had become their leader by surviving an endurance test which involved balancing a tree-trunk on his shoulders for longer than anybody else. When the Spanish finally captured him, Fresia's fury was such that she had dashed their baby to the ground, saying that she could not bring up the child of a weakling who had allowed himself to be taken by the enemy. Caupolicán had then been impaled on a stake, his insides shredded, writhing into death. Fresia's scornful reaction seemed a little harsh to Joe, given his final agony.

Joe drifts into sleep and begins to dream – of a starlit forest clearing and a man whose veins are bulging as he bears the weight of history on his shoulders. Outside, the river flows down from the mountains and the rats scamper in and out of the shadows where Pedro de Valdivia once stood with Inés de Suárez. It swirls alongside the walls where, centuries later, bright clenched-fist murals briefly erupted until bodies were tipped into its shallow waters and the murals obliterated. It trips by the Forestal Park where Pablo Neruda and Matilde Urrutia strolled together as young lovers, where bodies still move and limbs entwine in the moonlight. It ripples past streets bearing the names of both Mapuche warriors and *conquistadores*, spills by the Bellas Artes museum and the Mapocho station, courses alongside the statues of men who raised their swords in the many battles that stretched still further the length of the *dulce patria*. Conquest and resistance, honour and treachery, severed heads and discarded bodies – the brown river of drowned cats purls through the dreaming city, oblivious to all the detritus, the broken fragments, the fluvial deposits of history.

You Again

'The problem with your father is that he was really a romantic,' Guillermo Castillo said as he poured his niece a glass of beer. 'In spite of his misanthropic leanings.'

They were sitting beneath a large parasol on the roof terrace of Guillermo's flat. It had been a clear day and in the distance the sun threw a smoked-salmon glow on to the white peaks of the mountains. Guillermo was holding a small party for some fellow academics and Fresia had helped him to set out plates of salami, bread and olives, wine and whisky glasses, carefully arranged napkins. She had also leaned precariously over the railing to grab a cable fed up from the living room so that they could make hot dogs on an electric barbecue. Guillermo loved gadgets and had triumphantly returned with the barbecue after a trip to Canada where he had given a paper at the University of Toronto on patterns of residential segregation in Latin American cities.

'He got very depressed by the war in Yugoslavia and he had a very hostile reception to some of his work.'

Papi, are you awake? Is everything . . . The body slumped down on the desk, sticky patches on the sleeves of his cardigan, hand on a copy of his new and undoubtedly controversial manuscript, head turned sideways, glasses skewed across his face, that grotesque expression, the red drip on to the floor, somebody screaming.

'The last time your father was here,' Guillermo said as he fiddled with his barbecue, 'he had a terrible argument. It was with Rodrigo Petrovic, I think. They had known each other for years. Petrovic was making fun of nineteen-seventies intellectuals – the way they used to come to blows over Marxist abstractions. And although your father hated that kind of sterile jargon as well, he just went crazy and said that he had preferred Rodrigo when he was young and had some passion about ideas and wasn't a government hireling.'

'He upset everybody,' Fresia said. 'Even my brother Alex. And

16

you know how good-natured he is. Just because Alex is doing his Ph.D. on sustainable development.'

'Well, Petrovic got pretty angry,' Guillermo inspected and prodded the barbecue as if it were capable of biting him. 'He said that Ricardo was a nihilist maverick without a home and that even the Communist Party hated him and would have nothing to do with him.'

'Poor Dad,' Fresia said sadly. 'I think he was all too aware of that.'

Tongue hanging out strangely like a cat at a bowl of milk. Spatterings of crimson on the postcard of the Delphic Sibyl, the map of Latin America, the photo of her mother receiving her diploma, the brightly painted wooden Simón Bolívar beside a printout of his lament:

He who serves a revolution ploughs the sea.

Her father had taken them to see the house in London where the liberation of the continent was planned. Fresia still carried with her the photograph of a seven-year-old girl with plaits and a cheesecloth shirt standing with her brother and father outside the house in Grafton Way where the flamboyant sexual extrovert Francisco de Miranda had lived. Here Miranda had entertained the highly-strung Simón Bolívar and taught mathematics to a lonely young man called Bernardo O'Higgins. Fresia and Alex had been far more excited about the trip to the zoo which followed. At the zoo, he had shown them the caged animals from their native land, the condors, chinchillas and pudus, complaining angrily about the size of the condor's cage. Afterwards they had pestered him to take them to a Wimpy bar and although her father had grumbled that the food was a gringo atrocity, he had taken them to eat burgers and chips in Camden Town. She had slept happily under his arm on the train back to Oxford while he stared through his coke-bottle glasses at the countryside flashing past the train window.

Thinking what?

Guillermo ruffled Fresia's hair and put his arm around her shoulders. She smiled up at him. Her uncle had been working in Nairobi when she was last in Chile. This was a shame because he was easily her favourite relative and his presence would have made her stay far more bearable.

Her father had sat on this terrace with his brother looking out at the very same view, at the distant mountains. She could imagine them now, the two brothers, the hedonist and the depressive. In spite of their differences they had been very close and she heard

17

them laughing at some mutual acquaintance, somebody else who had sold out, academic charlatans. She imagined Guillermo and her father choking with laughter, Guillermo slapping his brother on the back, still chuckling as he went downstairs to fetch a new bottle of beer, her father suddenly alone staring out at the mountains.

'You know that we don't have mustard for the hot dogs,' Guillermo murmured, now holding his chin and surveying the table of food.

'I'll go and get some,' Fresia said.

'Get another bag of ice as well,' her uncle said.

Fresia hummed to herself as she walked down the quiet, leafy street, the breeze on her face, the early-summer light so different from London. A dog lay sleeping by the step of the corner grocery store which was run by a bad-tempered, middle-aged snob of a woman, together with her sinister-looking son. Guillermo hated the owner because she always put up a picture of the right-wing candidate at election times. Fresia liked these little shops though, with their bottles of coke, ice-cream freezers, sliced ham and cheeses in glass cabinets, eggs wrapped in newspaper, cartons of long-life milk, a lollipop tree by the till. The smell reminded her of family holidays at the beach in Italy, walking with sandy feet, pleading for ice-cream.

Fresia picked up a plastic mustard dispenser and a bag of ice which she hung over her arm but then moved as her arm grew numb. The man being served in front of her was foreign and was being treated rudely by the shop owner who was pretending not to understand as he asked for cigarettes.

'Marlboro Lights,' the man repeated.

'*Cómo*?' the woman said with brusque impatience and hand on hip. '*No te entiendo.*' Fresia winced at the rudeness.

'Marlboro Lights,' the man repeated more slowly and in a perfectly acceptable accent.

The woman took down a packet of red Marlboro. The man looked at them, hesitating.

'I'm sorry,' he said. 'I wanted Marlboro Lights.'

The woman pretended she had not heard and the man shrugged and handed over a thousand pesos for the cigarettes he did not want. Fresia felt a flash of impatience.

'You've given him the wrong cigarettes.'

'I can't understand him,' the woman said again rudely, reaching without looking for a pack of Marlboro Lights.

'Yes you did,' Fresia replied sharply.

'It's OK, it doesn't matter,' the man turned to her and she dimly remembered his face but could not tell from where. He was dressed in a style she liked – carefully but comfortably in a blue shirt, open at the neck to reveal a silver chain, white trousers and sandals. He smelled clean – of cotton and a light perfume – and his appearance suddenly reminded her of everything she did like about summer in London, the way people enjoyed the small quota of sun that they were allowed.

The man obviously recognised her as well because his face lit up.

'It's Fresia!' he exclaimed, switching into English. 'Remember . . . the plane . . . I sat next to you. There was the terrible turbulence.'

'Oh yes,' Fresia also spoke in English. 'How strange. What are you doing here?'

The shop owner put her hand on her hip and looked at Fresia as if she must have failed to see the sign on the door barring entrance to prostitutes: conversing with the foreigner and in his own language!

'Do you have a problem, Señora?' Fresia asked coldly. 'Apart from needing to syringe your ears.'

The man let out a burst of laughter and the shop owner gave them a disdainful look and retired, muttering under her breath, to the back of the shop where a TV was showing a Brazilian soap opera.

'What a horror that woman is,' Fresia said when they emerged back on to the sunny street. 'Did you tell me your name?'

'I'm Joe MacMillan. Good to make your acquaintance again, Fresia.'

'So what are you doing around here?' Fresia asked.

'I'm going to a sort of cocktail party. I don't really want to go but I was invited by this sociologist I need to speak to. I find these things pretty boring. It's just academic networking to be honest.'

'Really?' Fresia smiled at him.

'Yeah, it'll probably be a lot of snobby bastards competing about who's been to the most conferences. There are some decent Chilean academics but a lot of them are rubbish – care more about their office comfort than their research. And this Guillermo Castillo didn't sound like he could run a bath. Took him a while to remember his own address. I just hope there's plenty to drink.'

'I'm sure there will be,' Fresia said smoothly.

'Well, I think this is number 1540? Hey, that's a coincidence! The year Pedro de Valdivia came to Chile . . .'

'Amazing,' Fresia said.

He hesitated before the entrance to the apartment block as if this time they might exchange addresses. Fresia took out her key.

'Another coincidence,' she said. 'I live in these flats as well.'

'We'll end up going to the same party next,' Joe said.

Fresia grinned. 'Now that would really be too much,' she replied.

'Your father was at Oxford,' Joe said. It was a statement rather than a question.

They were standing on the balcony gazing out at all the constellations of lights from the buildings of Providencia. Joe had been startled and then mortified when she had accompanied him to the front door.

Fresia nodded.

'I saw him give a brilliant seminar once.' Joe poured more pisco into his glass. ''Utopians and Turncoats', he called it. Really original but it pissed everybody off. He was very funny though. And when some of the more lunatic questions came up, he would nod politely but he looked as if he were trying to stop himself from laughing.'

Fresia said nothing. She knew that expression well. The fascist shop owner and her creepy squinting son were alive. Her father wasn't.

'What about you?' Joe said. 'Did you study?'

'Photography,' Fresia replied. 'At the London College of Printing.'

'Never tempted by academia?'

'No,' Fresia said.

She remembered the house in Stockwell where she had lived with Mark, she remembered, with a pang that was half nostalgia and half relief, the steps leading up to the front door, the smell of damp in the entrance hall, the bicycles on the ragged carpet, the flyers for minicabs, takeaway pizzas and curries. Her mother had come to visit her, had looked around and raised her eyebrows.

'All I care about is your happiness,' her mother had said. 'Are you happy here, darling?'

Well, she had not been unhappy. Mark was a musician whose band made most of their money playing cover versions at the weddings of university friends – 'I Believe in Miracles' for thirty-somethings taking the inevitable next step from mortgage to matrimony. Sometimes Fresia would also do the photos at these events – relatives in hats smiling grimly towards the camera as they seethed with anger at some perceived slight received through the seating arrangement.

Mainly, though, she had worked on a freelance basis for local papers and magazines. *OK, just one more roll now, drop your shoulder a little, turn to the side, that's it, a bit less serious, come on, laugh for me.* And she would cross her eyes and do a send-up laugh, emphasising that she understood that it was all quite ridiculous, which always succeeded in making them laugh as well. Her job did not give her great financial stability but it provided her with an easy and tolerable equilibrium until the Christmas when she had returned to her parents' home in Oxford and that equilibrium had disappeared for ever.

Selfish, Mark had called her when she told him that she was leaving. He had raged, he had pleaded, he had wept. Hadn't he consoled her, cared for her, comforted her? Perhaps he was right. She did have a selfish side to her and she was glad that she did. Otherwise, she might still be walking hand-in-hand with him on the way back from the pub, held firmly in the web of familiarity and comfort which he had so carefully spun.

The young woman who had introduced Joe to her uncle wandered over. Magdalena was holding a napkin-cradled hot dog in one hand, a glass of golden whisky in the other. She was skinny with a big mass of unruly hair which, from the back, made her look rather like a gonk. But she had bright, fierce eyes and an attractive laugh.

Joe explained how they had met on the plane.

'Are you going to stay here now you're back?' Magdalena asked Fresia.

Fresia shrugged. 'I don't know. I want to travel. To get to know the country better.'

She wasn't sure if this were true. It seemed like the kind of thing one should say, the kind of thing one should want to do. But she was safe here, sitting out in the warm late September sun on the beautiful roof terrace, passing the afternoons reading or staring at the sky, listening to Coltrane and Miles Davis, Beatles and Bob Dylan CDs from her uncle's collection, padding to the shop to buy bread and cheese and pâté, talking softly over a beer at night. She had her own room with a single bed and a TV set right next to the roof terrace where she felt utterly alone and self-sufficient. She watched the late-night news in bed, got up to make coffee in the mornings, sat barefoot in the early sun, curling her toes and staring at the mountains.

Fresia knew that this situation was not tenable as a long-term strategy but she was grateful to her uncle for not commenting on it and leaving her to her own devices. He gave her papers to translate so that she could earn a little extra money but she hardly needed it as she had few expenses and still had money from her father's will.

Guillermo came over and patted them all affectionately. This bear-like gesture nearly had the effect of swatting the diminutive Magdalena over the balcony. Guillermo teased her about her persecution of harmless old torturers and Magdalena told them about one such shady figure who had once been a torturer and who now ran several businesses but whom nobody seemed to want to talk about.

'Everybody's more worried about this boy who's disappeared,' Guillermo said.

'Nobody would worry about him if he wasn't rich,' Magdalena said.

But Fresia remembered the mother's grief-ravaged face from the TV, the way she had pleaded for her son's return and thought that, even if true, this was a lame thing to say.

Guillermo told Joe that he wanted him to try a bottle of Chilean Cabernet Sauvignon and tell him if it wasn't the best wine in the world.

Fresia could see that her uncle liked Joe.

'Well, if you insist,' Joe winked at Fresia.

Later that night, after the wine had been drunk, after they had joked about whether it was insolent, impudent or a slippery cat of a wine, and Magdalena had dragged him off before they opened another one to settle this once and for all, Fresia lay in her bed staring at the ceiling. She felt suddenly the strangeness of her position so far away from everything she had ever known, so far from her real country. It seemed to her that Joe was more at home here than she was, knew Chile much better than she did. She wondered idly for a second whether he also knew that sharp-tongued Magdalena was in love with him.

Her mind drifted to England – cycling on dark, autumnal nights in Oxford across Magdalen Bridge, the punts and boats tied up and bobbing on the river below. She remembered the journey with Mark to see his family in Cornwall, the little train to St Ives, the crooked streets, the light over the sea, New Year surfers like seals in the waves. She remembered running, laughing, for her front door in London as fat drops of spring rain began to drill the streets. She had given it all up for this elongated country at the end of the world, for this city beneath the mountains.

22

And yet what had she given up? What did she have that she had renounced? There was her work, of course, and sometimes she would take her unused camera out and turn it around in her hand, sniff the plastic case, look through the lens up at the mountains or at the children playing beneath her. When people had asked her why she was going she had not really known what to say. She had just felt this sudden desperate need to leave, to do something different, to reconstruct her life. She had been able to see the road ahead and while it was not unpleasant it was impossible to countenance as a vision of her future. And then there was her father and that had changed everything. So she had returned to her father's country to get away from her father and the last image she had of him. She had fled with no guarantees, she had begun a new voluntary exile in the land of her birth.

Now she lay in the dark while a sudden fear and loneliness gripped her heart. All around her were the things she had brought with her: her camera equipment; CD player and box of CDs; a book of Tina Modotti photographs; a picture of a small girl with plaits and a cheesecloth shirt beside a blue plaque on the wall of a house in London. Why had she come here? She didn't even like the country very much; she thought that most Chileans were two-faced hypocrites. Her journey was not bravery but folly. You don't change your life or acquire depth and purpose by moving continents. She watched the shadow of a moth behind a curtain and thought about her mother waving goodbye to her at the airport. England had followed her silently but – until now – not particularly insistently. She lay in her single bed watching the desperate shadow games of the light-tortured moth. Then she closed her eyes.

So Fresia drifts into sleep while thousands of miles away her ex-boyfriend Mark stares at a photograph of a good-looking couple laughing in St Ives, spray flying up from the harbour walls. And Joe and Magdalena walk the few blocks back to the flat where Magdalena will lie awake in the living room, tracing patterns on the wall, feeling the blood pulsing in her fingertips, alive to every possibility of movement.

To the south of the city, in one of the poor neighbourhoods which lies towards the end of the potholed Avenida Santa Rosa, there is a tiny house which has been the centre of frenzied attention over the last few days. Ice-cream sellers call out that they have pine-apple, chocolate and *chirimoya*, children shriek and leap star-shaped for the TV cameras, mothers watch anxiously for rats in the shadows.

Hail Mary full of grace . . .

Our Lady of the shantytown – for whom is she weeping? For the thirteen-year-old girl whose belly is swollen with her uncle's child? For the young robber on the pavement looking up through fading eyes at the policeman who has just shot him? Perhaps she weeps for the distraught mother in Chillán whose son did not come home from his night out with friends, perhaps for all the tired faces and sore feet that will, nevertheless, come in their thousands, will flock down unpaved streets past TV vans and – if they are lucky – be interviewed by pretty young journalists of the type that Magdalena both despises and envies. They will come here with their everyday tragedies, they will plead in silent desperation for intercession, lifting their aching hearts to the sacred paradox of the Virgin Mother. Surely she weeps for them, surely she will help them, this little plaster miracle whose hands are piously clasped to heaven and whose chalk-white cheeks are stained with hot scarlet tears?

Pink-lipped Razor Clams

A warning horn wailed at the Santa Lucía Metro station as the doors closed on one of the blue trains purchased from the Paris Métro. Joe had allowed a little time to elapse after the party and then he had called Fresia. She had seemed pleased to hear from him and they had arranged to meet up – there was a Buñuel season at the Normandie Cinema and they were going to see *The Discreet Charm of the Bourgeoisie*.

Joe glanced at his watch and, as he did so, Fresia appeared in front of him. She pulled a face of wry apology and explained that she had had to wait for Guillermo.

Joe was secretly quite relieved that they had missed the film and they walked alongside the Mapocho river and crossed over the bridge into the Bellavista bar and restaurant area, passing hippies squatting with their rugs of jewellery and drinking from cartons of red wine. At the foot of Pío Nono Street, the San Cristóbal hill rose up above the city, elevating its white statue and ruby-studded television aerial above the smog and interference. Roads curled around the hill to the open-air swimming pools and old zoo on its slopes. Pablo Neruda had owned a house near by when this was a genuinely bohemian area; Joe had gone there with Magdalena and they had wandered through rooms which, after the coup, had echoed to the sounds of soldiers' boots and splintering glass. Now, couples were sitting outside cafés cupping their hands beneath bulging hot dogs, drinking giant glasses of beer mixed with Fanta. A few pale-skinned backpackers studied *Lonely Planets* and *Rough Guides*, pushy waiters tried to hustle people into their establishments.

They cut off Pío Nono on to a quieter and darker road. And there in the shadows a man was pinned against a wall while another man held a knife at his throat and his accomplice frisked his pockets. The man with the knife appeared to be whispering threats to their victim in order to pass the time.

'Hey,' Joe said out loud.

All of the men in the shadows turned and stared at him. They were frozen in their gestures of menace and terror like a choreographed street-fighting scene. The man with the knife said,

'You want something, *huevón*?'

The man being mugged was wearing a well-tailored suit. His face was a white blur of fear. Joe stepped forward.

'Leave him.'

'Check the gringo, *huevón*,' said the man to his accomplice. He stepped towards Joe who bared his teeth and said quietly in English,

'Come on then.'

His adversary understood the invitation, twisted the knife by his thigh a couple of times. He was wearing stone-washed jeans and chunky black-and-white trainers.

'Joe, he's got a knife,' Fresia said.

'I know,' Joe said, staring at the man and sensing that he had already caused a tiny doubt in his mind. He knew that the man did not want to use the knife here, but might if he could not see another option which also left his pride intact. It had all got too messy because Joe had faced him down.

The accomplice said something quickly and the knifeman turned. Another couple had entered the street from the opposite end and were walking towards them. In a building opposite, one of the windows suddenly filled with light and a woman pulled the curtain back and peered out. The two muggers glanced at the window, at the approaching couple, back to Joe. Then they picked up the briefcase, which obviously belonged to the man, and began to walk slowly towards Joe.

Joe stood his ground and the mugger came right up to his face. He looked down at his knife and then he laughed.

'Hooligan,' he said in English. 'English hooligan.'

He pronounced it *kooligan* and Joe fought a desire to laugh. Instead he raised his eyebrows like a batsman who has just avoided a vicious bouncer from a feared fast bowler. The man feinted as if to jab him with the knife and Joe recoiled. The man laughed and said, '*Ciao*, hooligan,' and they sauntered off.

Fresia went to the man who was standing against the wall. 'Are you OK?' she said, taking his arm.

'Yes,' he answered. 'I think so. They haven't hurt me.'

But he suddenly started to shake quite violently, his body almost spasming.

'I'm sorry,' he said. 'I don't know . . . it's just . . .'

'It's OK,' Fresia said and put her arm around him. 'It's shock.'

Joe stood apart for a moment, watching as Fresia held the man. He guessed that he must be in his mid-forties. He was wearing an elegant suit, his face was angular, handsome, intelligent. Making an effort to compose himself, he turned to Joe and said in perfect English:

'I think they mistook your nationality. Aren't you a Scottish hooligan?'

Joe nodded, surprised by the slight upper-class intonation. 'But you're English?'

'On my mother's side. My name is Roberto Walker. Thank you. I need a drink and if you have time I would like to buy you one. They missed my wallet.'

'What about your briefcase?' Fresia asked.

The man laughed, normality returning. 'I think they might be disappointed. Unless they're fans of the novelist José Donoso. It contains an article I was writing on him and I have that on my computer at home. The only loss is the briefcase and I wasn't so attached to it. But I really am grateful to you. How about that drink? If you want to be alone together I shall understand, of course . . .'

Joe glanced at Fresia who said, 'We're just going round the corner, aren't we? I think we all need a drink.'

'Bellavista has changed,' Roberto Walker said as they drank cold wine and picked at plates of tapas. They were sitting at a pavement table. Fresia had suggested that they take a table inside in case their assailants returned but it was a warm evening and the restaurant was filling up.

'They won't bother us here,' Joe said. 'Unless they get upset by his interpretation of José Donoso.'

The waiter brought some more plates of food in earthenware bowls – potato tortillas and chorizo and *machas* with Parmesan cheese.

'I love these,' Fresia said, picking up one of the delicate shellfish, pink and flat like a little cat tongue.

'As long as they're cooked properly . . .' Roberto tried one and smiled to show that it was.

'What are they called in English?' Fresia asked. 'Do they even have a name?'

'Pink-lipped razor clams,' Joe said, spearing one with his fork.

'Are they really?' Roberto said. 'And we just call them *machas*.'

'Do you live around here, Roberto?' Fresia asked.

'Oh no. I live up in the mountains now. Do you know the Cajon del Maípo?'

Fresia shook her head.

'It's the valley just outside the city which runs through the mountains up to the border with Argentina,' Roberto said. 'There are several villages. I live in one of the smallest.'

'It's where they ambushed Pinochet once,' Joe said. He looked at Roberto, watching for his reaction.

'Yes,' Roberto speared a *macha*. 'They had very bad luck and he had a very good driver.'

'So what are you up to in Bellavista then?' Fresia asked.

'I was looking for somebody,' Roberto said.

'Didn't they turn up?' Joe beckoned for another bottle of wine.

A look of fatigue suddenly flickered across Roberto's features. He rubbed his eyes. 'No, it was a complete waste of time.'

He reached into his pocket and took out a photograph. 'That's my nephew.'

'The boy from Chillán!' Joe exclaimed.

'Pablo,' Roberto said. 'We got some information that he had been seen in Santiago hanging out with some *artesanos* in Bellavista. Sadly, the people I went to meet were more interested in the reward and then I bumped into those two, who decided that they would just go straight for the reward.'

He put the photograph away in a manner that suggested he no longer wished to discuss it.

'Have you really never been to the Cajon del Maípo?' he asked Fresia.

'Well, I'd only been once to Bellavista before tonight. I was brought up in Britain.' She gestured to Joe. 'He knows this city much better than I do. Really, he's more Chilean than I am.'

'But you are Chilean?'

'I was born here. I've lived all my life in Britain though.'

'Ah,' Roberto said. 'Your parents left . . .'

'After the coup,' Fresia finished it for him. 'I was born a short time afterwards actually.'

Roberto studied her for a moment. Then he laughed.

'Not very convenient for your poor mother. Well, you must get to know the Cajon del Maípo. Why don't you both come up? I usually have people round for a barbecue on Sundays. Not this Sunday because I have to go to Chillán and visit my sister for a few days. But any Sunday after that. Just drop by if you feel like it, it's quite informal.'

Joe hesitated. He was about to make a polite excuse when the tables and chairs began to vibrate, the glasses to clink, the cutlery to jerk across the table. Inside, the diners froze. It was as if a séance had just begun to get interesting, the ouija boards to spell out their spirit messages. A single fork dropped to the floor. A dog barked. Then the rumble stopped.

'An earth tremor,' Roberto said calmly, picking up the fork and wiping it with his napkin. 'Quite strong. We're overdue an earth-quake.'

Joe looked at Fresia whose eyes were glittering.

'That was incredible,' she said. 'I'd love to be here when there's an earthquake.'

Roberto regarded her with mock puzzlement.

'I doubt that somehow. Well, I can't promise an earthquake but we'll have a very good barbecue. Will you come up?'

He was talking to both of them but still looking at Fresia.

'It would give me the chance to get to know the Cajon del Maípo, ' Fresia said. 'You'll come too, Joe?'

'I'm not sure,' Joe said. 'I sometimes play football on Sundays.'

'Well, here's my address and number,' Roberto took a card from his inside pocket. 'It's very easy. You have to get to Puente Alto and take a *collectivo* from bus stop 37, that goes as far as San Gabriel. It'll only take about an hour or so. Ask the driver where to drop you.'

He held the card out between them, playfully moving it to and fro as if unsure which of them to give it to.

'You take it,' Joe said to Fresia.

Fresia took the card. Roberto Walker stood up.

'Well, I must go. Joe . . .' he held out his hand '. . . thank you again for saving me. Fresia, I hope if there is an earthquake you won't be crushed. I may see you both one Sunday. Bring your swim-ming costumes if you do come. I have a pool.'

He walked inside to the bar and beckoned the waitress, handing her some money. She looked over at their table, smiled and nodded. Roberto hailed a passing cab and she came outside with two *caipirinhas*, lime glinting through crushed ice.

'The gentleman paid the bill,' she said. 'He said to bring you these.'

'What did you think of him?' Fresia asked Joe.

29

'I think he's dodgy. I think there's more to him than meets the eye.'

She frowned. 'Why?'

'Just a hunch, I guess.'

'I don't see how you can say that.' She was almost irritated.

'It's a bit weird, isn't it, wandering around Bellavista like that?'

'Not if you're looking for somebody.'

Joe shrugged. 'Oh well, I suppose we won't find out now.'

'Unless we go to his barbecue.'

'You really want to do that?'

'It would give me a chance to see the Cajon del Maípo.'

They drank more *caipirinhas* and Fresia asked Joe about his work. He told her about the September 11th attack on Santiago by the local chief Michimalonco while Pedro de Valdivia was out chasing an army of shadows. The Spanish had been surprised by the determination of the attacking hordes who had set the nascent city ablaze. He told her about the seven hostage princes decapitated by the sword of Inés de Suarez in order to discourage the attackers; the single surviving chicken scratching in the burnt-out ruins that the Spanish christened Eva.

They were soon quite drunk and Fresia dragged Joe to a *salsateca* where they danced badly and met a girl from Preston who was a dancer on a cruise ship. She was a tough, bright girl with a loud laugh and an engaging persona that masked a certain restlessness, an impatience, disruptive tendencies. Joe had met women like her before; there was a ripple of anger in her brashness, unpredictability. She said that she would never go back to Preston.

'Ten years,' she said as if it were a decade too few. 'That's how long I've managed to stay away from that fucking dump.'

Gillian had been all over the world – floated down rivers in Thailand smoking opium, worked in strip clubs in the Zona Rosa of Mexico City. She had been to Chile several times before and was not short of opinions on the subject, dissecting it with malicious glee. She had picked up her current partner in the *salsateca* the night before. Diego was a stupid, good-natured PE teacher from Iquique who spent a lot of time explaining to Joe that, while there had been some excesses under Pinochet, the General had saved the country from lawlessness.

It was 4 a.m. when Joe and Fresia staggered home along Bellavista, past the shops which sold artefacts from lapiz lazuli: bracelets, necklaces, rings, wine goblets, clocks, a giant copper owl with lapiz-lazuli wings and red stones for eyes. As they crossed a small street, they saw two olive-uniformed policemen facing a third man among the shadows. Every now and again, one of the policemen would aim a kick at the figure or launch sudden jabs with a truncheon. There was a sinister laziness to their assault. They would stop, address a few words to each other, then to the figure in the shadows, then they would swing a boot or jab with the stick. Joe hesitated and one of the cops turned to look at him. So did the victim of the assault.

'Hey, English hooligan. Aren't you going to help me as well?'

He started to laugh and the cops stared at them as if asking whether Joe would like the same treatment. Fresia pulled him on.

'Don't,' she said. 'You can't do anything.'

They crossed to Providencia, reaching Fresia's turning first where they both stood awkwardly on the corner.

'I really enjoyed myself tonight,' Fresia said. 'I haven't been out like that for ages.'

'Me too,' Joe said.

Joe very nearly suggested that they carry on to his flat but something stopped him. More than anything he didn't want to appear vulgar and obvious. They stood for a moment longer and then she laughed.

'I'd better go in or the neighbours will start to talk. Call me,' she turned, waving as she went.

Joe continued down Providencia, past darkened patisseries and half-shuttered bars where exhausted waiters were sweeping up cigarette butts and wiping abandoned tables. He lit a cigarette he did not want for company, thinking about the truncheon jabbing into the shadows, the green uniforms with their brown leather holsters, the mocking laughter of the man in the shadows.

The Hand of God

'Good afternoon, ladies and gentlemen, I'm sorry to interrupt your journey but I want to ask for a little compassion for my friend who you can see in front of you . . .'

The voice came from the back of the bus heading down the Avenida Santa Rosa. Joe turned to the speaker with the rest of the passengers and then back to the front of the bus. He began to sweat as he saw the hand. It was hugely distorted, puffed up as if it had been stung by a giant bee, fatter than a boxing glove, bigger than a baseball mitt; it looked too heavy for the slender wrist supporting it.

'As you can see, my friend suffers from a terrible deformity. This means that he cannot work. Look at that hand, ladies and gentlemen . . .'

Joe could feel the collective tension, his own panic rising. He swallowed and tried to control his breathing. The man at the front obediently held up the enormous hand as if he and his partner were about to auction it off. It had no fingers and a single thumb which was bigger on its own than the average normal hand. A woman went pale and turned to look out of the window, holding her neck. A child stared in amazed fascination.

'So if you could spare a few pesos for my friend . . .'

The man began to walk down the bus. Joe struggled in his pocket to find some change. Then he realised to his horror that the man was holding out the deformed hand to receive the money. He wanted to put the money back in his pocket and turn away but knew that he could not do this.

The man drew level with Joe; he had seen him reach into his pocket. The hand was huge, grotesque, inhuman. Joe stared down at it. The flesh on the palm of the hand was soft and puffed outwards. If he just dropped the coin it would roll off on to the floor. He looked up at the hand's owner. The man was only young, in his mid-twenties maybe, and was regarding him calmly. Joe was almost paralysed by his disgust and pity.

'Thank you,' the man said, waiting patiently until finally Joe managed to half drop and half place the hundred pesos on to the monstrous hand. With his good hand, the beggar transferred the coin into his jacket pocket and moved on.

Joe looked out of the window. He was in the middle of nowhere. He could feel the onset of a panic attack and struggled to control his breathing, humming to himself which often worked. He thought about other things: about his night out with Fresia, the man whose briefcase had been stolen, the missing boy.

Magdalena was waiting for him when he got off the bus and they made their way through the dusty, unpaved streets of Villa Caupolicán to where Lalo lived. Some of the young girls who passed them recognised Magdalena from the sex education classes and nodded to her. One of them – on whom the classes had clearly had little impact – glanced down at her belly and blushed. The rest giggled loudly when they looked at Joe.

Villa Caupolicán was a mixture of two types of housing – blocks of low red-brick basic flats formed one part of the shantytown, while the other consisted of wooden houses with a tiny kitchen and toilet unit attached to the front, courtesy of a government slum-upgrading initiative. Lalo lived in one of these self-built properties – some of the houses were quite solidly constructed, one even had two storeys. Others were little more than shacks, patched up with cardboard and newspaper to keep the cold out in winter. All of the houses were protected by fences and gates; a few of them sold cold drinks, loose cigarettes or cherry-flavoured ice from behind the protective bars. The street was filled with kids and packs of mangy dogs, loud *cumbia* thumped out of open windows and a few women turned hoses on to the street outside their yards. A gang of squatting-and-standing-smoking-on-the-corner youth appraised them as they passed but then they recognised Joe and nodded at him.

They arrived at Lalo's house which was on the corner and stood out from the rest because it was painted purple.

'*Alo?*' Magdalena called, standing outside the fence of Lalo's yard. Joe had quickly learned not to pass through and knock directly on the front door. You had to wait for your invitation.

Lalo emerged from his front door grinning at the sight of Joe and Magdalena. He opened the gate to his yard and held out his arms with pleasure. He was a big, curly-haired, intelligent man. Fundamentally good-natured, Lalo also had a fierce temper when provoked. His favourite younger sister had once turned up weeping with a black eye, and Lalo had gone round to her house, dragged his brother-in-law into the street and beaten him unconscious. It had taken Ximena and Joe some effort to drag him off before he killed him.

'Hey, my number eight has returned. Now we can get rid of that useless *flojo* Wilson. Pablito, go and buy a bottle of coke and some cigarettes from your Aunty Loreto's.'

'*Hola, Tio,*' shrieked Pablo at Joe before streaking off pursued by five other screaming children and a barking dog, dodging around a bus that was grinding through the narrow streets.

'Come in, come in,' Lalo ushered them into his tiny living room with its flimsy wooden walls. Joe waited to be invited to sit down, looking up at the image of Salvador Allende and the text of his farewell speech that accompanied it.

This is the last opportunity on which I shall be able to speak to you . . .
Joe knew the speech by heart.

They have the force. They can overwhelm us. But neither crime nor force can halt a social process. History is ours and it is made by the people.

Lalo had been a member of the Manuel Rodríguez Patriotic Front during the nineteen-eighties. He had been imprisoned and tortured following the failed attempt on Pinochet's life when members of the group had lain waiting for his convoy with rocket launchers in the Cajon del Maípo – the river valley through the mountains just outside Santiago. Lalo was lucky because most of his friends had been killed in the subsequent 'Operation Albania' massacre when Pinochet's agents had entered houses and executed the inhabitants in cold blood. Joe had always assumed that it was Lalo's involvement with the FPMR that caused him to him to walk with a limp but Ximena had told him once that her husband had actually shot himself in the leg when he was drunk.

There were two other rooms at the back of the house – one for Lalo and his wife Ximena, the other for their two young children, Pablito and America. Their sixteen-year-old son Lucho slept in the living room. Joe had known Lucho since he was a kid; he still had a luminous moon that Joe had bought for him because of his fascination with the stars and the planets. He was fine-featured – a local heart-breaker, but recently he had taken to smoking *pasta base*, the cheap cocaine derivative that was popular in the shantytowns of the city's periphery. He hardly spoke to Joe any longer.

The front door opened and Chelo and Nacho poked their heads

round. Chelo was the team captain and his best friend Nacho was the goalkeeper.

'Hey,' Chelo grinned and high-fived Joe. 'That means Wilson's sub.'

Joe liked Chelo but treated him with caution. He was a local criminal and Lalo had had to fight hard to persuade him to participate in the club. Lalo had also told Joe that the last person to cross Chelo had been found by a Canadian rafting group floating in the Maípo river. He had had a big drug problem but had recently cleaned up.

'Make sure those idiots bring their money for the bus,' Lalo told them.

After the game, the bus made its way back through the darkening streets of Santiago's southern periphery. Spirits were high because they had won 3–0 and Joe was happy because he had scored the last goal. This meant that they had gone two points clear of Nueva Estrella, their bitter rivals for the local championship, who had only managed to draw. The players teased Wilson, the substitute, that he would never start another game for the club while Joe was there. Joe tried to smile apologetically but received an angry scowl in response.

'We're good enough to win this league,' Joe said cheerfully to Lalo. 'If we carry on playing like that.'

Lalo sighed and glanced at the boys laughing and teasing each other in the back of the bus, passing bottles of beer between them and smoking Belmont cigarettes, leaning out of the window to whistle at passing girls.

'If we win this league,' he said, 'then our problems may be only just beginning.'

The night was warm and they sat in Lalo's living room drinking beer with the front door open on to the yard. The air was cleaner here in the south of the city and the sky above the mountains was streaked with pink. Somebody called to Lalo from outside and he exchanged a glance with Ximena, sighed and got up. Before long, they heard the sound of raised voices, an exchange of insults so rapid that Joe could not keep up. One of the shrillest and most abusive voices belonged to a woman. *'Comunista de mierda,'* the woman shouted on several occasions. Fucking communist. Joe could also hear Lalo swearing, which was unusual because Lalo was a man who was proud of his self-education and usually avoided bad language.

'What's going on?' Joe asked but Magdalena shhhed him.

They heard footsteps and Lalo came back inside, bringing with him two people – a man and a woman – who seemed both awkward and defiant. The woman was tall with blonde highlights in her hair and folded her arms aggressively. Lucho came out of the back room and stood staring at the visitors with his arms also folded and a blank expression on his face.

'Joe,' Lalo said, 'I want you to give these people the money.'

'What?'

'The money. Give them the money. Don't worry, they're from the Executive Committee of the club. Give them all the money you were going to give to me.'

Joe thought that Lalo must be angry with him from the look of fury on his face.

'I don't know what you're talking about.'

'Yes you do, *huevón*. The money you brought from England that you were going to give to me.'

'There isn't any money. I didn't bring any.'

Lalo turned contemptuously to the couple.

'You see.'

They stood for a second longer and the woman looked at Joe with an expression which made him uneasy. He shrugged to show that he had no idea what was going on but she continued to stare at him with a strange kind of hostility and contempt.

Ximena banged a pot down angrily in the sink and stared at the ceiling. Then she came to the front door and said, 'Get out of my house.'

The woman looked at her and laughed. 'You won't get away with it, we'll make sure of that.'

'What was that all about?' Joe asked. The encounter had been unpleasant, almost frightening.

'Those are two members of the club's Executive Committee,' Lalo said, lighting a cigarette. '*Were* two members, I should say, because they were voted out at the last meeting. The guy I've known for ages, we were in the Party together, now he mixes with that woman and her group. She has links to right-wing parties, the UDI in particular. People like her because she can get them material for their houses and jobs sometimes. He's a *cahuinero* – always starting rumours and spreading gossip because he thinks he should have been president of the club.'

'People are frightened of them as well,' Ximena said.

'And what was all that about money?'

'Sorry about that. They've started a rumour that you've arrived with money for the club from England but that I've taken it all to buy a new house.'

'That's ridiculous.'

'Yes, but in a place like this rumours spread very fast. It happens all the time and it makes it really hard. People are always prepared to believe the worst.'

'Sometimes,' Ximena said, 'I just think we should give it up. Let them run things and get on with our life. It's too tiring. As if we haven't got enough problems.'

'They want you out of the club?' Joe was amazed. 'Why? After all you do for it?'

'Because often,' said Magdalena, 'if you give somebody your hand, the next thing they'll do is grab your arse.'

Somebody else shouted from outside. Joe raised his eyebrows at Lalo but he laughed.

'Don't worry,' he said. 'It's just Jaime. They'll all have heard what happened.'

A stream of people followed the unexpected visitors to express outrage, add their opinion or simply find out what had taken place. In the end, Lalo took Joe and Magdalena to wait for their bus back to La Florida where Magdalena lived. He always waited with them at night and Joe felt more secure for his doing so. He could walk about quite freely during the day because people were used to his presence but at night the atmosphere grew more volatile.

As they stood waiting, they heard the sharp crack of gunshot from a couple of blocks away. Lalo smiled sadly.

'There goes our centre forward.'

He waved at them as their bus headed away through the streets of the shantytown which, in spite of the late hour, were still full of people.

'Poor old Lalo,' Joe said to Magdalena.

She shrugged.

'He can look after himself. But it's getting worse – some of these people would sell their grandmother for a free *empanada*.'

Magdalena lived on a quiet street of identical lower-middle-class houses. The front garden was carefully tended and Magdalena's disagreeable anarchist sister Liliana was sitting on the patio with her feet on a chair in front of her, keeping her revolutionary wrath warm by reading *The Open Veins of Latin America* for the fifteenth time while eating a tub of pistachio ice-cream.

'You're late,' she said, glancing up from her book.

'Sit down, sit down,' Magdalena's tiny, good-natured mother Amanda gestured to the table set with two places for Joe and Magdalena. 'Liliana, don't eat all that ice-cream! You must leave some for Doctor Joe.'

Liliana grinned malevolently and pirouetted to show Joe the tub with a tiny bit of ice-cream left which she scooped out and slowly licked off the spoon.

'What did I do to have such terrible daughters . . . you can go out and buy me some more in a moment.' She looked adoringly at Liliana who disappeared into the room she would share that night with her sister because Joe would be given Magdalena's room. 'Now, Joe, have a little bread with *aji* while I warm the soup up.'

Magdalena offered Joe the chilli sauce and the basket with the bread in it, fluttering her eyelashes in mockery of her mother's deference to the visitor.

'It smells wonderful,' Joe said as Amanda put a bowl in front of him. He bowed his head over it, inhaling the odour. It was the classic Chilean *cazuela* – a soup of chicken, sweetcorn, pumpkin, green beans and potato, covered with a light sprinkling of coriander and accompanied by a tomato and onion salad. There was nothing better to eat after the bottles of beer he had drunk. After eating, Joe and Magdalena sat out on the patio for a while.

'Have you seen that girl again?' Magdalena asked.

'Which girl?'

'Which girl! Guillermo's little niece.'

'Oh. Yeah, we went out for a drink. We're going up to the Cajon del Maípo soon.'

'Lovely,' Magdalena exhaled a stream of smoke into the air. 'You like her, don't you?'

'No,' Joe said. 'Not in that way anyway.'

'Right,' Magdalena said, flicking her cigarette away.

'Really,' Joe said

But Magdalena was right. Joe did like Fresia, had liked her since he saw her tying up her hair on the plane, staggering under the weight of her rucksack at the airport. There are some darts that enter with little more than a pinprick but that can – especially when left unattended – lead to all kinds of confusions and complications. Magdalena knew this better than most.

Back in the living room, Señora Amanda was sitting in front of the TV, nervously chewing her fingernails. She was watching a programme which specialised in reconstructing real-life crimes. This week's case concerned a madwoman who had abducted a mother and baby in the street, beaten the mother unconscious and then thrown her into a cesspit in the garden so that she could bring up the baby.

'*Maaala!*' Señora Amanda repeated with incredulous relish every time the mad-eyed baby-thief appeared. Joe and Magdalena laughed at the actress who was pulling out all the stops short of foaming at the mouth to alert the audience to her character's deranged mental condition.

'Look how it cries for its mother,' Amanda shook her head sorrowfully.

'Huh,' Magdalena snorted. 'That's what this society is like. If you don't have a baby you're not a real woman. No wonder she went mad.'

'You were a lovely baby,' her mum said. 'Sweet, good-natured, never cried . . .'

'Shut up, Mum!'

'I bet you wish now that somebody had stolen her,' Joe muttered and Magdalena hit him with the cushion.

'Would you like a little pisco, Joe?' Amanda asked him and Joe grinned and nodded.

Later that night, Joe lay in bed and listened to the sound of the two sisters giggling and shhhing each other next door. He examined Magdalena's books: Neruda's *Canto General*; the poems of Gabriela Mistral; three volumes of Carlos Marx and Frederico Engels; *Jonathan Livingstone Seagull*; *Men are from Mars, Woman are from Venus*. There was a scroll on the wall with an embroidered Che Guevara, a picture of John Lennon with the lyrics of *Imagine*. On the bedside table, there was a Walkman with a couple of Silvio Rodríguez tapes scattered about.

Joe took down the copy of *Canto General* and found the poem which Neruda had written for Pedro de Valdivia. The poet was not keen on either the *conquistador* or his mistress, Inés de Suarez – describing them respectively as the intrusive captain and the infernal harpy who filled the country with death, solitude and scars. Perhaps this was true, Joe thought, but they also bequeathed Neruda the

39

language with which to berate their cruelties. And the two black-haired sisters whose sudden laughter he could hear through the thin walls of the neighbouring room, the warm-hearted Amanda snoring in her solitary bed, were they not also born out of the irreversible dialectic of conquest? Joe put the book down on his chest and closed his eyes, feeling the weight of the book rising and falling on his chest, listening to the neighbourhood dogs barking as he slid into sleep.

Plastic Dolphins

'Does this guy want to kill us?' Fresia murmured to Joe as their collective taxi overtook a lorry on a curve in the narrow road at seventy miles an hour. This was only the second time she had been in a *collectivo*; she had always found them intimidating, never quite understanding how they functioned. Once she had hailed one thinking that it was a normal cab and had been outraged when somebody hopped in alongside her. Startled and then amused faces had greeted her protestations that she had hailed the cab first.

'Turbulence, earth tremors and now a psychotic *collectivo* driver – remind me never to travel with you again . . .'

It felt strange to be leaving Santiago behind them as they headed out of the city towards Roberto's village in the Maípo valley. Fresia had followed the case of the missing boy with particular interest since their unusual meeting with his uncle in Bellavista.

They had taken the Line 5 Metro to La Florida, a bus to Puente Alto, and now their *collectivo* was speeding with kamikaze abandon up into the river valley. The sky became hard blue as the air freed itself from the contamination which gripped the city, the mountains sharp, untainted by haze. They drove through little villages with grocery stores, signs for camping, rafting and cabin hire. The other woman in their taxi held a cake-box on her lap and seemed unconcerned at both the speed and recklessness with which they were being driven. To distract her mind from thoughts of oncoming lorries, Fresia stared out at the mountains with their shaded layers of rock which reminded her of the test-tube of coloured sand she had once brought back from a school trip to the Isle of Wight. Her brother Alex had smashed it during an argument. She remembered looking desolately at the broken glass in the muddled-up sand, the obvious irreparability of it.

She glanced at Joe who was also staring out at the mountains with his chin in his hand. They had met up a couple of times since their evening together in Bellavista, sitting out on Guillermo's roof terrace chatting until late into the night. She liked him for his enthusiasm and his energy, the way in which he would talk to her uncle, the two men laughing at figures from Chilean history as if they were real. He had his own voice, an original personality, impatient and quick-witted. In spite of his outward confidence, however, there was sometimes a nervous quality, a restlessness about him. He had told her that he sometimes got panic attacks, insomnia, strange dizzy disembodied sensations where noises became very loud and nothing seemed real. She saw it from time to time in the way that he drank and smoked – rather driven and compulsive, as if fending off anxiety, reassuring himself, giving himself props.

Standing at the entrance to her apartment block, Fresia had wondered if Joe was going to make a move on her. She was glad now that he hadn't but knew that she would almost certainly have gone on to his flat if he had suggested it. He was attractive and good company and it had been a while now since she had slept with anybody and much longer since she had slept with somebody other than Mark. That had been an actor she was photographing in his flat one afternoon. She had never seen him again – apart from in pictures or on TV – nor told Mark, which gave it an illicit thrill far out of proportion to the pleasure she had received from the act itself.

They circled the large and featureless town of San José de Maípo, where the taxi driver lingered in vain for more customers, and then returned to the winding mountain road where stallholders adver-tised candles and honey and walnuts. The valley seemed to be pressing in on them now. At the tiny settlement of Melocotón, Joe showed Fresia the ranch from which Pinochet had left one Sep-tember afternoon in an armour-plated Mercedes-Benz, ignorant of the fact that several miles down the valley a group of young men and women were waiting, chewing their lips and fingering LOW rocket launchers. The woman with her cake-box got out and said goodbye to them. 'Bring me the head of Alfredo García,' Joe mur-mured as she walked off. Finally, they arrived at a small village and the driver stopped and pulled over by a grocery store.

'Ask in the shop,' he said. 'They'll give you directions.'

The heat was dry and pressed hard against the skin. The air smelled of sand and pine.

They wandered to the grocery store past four-wheel drives with canoes piled on the roof. Parents sat drinking cokes on the seats under a parasol while their fair, light-skinned children squabbled over the ice-cream cabinet. Watermelons lay stacked on the shelves like green munitions, some split in half with an old machete which still rested on the shelf beside them. A couple of identical round-faced twins were serving and Joe bought some cigarettes and lemon sodas while Fresia asked for directions.

'Don Roberto? He lives on the other side of the river. You have to ask the woman in the camping lodge for the key to the bridge. Oh, and if La Señora Barbara is there, could you tell her that I've had a word with Bernardo about the dog and told him he must tie it up.'

'She sure hates that dog,' said the other twin.

Fresia and Joe waved goodbye and wandered down the street, which led to the river whose ceaseless flow they could now hear through the pines. A pair of dark-skinned rural workers sat in the shade smoking and passing a bottle of beer between them.

The sulky woman in the office of the camping lodge denied all knowledge of a key to the bridge.

'It might be open anyway,' she said in a tone which meant that it certainly wouldn't be.

They walked along the side of the deep ravine until they arrived at the point where it was spanned by a precarious rope bridge. The entrance to the bridge was controlled by a gate with a heavy padlock. They could see a couple of secluded houses across the river, one of which must belong to Roberto Walker.

'What shall we do now?' Joe said.

'Fuck knows,' Fresia stared at the padlock.

'Maybe we should go back and ask the woman in the lodge who else might have the key.'

'She wasn't very helpful.'

They sat down by the entrance to the bridge, letting the sun warm their arms. Joe lit a cigarette, waved it at the flies and watched the families by the picnic area in the woods, the wall of rock rising steeply up on either side of the narrow valley.

'It's fantastic here,' he said. 'We'll have a picnic if we can't get across. I'll go to the shop and get some bread and cheese.'

He sounded as if he rather hoped that this was the case but then they both turned as a man emerged from the pines and walked down the path towards them. He was tanned and lean, with almost unnaturally blue eyes. Fresia guessed that he must be in his early forties. He was wearing beige leather trousers with tassels and a pair of cowboy boots. A knife hung from his belt.

'Let's ask Crocodile Dundee,' Joe said.

The man appraised Fresia rather shamelessly as he approached.

43

She looked back at him. He was handsome in a rather too arrogant, humourless way.

'Hello,' Joe said. 'Do you know how we can get across the bridge?'

Beige leather glanced at him dismissively without saying anything and Joe rolled his eyes at Fresia. Then their new acquaintance suddenly leapt on to the gate to the bridge and began to climb it. It was dangerous because on either side of the gate there was a long, steep drop down to the fast-flowing river. He began to edge his way around the side, putting one of his feet on to the other side of the gate and swinging himself out and round. Then he dropped on to the bridge. He looked at Fresia as if seeking approval for his athleticism.

'Da-da,' Joe sang a little mock fanfare.

'Are you going to Roberto's?' the man asked, looking askance at Joe.

'Yes,' she said.

'Wait. I'll be back with the key.'

He said this in the tone of one used to giving commands, a man who took himself immensely seriously.

'OK, copy that,' Joe said in English and Fresia nudged him in the ribs.

The man jogged away and Joe and Fresia both laughed as they watched him cross the bridge, which swayed alarmingly. When he reached the other side, he began to climb the hill at the same pace. They sat down and Fresia threw pebbles at an empty Sprite can.

The figure that returned to unlock the gate was not running. Joe and Fresia stood up and shaded their eyes from the sun as they watched the man crossing the bridge. Roberto Walker was no longer wearing a suit but faded Levis, white espadrilles and a T-shirt. His arms were golden-tanned and he seemed relaxed, elegant, at ease with himself.

'I told the woman in the lodge you might be coming . . .' he said. 'I'm sorry you've had to wait.'

'It's OK. That guy climbed over the gate.'

'His mother will kill him if she finds out he still does that. He is my neighbour, Tulio – his family own half of the land around here. Actually, you had better be careful, Fresia. He is also the village Don Juan and I think he has already taken rather a shine to you.'

'Not my type, I'm afraid,' Fresia said.

'And I thought it was me he fancied,' Joe said.

Roberto threw his head back and laughed.

'I'm not sure whether such an idea has ever entered his head.'

Joe and Fresia followed him across the slatted rope bridge which began to lurch and sway under their weight. Fresia glanced at Joe and rolled her eyes.

'Here we go again,' she said.

They climbed the hill until they reached a gate which opened on to a narrow path overhung with vines. On a pretty veranda shaded by an apple tree, a table and chairs presented a still life of interrupted reading – a pair of sunglasses, an empty china teacup and a collection of Alice Munro stories.

'You read in English?' Fresia said.

'Yes. My neighbour Barbara is English. She gets books sent from England and then she passes them on to me. I have become rather a connoisseur of Canadian writers recently.'

The path continued past the veranda and around the side of the kitchen to the back of the house through some cherry trees with hammocks slung between them. Fresia could hear voices, a sudden peal of laughter and then they emerged into a large garden. Both Fresia and Joe paused.

'Oh,' Fresia said.

Lemon, cherry, walnut and apricot trees surrounded a large green lawn, butterflies flickered in the flowerbeds. Small wet footprints marked the edge of a swimming pool with coloured floats and inflatable toys bobbing on its shimmering blue surface. Some children were playing in the water, squealing as they tried to climb on to a lipstick-pink rubber ring. By the side of the pool a diminutive tomato plant was weighed down by a single large fruit. It was as if the plant were indulging in a self-deprecating joke with the other trees. Beyond the splashing children, towards the end of the garden there was a secluded barbecue area with wooden benches and chairs arranged underneath a plum tree. Smoke was peeling off and up towards the mountain which suddenly seemed to be looming over them – a massive wave about to break. A man stood at the barbecue with apron and tongs. The group sitting at the table turned their faces to see the new arrivals.

Roberto Walker introduced Joe and Fresia. Barbara the supplier of books was a tall, blonde, elegant, Englishwoman who spoke Spanish with a near-perfect Chilean accent. She wore a blue sarong and played with a large necklace. Sitting next to her was Valentina, a strikingly beautiful, amber-eyed Chilean woman in her early forties.

She was an actress and was currently playing Regan in a production of *King Lear*. There was an obvious flirtatious intimacy between the two women which made Fresia immediately wonder whether they might be lovers. The man with the tongs was Pancho – he was a novelist. He was small, dark and bearded, with the face of a slightly self-satisfied joker. His wife Carmen seemed more reserved, unlikely to offer strong opinions but certain to hold them. Fresia guessed that she was the kind of woman who would scold her husband privately and yet be highly sensitive to any perceived criticism of him.

Joe and Fresia sat down and accepted a pisco sour and Joe immediately lit a cigarette even though he had just put one out. Fresia shifted in her chair as she felt Tulio, who was standing chatting behind her, move his little finger against her shoulder.

'I'd like to read you my poetry some time,' he murmured.

'Did you bring your swimming things?' Roberto asked them. 'You could have a dip before lunch. Just go into the house to change.'

Roberto's house was cool and shady; it smelled of casual wealth and old comfortable furniture. Fresia inspected the living room while Joe changed in the bathroom. It was a spacious room which Roberto obviously used for work as well as relaxation. There were soft, sinking sofas, ageing armchairs, a small portable TV in the corner which announced that its owner was relaxed about the medium – neither immune to its appeal nor dominated by it. A desk with stacks of paper, news clippings and a feather-light silver laptop computer stood by an open window through which the mountain loomed in the background and a hollyhock swayed as if trying to sneak a glance at the piled documents. A laughing young man looked out from a framed photograph but it wasn't the missing nephew. A small CD player stood on a bookshelf with a collection of jazz and classical CDs as well as Chilean folk music. There was a picture of the singer Violeta Parra on the wall bending over her guitar, above her declaration: *I sing of the difference between the true and the false.*

More than anything else, though, there were books: on shelves, stacked on a large mahogany table, piled up by the side of the desk. The smell of books was everywhere. There were books on literary theory, on art, on politics and history. There were slim volumes of poetry – Neruda, Yeats, Baudelaire – and there were novels in both English and Spanish. Roberto obviously liked García Márquez and Fresia commented on this to Joe as he emerged from the bathroom in his swimming trunks and unbuttoned shirt.

46

'I think Márquez is one of the most overrated novelists in the world,' Joe said. '*Love in the Time of Cholera* was nonsense, a nothing book. Vargas Llosa is a much better writer in spite of his rubbish politics . . .'

'You didn't even like *One Hundred Years of Solitude*?'

Both Joe and Fresia jumped as they turned to see Roberto standing in the doorway.

'Yeah, OK, it's not bad,' Joe said, recovering quickly. 'But I still think Vargas Llosa is a far better writer.'

'You still don't know who killed Palomino Molero?'

Joe laughed. 'It's not always necessary to know the perpetrator of a crime.'

Roberto raised his eyebrows. 'Not usually a problem in this country.'

'I like them both,' Fresia said.

'Wimp,' Joe said.

Fresia went into the bathroom and started to undress, sliding off her flip-flops and feeling the cool white tiles under her bare feet. She took out the swimming costume she had bought while shopping with her mum in Oxford Street on one of her last days in London. She laid it on the toilet seat and stared at it for a moment. They had eaten cakes in an Old Compton Street patisserie and then crossed the road to the hairdressers where her mother had read *Hello!* and *OK!* while Fresia had her hair cut. 'Chile,' sighed Claire – Fresia's friend and hairdresser. 'You're so lucky, I hardly ever get to go on holiday.' Fresia felt a pang now as she thought of Claire who – when not out misbehaving at night – was, in fact, virtually always on holiday.

Fresia sighed, unzipped her skirt and let it drop to the floor. As she took her T-shirt and bra off, she noticed in the mirror that there was a small open window looking out on to the passage. It would be possible for somebody to see her reflection in the bathroom mirror through the window so – worried that Tulio might be prowling about – she moved quickly to shut it. The window was wedged open with a piece of wood and as she removed it, Roberto Walker came into the passageway from another room. Did she hesitate, did she hesitate? If she did, it was only for a second but it was enough time for him to glance up and see her. She quickly shut the window. Did she hesitate? More importantly, did he think that she might have hesitated?

Splash! Fresia slid into the cold water of the pool. She swam vigorously to warm up and then floated, watching a scarlet butterfly flitting promiscuously between the roses, the mountain above them. This was pure freedom, this moment of suspension in the cool blue water, paddling with her hands and feet, murmurings and laughter from the table in the garden, the glare of the sun, smoke rising, a single reddening tomato, a flickering dragonfly.

The back of her head bumped a float. A little girl with plaits was clinging to a blue, smiling dolphin.

'I like your plaits,' Fresia said, standing up in the water.

'Why do you speak like that? Where are you from?' the child asked.

Fresia smiled at the child's directness.

'I'm a mermaid from under the sea.'

The child giggled. 'No you're not.'

'Oh yes I am. I swam all the way from England.'

'Where?'

'England. It's another country.'

'Are you Chilean or English?'

'Both. Neither.'

The little girl laughed again and twisted her plait. 'You can't be both and neither. That's stupid.'

'You're right. OK, I'm English.'

'Is England a long way away?'

'Yes,' Fresia said. 'Yes, it's a very long way away.'

'Further than Concepción?'

'Oh, much further.'

'Why do you live there?'

'My parents took me there when I was even younger than you.'

'How old are you?'

'I'm twenty-nine. How old are you?'

'I'm eight. Why did your parents take you so far away?'

'Because there were people here who wanted to hurt them. So they had to go away.'

The little girl considered this.

'That's sad,' she said finally.

'Yes it is,' Fresia said. 'It is sad. But it was a long time ago. Shall I pull you?'

And she rolled on to her back and pulled the dolphin along while the little girl laughed and then Joe swam over to chase the dolphin and make the child scream with delighted, terrified laughter by pretending to be a shark. Roberto came to the edge of the pool and smiled as he watched them playing. Fresia looked up beyond him to the mountain which had been in this place for millions of years, which had been here before the first humans arrived in America, either (depending on your favoured theory) from the north through the Bering Straits or in boats from Polynesia to the west, or across the ice-packed southern oceans from Australia.

The mountains loomed over the people swimming and talking and cooking in their gardens just at they had loomed over Picunche tribespeople and *conquistadores*, patriots and royalists, communists and fascists, exiles and returnees. Under their shadows, men had kicked their human cargo out of a pick-up truck, stood smoking casually with guns and shovels and a canister of petrol. 'Whistle, arsehole. Whistle *Venceremos*.' And they had laughed together at how they were making these *huevones* whistle the battle hymn of the old government, a song called 'We Shall Win' when here they were, clearly in a state of the most abject defeat. And those about to die – bemused and terrified by the sudden removal of everything that had made them safe from such persecution – had whistled the familiar tune and perhaps it even consoled them in those final moments as they stared up at the immense facticity of the mountain which had outlasted them, just as it would outlast their executioners, the humans playing at mermaids and sharks in the pool, the little girl with pigtails and a plastic dolphin.

'Why Chile?' Valentina asked Joe when he had explained what he was doing in the country. 'Why did you become interested in Chile in the first place?'

Joe paused with a chicken drumstick halfway to his mouth. Everybody was listening to him.

'When I was a kid, my granddad told me stories about Chile. He had fought in the Spanish Civil War and was active in his union. He helped Chilean refugees when they arrived in Scotland. I became kind of obsessed with Allende, I used to dream about him.'

'And you made it your career?' Pancho said.

'Well, there's not much that Chile can't teach you about the twentieth century,' Joe said.

Fresia suddenly imagined him standing in a lecture room.

'Did your grandfather teach as well?' Barbara asked him.

Joe glanced at her. 'He was a miner.'

'Really?' Barbara said.

'No, I'm lying.'

49

Fresia was taken aback by his sharpness. She watched him splash more yellow-white pisco into his glass, reach for the Coca-Cola.

'He must have been an extraordinary man,' Barbara blithely continued.

'Only if you think it's extraordinary for working-class people to read books or take an interest in politics or believe in education.'

'No I don't think that,' Barbara flushed slightly.

Joe shrugged. 'That's a lot of people's attitude. My grandparents believed in education; they sent my mum to university. What does that make her? What does that make me?'

Drunk, Fresia thought.

There was silence for a moment. Barbara toyed with her necklace. Valentina studied Joe solemnly, her eyes as large as eggs.

'Well, I'm not sure what it makes you,' Pancho said. 'But I think you are a little greedy.'

'Oh yeah? Why's that then?' Joe asked, balling his fists. Fresia glanced anxiously at him again.

'Most lonely children are satisfied with an imaginary friend to play with. You gave yourself a whole country.'

And everybody laughed.

Fresia turned to Roberto. 'Has there been any news about your nephew?'

'No, I must call my sister,' Roberto said, looking at his watch.

'Does nobody have any idea what happened?' Fresia asked.

'This time we *don't* know the perpetrator,' Roberto said. 'Pablo was in a bar with a girl, then he left for a disco and nobody has seen him since. And now they keep finding bodies but it's not him . . .'

'I saw that,' Joe said. 'They found another one in a lake the other day.'

'Who are they then?' Fresia asked. 'Not one of the disappeared?'

'That's the worst thing,' Roberto said. 'Nobody seems to know.'

'Or care,' Pancho said. 'The minute somebody says that it's not Pablo Errazuriz everybody loses interest. Perhaps it's only a woman. Or a kid from a shantytown.'

'Your sister must be in a terrible state,' Fresia said.

Roberto said, 'I have never seen a human being suffer as Gilda is suffering. Pablo was her favourite child. I'll probably go and see her again for a couple of days next week.'

'I'm going to the south soon,' Joe said.

'Are you?' Fresia was startled. 'For how long?'

She was disturbed at the idea of Joe going away, had grown used to his company.

'I don't know,' Joe said. 'I'm going to do some work at the University of Concepción. Visit some places in the Arauco region. You should come and visit while I'm there.'

'Maybe I will,' Fresia said. 'I would like to see where I was born.'

Afternoon began to slide into evening and Roberto collected lemon verbena from the garden to make tea. The sun disappeared on a light breeze, Fresia put on a sweatshirt. She tapped her wrist at Joe to signal that they should think about the return journey.

'You can both stay here,' Roberto said.

'But I'm driving down to Santiago tonight,' Valentina said. 'I'll take you. You don't need to go now.'

She was strumming gently on a guitar and the dying embers from the barbecue patterned the light across her face.

'Sing,' said Barbara, putting her hand on her arm. 'Sing for me before you go.'

Valentina looked down at the guitar curving easily around her crossed leg. She brushed a dark curl from her face and then she began to sing an old Violeta Parra song.

Corazón contesta
Porque palpitas asi
Porque palpitas?

And Fresia felt her own heart thumping and tears pricking at her eyes because Valentina had a lovely voice which rose like smoke into the night air and it had been one of her father's favourite songs: *Tell me, my heart, why you beat like that, why do you beat*? A watermelon wound, eyes that would never see again, blood on the manuscript. And now here in this valley, hemmed in by the mountains, the river flowing over rocks, and that voice, the human voice rising into the night air, the human heartbeat, the human lament. Because Violeta Parra – like Fresia's father – could go on no longer. Alone in the tent she had hoped would be a centre of popular art and surrounded by the indifference of the general public, she blew her brains out and stopped her heart from beating. *Tell me why you beat, like a little ship on a violent sea, like a vibrating bell, why do you treat me as the jailer does his prisoner*?

Valentina put down the guitar and a solitary tear dropped on to Fresia's hands which she held clasped tightly in front of her. When she looked up, she saw that Roberto was watching her and something old and familiar, wanted and unwanted, twisted inside her.

'What does Roberto Walker do?' Fresia asked Valentina as they drove back down to the city through the dark valley. Joe was sitting in the front, Fresia in the back. She loved driving in the darkness like this, warmth and enclosure, like rain on canvas at night.

'Well, he writes for newspapers and magazines. He does lots of reviewing, sits on juries for poetry prizes, lectures at the Catholic University. He comes from a very wealthy family. His mother's family are landowners. They own land in the south. And his father's family made money out of the privatisation of the banking system after the coup. His mother was the black sheep, had lots of lovers and wrote poetry. The children use the mother's surname.'

'Why?' Joe asked.

'Because it's English. They are really Rodríguez Walker and not Walker Rodríguez. Pancho always teases Roberto about it.'

A pair of truck lights lit up the curve of a road some way from them and then disappeared, the mountains were dark shadows, the river invisible now.

'He has a lovely house. It's such a beautiful place,' Fresia said. It seemed to her that Roberto was one of those people who carry a kind of quiet humour and reassurance with them. His money helped him to sustain this, of course, but he appeared at least to have done something graceful with it.

As if she knew what Fresia was thinking, Valentina said, 'Yes. It has an energy. Roberto worries about his wealth like a classic intellectual. But he could never give it up because it gives him freedom. He was able to study literature at the Catholic University, do his thesis at the Sorbonne in Paris.'

'There are worse things to do with your money, I suppose,' Joe said.

'Oh well, Roberto's not vulgar or a fascist like some of his relatives. And he's generous. Not just with his money but with people. It's easy to make fun of him as Pancho always does. But he's a good man.'

'He has a son?'

Valentina glanced at her. 'Why do you ask?'

'I saw the photo on his desk. I just thought it might be . . .'

'Ariel. He's in Paris.'

Fresia remembered Roberto as they had walked down the dark

hillside towards the bridge. He had steadied her arm on the narrow path and as they had come to the bridge he had touched her hip.

'Come and see me again.'

She had not been able to see his face properly in the darkness. His touch had been light but suggestive and suddenly on the dark path she had felt that stab of desire again, had wished that they had been alone at that moment.

The truck whose lights they had seen earlier rushed past them, almost making the car shake. Just the slightest contact, the smallest misjudgement on the part of either driver and they would have flown into the river below. *We are always so close to death*, Fresia thought almost nonchalantly. Valentina pushed her hair from her face and raised her eyebrows.

Now they were driving into the city again. There were McDonalds and Kentucky Fried Chicken restaurants, Blockbuster Video rentals, buses thundering towards the centre, low-rise red-brick housing projects with washing hanging in dusty courtyards. And far away, at the end of the Avenida Vicuña Mackenna, were the lights of the Plaza Italia and the San Cristóbal hill, its blind white statue staring sightless over the city of smog. Fresia looked at Joe whose head was resting against the window and whose eyes were closed. Valentina chuckled and said, 'I think he is dreaming.'

Night-train

'There's a big history with this team from San Bernardo,' Lalo said as they ate roast chicken and mashed potato in his house before the game, the TV news on in the background. 'I'm going to have to keep an eye on one or two of the players.'

'Why is there a history?' Joe asked. It was an important game, which they had to win to stay in touch with their rivals Nueva Estrella who they were playing in their final game. Lalo's biggest fear was to go into that game having already lost the championship.

'When we played them last season there was a massive fight. Players, supporters, it really kicked off. Some of their lot went away and came back with guns . . .' He grinned at Joe over his drumstick. '. . . there was a bit of shooting.'

'Oh right,' Joe said casually. 'And are they the same players this time round?'

Ximena laughed.

'Well, more or less,' Lalo said. 'Apart from the players who were suspended for the whole season for trying to shoot our goalkeeper. I've never seen that fat bastard run so fast in his life.'

'Don't worry, Joe,' Ximena said, handing Joe the tomato salad, '. . . they must have been pretty bad shots if they couldn't even hit Nacho's arse. I hope they're never called upon to defend the country.'

'They had a bad attitude towards us,' Lalo said, 'because of where we're from.'

'I suppose,' Ximena said, 'that it didn't help when some of their stuff went missing from the changing room. Or when Juanito told their captain that he had had his sister the night before and paid her with a cigarette.'

'No, that didn't help,' Lalo agreed. 'There'll be none of that this time round. We've got to be focused. If we win the championship, we can use the prize money to buy a new kit for the regional cup. This club can really go places.'

Joe's attention was suddenly caught by a report on the TV about the missing boy in Chillán.

'I met his uncle the other day,' he said.

Ximena turned the volume up. The police were investigating a possible love-triangle scenario. They were interrogating a boy who had been dating the girl who was the last person to see Pablo on the night he disappeared.

'Some of those rich kids are real psychos,' Lalo said. 'But if they're guilty they'll still get them off somehow. What's the uncle like?'

'He's very handsome,' Ximena said. 'I've seen him on the news a couple of times. With his sister.'

'More handsome than me?' Lalo asked, and she laughed and ruffled his hair.

'Impossible.'

'He's not that handsome really,' Joe said. 'He's quite old.'

'Really?' Ximena asked. 'He only looks like he's in his early forties.'

Joe shrugged. 'I don't know how old he is. He's got a great big house in the Cajon del Maípo with a swimming pool.'

Ximena looked at him quizzically. 'So?'

'There's something funny about him, that's all. He made money out of the privatisations after the coup.'

'Maybe that's got something to do with the boy's disappearance,' Lalo said.

'Maybe,' Joe agreed.

'I don't think so,' Ximena said. 'I've seen him interviewed. He was *simpatico*.'

They finished eating in silence, watching a report about a psychopath who had hacked an entire family to death in Arica, and then Joe wandered outside to where players and their families were waiting to get on the bus. Out of the corner of his eye he saw the woman who had come round and screamed about the money he had supposedly brought from Britain. She was standing hosing down the pavement and seemed to jerk the hose towards him as if she wished that the water could reach him. Joe was relieved to see Chelo and Nacho the goalkeeper, who always travelled to the games in Chelo's car. The car was parked behind the bus and the two friends sat in the front preparing themselves by drinking a beer and sharing a joint. Marcos, the team's star player, was sitting in the back with Wilson – the player whom Joe had displaced. Wilson turned away and stared sulkily out of the window when he saw Joe.

'Hey, Joe,' Nacho offered him the reefer through the open window. 'Wanna come with us? There's room in the back.'

'And if there isn't, you can always have Wilson's place,' Chelo said.

'It's OK, thanks,' Joe said, declining Nacho's reefer. 'I'll go with Lalo on the bus.'

'So, was there a gun battle at the game?' Magdalena asked.

'No,' Joe said. 'Although there was nearly a riot because we only scored with a few minutes to go and they claimed it was off-side.'

It was a hot evening and they were sitting in the Plaza Brazil drinking beer and eating *empanadas*. After the game, Joe had had tea with Ximena and Lalo and then taken a bus from Villa Caupolicán into town where he walked down one of the long streets heading away from the busy centre towards the run-down sunset west of the city. The large doors along the street opened on to shabby *conventillos* – crumbling, high-ceilinged, colonial tenement buildings built around courtyards which would have been long-gentrified in London. Offers of substantial renovation subsidies, however, had still failed to overcome the stigma of these conveniently located houses with their suggestion of age, of history, the rebellious and promiscuous rabble. Now, flashy apartment blocks with balconies were springing up around the fashionable and bohemian Barrio Brazil; brand-new flats, the sign of social arrival. Even these, however, would never attract the real bourgeoisie, whose neurotic obsession to be among their own kind was undiminished by either time or fashion and whose talons would remain forever clasped to their traditional perch in the north-east of the city.

Magdalena had brought Vasily with her, a young computer specialist from Guillermo's research institute. Vasily was from La Pincoya – a tough shantytown on the outskirts of the city. He was good-looking, tall, with long hair and a tattoo of Che Guevara on his arm, and he hated the police more passionately than anybody that Joe had ever met.

'What does La Pincoya actually mean?' Joe asked Vasily.

'A mermaid from the island of Chiloé,' Vasily mumbled through a mouth full of *empanada*. 'Brings you luck.'

'Here comes your little girlfriend,' Magdalena said to Joe as Fresia waved from across the square.

'Is she your girlfriend?' Vasily asked.

'No,' Joe said, glaring at Magdalena.

'You're Guillermo's niece?' Vasily asked Fresia when she sat down and ordered a beer. 'The one from England?'

'An exile,' Magdalena said flatly.

Fresia glanced at Magdalena. 'That's right,' she said. 'Well my parents were exiles.'

Fresia turned to Joe who had remained quiet during this edgy introduction. He was staring at one of the palm trees in the square where some kids were launching a little purple kite.

'How is the lovely Inés de Suarez?' she asked him.

'What? Oh, she's looking after her chickens and worrying about Pedro de Valdivia.'

'Why, what's Pedro up to?'

'He's down in the south setting up forts and chasing after Lautaro who will eventually set a brilliant trap to capture him.'

'Poor Pedro.' She grinned at him, picked up Magdalena's cigarette box and turned it round and round in her hand.

Could you feel pity for Pedro de Valdivia, the man who (according to the case for the prosecution at least) covered the country in solitude and scars? Christmas Eve, the desolate smoking ruins of a fort, wave after wave of attacks, the summer sun beating down on the small group of *conquistadores.* Horses were their strength and Lautaro knew this. Having grown up in the stables of the Spanish he also knew the smell of horseshit, he knew the difference between a man and the horse that carried him, knew that they were divisible, that the enemy was not a bearded centaur. *Bring them down,* he told his warriors, *we'll deal with them on the ground,* and so . . . a screaming rearing animal, the clash of armour on hard ground, a bearded armadillo spinning in the dust.

Did they make him drink melted gold to punish him for his avarice? Or bring him before the chiefs and berate him for invading their land until he was struck a massive blow from behind? Was there really a party in which the celebrating Mapuches drank *chicha* from his skull and made his ribs into flutes? Or did he crawl away unnoticed from the battlefield, to find shade beneath a monkey-puzzle tree and review the trajectory of his eventful, ebbing life? Did he think back to the harsh land of his birthplace in Extremadura, the slap of the Atlantic against a ship's bow, black-haired Inés with the city's conflagration gleaming in her bloody sword, a burning boat upon the beach, the flame-lapped sail of a vessel that would never navigate the long coastline, never return to the place where it all began in the City of Kings, the newly-founded empire of a brutal swineherd?

Was it the sound a bird made (Chi-le, Chi-le)? Did it cry out from the branches of the monkey-puzzle tree above the body of the dying Governor? Could you pity the invader, the torturer?

Perhaps he lay there contemplating the scars and the solitude, the mysterious exigencies of conquest that drove him first across the ocean and then on this final journey, beside the fierce mountains, the coves and inlets and bays, from the punishments of the desert to the volcanoes and lakes of the south. Perhaps in the end he sighed at the strange, violent, beauty of it all as the sun dropped slowly into the sea beyond the Gulf of Arauco, as his blood seeped into the earth he had invaded.

Or perhaps his teeth just went flying from his head as they whacked him on the head from behind when he was least expecting it.

Either way – poor old Pedro.

Joe looked at Fresia and smiled.

'I'm taking the night-train to Concepción on Friday.'

'Can I still come down and see you while you're there?'

'Of course.'

A long-haired figure with a guitar wandered over and started singing 'Ojala' by Silvio Rodríguez. Vasily scowled at him.

'Get lost,' he said. The singer hesitated so Vasily fixed him with a ferocious stare until the singer hurried to another table still singing, followed by his female companion shaking a hat.

'Don't you like Silvio Rodríguez?' Fresia asked him.

'Can't stand him,' Vasily said. 'I hate hippies and I hate all that hippie crap that Magdalena listens to.'

Magdalena glanced at Vasily as if such false consciousness were barely worthy of comment. Then she beckoned the waiter for another bottle of beer.

Santiago, San Bernardo, Rancagua, San Fernando, Curicó, Talca, Linares, Parral, Chillán, Nuble, Concepción.

Across the Maule, across the Itata rivers and down to the Bío-Bío.

Under the peaks of Tinguirirrica (4,300 m.), Peteroa (4,090 m.) and Campanario (4,200 m.).

The train to the south dragged itself slowly out of Santiago's Central Station and Joe waved goodbye to Fresia and Magdalena who had come to see him off. He watched them walk off together and wondered if they were going to start an argument but they were both laughing.

'I'll come down soon,' Fresia had promised. 'Do lots of work so that you can devote your time to entertaining me.'

'Come back soon,' Magdalena had said. 'You've only just arrived and then you rush off.'

Joe loved the train to the south, a journey he had made several times before. He had booked himself one of the wood-panelled compartments with a bunk bed and dropped his bag there before going to the restaurant car where he ordered a pisco with coke and a *churrasco* sandwich. He sat and read the paper, smiling at a story about the blood-weeping Virgin who had been discovered to be a fraud. The person responsible had had to flee their home after an angry mob had descended, determined to avenge the exploitation of their gullible faith. They had burned down the shack, and the Virgin – who had caused so much furore with her ruby tears – had disappeared in a brief crackle of flame, a twist of oily smoke.

There was also a small piece on yet another body which had been found in woods near to Chillán during the search for the young teenager Pablo Errazuriz. Some were saying that it might be the body of a union leader who had disappeared after the coup. Others claimed that the corpse probably belonged to the victim of an international gang (possibly Chinese or Israeli) stealing human organs from Chileans to sell to foreigners. Whether the body was one of Pinochet's victims or somebody whose kidneys had found a new home in Tel Aviv, it brought to eight the number of bodies found since the beginning of the search. None of them was Pablo Errazuriz.

The paper carried a picture of Gilda Errazuriz, the young boy's mother. Her face was quite destroyed by sorrow so it was impossible for Joe to tell whether or not she bore any resemblance to Roberto.

That night he lay on his bunk beneath a thin blanket watching the starry night, the lights from southern villages. He listened to Violeta Parra on his Discman – *cuecas*, waltzes, polkas, *tonadas* – the clapping beat of the south like the rhythm of the train through the night.

Da-dum da-dum da-dum da-dum

. . . *Blue violets for my sorrow, red carnations for my passion* . . .

Songs of lost and unrequited love.

He drifted in and out of sleep, strange anxiety dreams, sweat on his pillow, jolted about on the wooden bunk.

What is it with you and Chile, Joe?

The smell of coal-fires in an icy sky, the cawing of crows, starched sheets in strange rooms. When he was little he would lie in the dark and feel the noise growing all around him, the crescendo of the clock, the roar of his skin against the sheets. He remembered his grandmother stroking his forehead, his grandfather telling him stories about the life down the pit, about the battle of the Ebro, about a country so far away that it was right at the end of the world. And that was the story that had somehow caught and grown in the mind of a troubled and imaginative boy – the brave President in the burning palace, defying the tanks and the planes with his machine-gun.

And that story had shaped his life ever since, through his Ph.D. on the nineteen-eighties protest movement against Pinochet to his position as a young university lecturer and now here, lying on a bunk on a jolting train thinking about a girl who had been snatched up by history's tornado and dropped in a place thousands of miles away. It had brought him to the smell of morning coffee, the sound of shouted jokes between the conductor and the guard, the dawn rising over the river which had once been a frontier between two nations.

It was this land that had produced the miners who had arrived in Fife, the fleeing families for whom his grandfather had organised shelter and food, bringing stories of a faraway place between the mountains and the sea, of terrible loss, bewildering catastrophe.

The train crawled with a dreary slow movement as it approached the hook of land jutting out into the Pacific, the city of Concepción with its white-arched university, cradle of hotheaded revolutionaries who demanded *patria o muerte*, paying dearly later for their impatience. Beside the city lay the port of Talcahuano – famous for the variety of its brothels – where Joe had once spent New Year's Eve with some students from the University of Concepción. They had eaten *ceviche*, watched sea lions splash by the seafront fish market, staggered drunkenly down to the port to listen to the midnight hooting of moored ships as the sailors sent fireworks streaking from the decks to explode over the black sea.

To the south of the city, across the river, lay the towns of hard poverty – Lota and Coronel – where fish were hung out to dry outside flimsy beach shacks and the old coal-fields unravelled under the ocean. Families with German surnames once made their fortunes here, Communist organisers recruited members to the Party and skinny children fished for waste coal in the surf. And, beyond these, were the old frontier settlements where the Spanish built their forts: Los Angeles, Yumbel, Angol, Collipulli, Nacimiento, Mulchén and, of course, Cañete, where Caupolicán writhed on the stake, where Pedro de Valdivia tumbled from his horse into the dust.

All of this awaited Joe as he stared out at the morning sun and drank sweet black coffee from a plastic cup brought to him by the good-natured conductor.

The Mermaid in the Pool

Bowls of tomato salad and bottles of wine stood on the table in Roberto's garden beside plates of *humitas* – puréed corn, spices, herbs and garlic tied up and cooked like little parcels in the leaves of the cob.

'I haven't had one of these for ages,' said Fresia, snipping the string holding the package together and peeling away the long green leaves to reveal the savoury, steaming, golden treasure inside. 'Oh God that smells delicious, I think these really are my favourite Chilean food.'

She had woken that morning and thought about calling Joe. Then she remembered that he was down in the south and had felt a vague ache for company. *Come again,* Roberto had said. Contemplating the journey alone had been both intimidating and exciting but once the idea had entered her head she knew that she would feel dissatisfied with herself if she did not go. She had felt shy as she had walked across the garden and everybody turned to look at her. Then the little girl with plaits to whom she had spoken in the pool had run to her side and shouted, 'It's the English mermaid,' and walked across the grass holding her hand.

Fresia ate her *humita* hungrily while Roberto poured her a glass of wine.

'What's happening with your nephew?' Fresia asked him.

Roberto shrugged. 'My sister has started getting some terrible letters. People saying that they've got Pablo and describing what they're doing to him, taunting her that she won't recognise her son when they find the body. And then other people saying that he is only getting this much attention because he comes from a wealthy family . . .'

'Which is true, of course,' Fresia said.

Roberto glanced at her. 'Yes it's true. But writing such letters to a mother out of her mind with grief and anxiety is lacking somewhat in compassion.'

'Compassion,' Fresia echoed vaguely.

'It's not a quality that has a very good track record in this country,' Roberto said.

'It's not a quality that is very popular in many places at the moment,' she said.

She remembered her father one morning staring at a photo in a Sunday supplement. The photograph showed just the legs of a woman hanging from a tree somewhere in Bosnia. Twelve inches between the dangling feet, from which one shoe had fallen, and the forest floor covered in autumn leaves. He had torn it out and kept it by his desk.

Roberto jiggled the espadrille on the end of his foot. Behind him, Tulio was staring at her and making little gestures with his eyebrows towards the house as if suggesting that they should sneak off there together. Fresia ignored him – he was really starting to annoy her.

'Not all of the letters are from freaks though. Some of them seem more serious. I'm going down soon to help check out some of the rumours.'

The afternoon sun grew fierce and people wanted to bathe but Roberto's pool was full of kids from the village and he didn't want to tell them to get out. So they collected their stuff to go to the much larger public pool at the campsite across the river, which was owned by Tulio's family.

Fresia watched a tiny lizard, a flicker of brilliant green on the end of her white towel as she sat with Barbara by the pool. Tulio was reciting some poetry to a couple of Norwegian girls who were on a rafting trip. Pancho rolled his eyes and said that this proved that prose was a superior form of artistic expression to poetry. Roberto laughed and said that Pancho was a philistine and that nobody had to choose between the two and that poetry could not be held responsible for Tulio.

Barbara was an animated gossip and told Fresia that her husband was a very wealthy and charming diplomat who was incapable of sexual fidelity. During his posting to Chile, Barbara had liked the country so much that she had decided to stay. She also told Fresia that Valentina had had a relationship with Roberto Walker but that it had finished many years ago and that she and Barbara were now sort-of-occasional-lovers.

'It's all go up here,' Fresia murmured.

'Oh yes,' Barbara said cheerfully, turning her face to the sun. 'It's the mountain air. Why did your friend not come with you today?'

'He's in the south.'

After the train had departed, she and Magdalena had gone to a dingy bar near the Central Station. They had drunk cheap brandy and argued about whether exiles had had an easy life compared to those who stayed and fought the dictatorship. Their discussion had become animated enough to attract the attention of a group of men sitting at the next table who smirked and made lewd comments until Magdalena turned and said something quiet and vicious. 'Lesbians,' one of the men had muttered angrily but they left them alone after that.

'I rather liked Joe, ' Barbara said, 'even though he did jump down my throat. They can be terribly touchy, of course, the Scots. But I thought he was an interesting young man, especially if he comes from as poor a background as he says he does.'

Fresia was relieved that Joe could not hear this utter mis-representation of what he had said. She liked Barbara and thought she meant well, but she was still a monument to unconscious snobbery.

'I don't think that was quite his point,' she said.

'Perhaps that was my problem,' Barbara said. 'I couldn't really see what his point was. But never mind, there is always something lovely about somebody who has a passion and he obviously has a tremendous passion for this country.'

'Yes he does,' Fresia agreed.

'And what about you, Fresia?'

'What about me?'

'Well, what are your plans?'

Plans, Fresia thought. Plans were important, they gave life a structure. She thought about Joe's laptop, the pile of books and papers beside it, books about wild men and shamanism, the psy-chosexuality of violence. She had teased him and asked him if that was his idea of a bit of light reading and he had laughed and said that a lot of it was *pura paja* – post-modern wank. Sometimes she came round to find him reading in the half-light, immersed in his complicated worlds of semi-fictional historical figures; he would talk about Lautaro learning about the Spanish as he cared for their horses, the clever ambushes they laid. Now he had taken the train to Concepción to continue his work. Joe had a plan, a structure to his life.

'Fresia?'

'Oh sorry. Plans? I don't really have any at the moment,' Fresia said.

'You should try the skiing out here,' Barbara patted her hand kindly. 'There are some wonderful slopes. Around Chillán, for example.'

Fresia nodded dumbly and felt a sudden lump of sadness in her throat. Half-a-person? Was that what she had become? Sitting here with this woman she barely knew, talking about skiing – an activity which held no interest for her whatsoever. And suddenly she thought longingly of her camera equipment, barely used since she got here. That was what she did, what she was good at, she had to get back to that.

'Ah look,' Barbara pointed across the pool. 'The evil Regan has arrived.'

And she waved at Valentina who raised her arm in salute.

The sun began to disappear. Pancho and Carmen said they were driving back to Santiago, offering her a lift.

'Oh don't go now,' Barbara said. 'Valentina can take you down later.'

'I may not go later,' Valentina said. 'I'm tired. I might drive down tomorrow morning.'

'Well, I'm sure one of us can put you up,' Barbara said. 'Then, if you want, you can go down with Valentina in the morning. Or take a *collectivo* or whatever.'

'OK,' Fresia said.

She felt dizzy from the sun and did not particularly want to get in a car straight away.

As they walked back down to the river, they passed Barbara's house. Fresia noticed a gaggle of children and adults standing at the gates of her neighbour's property. Then she heard a whistle and a noise which sounded exactly like a steam train, which *was* a steam train.

'Ah, Javier is taking the train out,' Barbara said. 'You must see this, Fresia. My neighbour is a physics professor at the Catholic University. He's an absolute nut about trains. He built a model railway which goes all the way around our properties. It's rather wonderful.'

The children began to shriek as the hissing and puffing intensified and a little steam train appeared on a miniature track. There was just room on the small engine for a smiling waving man who looked like a Chilean Casey Jones in stripy overalls and goggles. The wagons behind were filled with delighted children. The man hunched up on the engine waved and blew the whistle as they passed and then the bonsai train puffed busily round and disappeared into a tunnel by the side of Barbara's garden.

Fresia felt a strange shudder as she heard the cries of the children from the train in the tunnel. She looked up at the mountains surrounding them, the cars heading back towards Santiago. The evening was cool; her shoulders and face were burned by the sun. The dog opposite raised its head from its paws but then slumped down again as if it could no longer be bothered to bark.

When they got back to Roberto's house, Fresia took a shower, letting the cold water run over her throbbing skin. When she came out of the bathroom, Roberto was making tea in the kitchen. Barbara and Valentina were sitting on the veranda.

'Feel better?' he asked.

'Better?'

'I thought you were a little subdued.'

'It was just the sun.'

She did, suddenly, feel strange and disorientated.

'You seemed sad.'

And Fresia felt the lump in her throat again, an agonising loneliness. How had she got here? What was she doing here with these people she barely knew? It was so foolish. She suddenly felt very dizzy. Roberto frowned at her.

'Are you OK? Look, let me just take the tea out to Barbara and Valentina. Why don't you go and sit in the living room for a while and I'll be right back.'

She went into the living room and wandered to the window by Roberto's desk. She looked again at the photograph of the smiling young man on the desk. A manuscript also lay there and beside it, face down, an open book of Neruda's poetry. The manuscript had some pencilled notes on it so she guessed that Roberto was correcting his own work. She picked up the book and turned it round. It was open at a poem called 'Fable of the Mermaid and the Drunks'. Fresia smiled as she read the familiar lines about a lost mermaid who strays into a tavern filled with drunken men who laugh at her and torture her with their cigarettes.

. . . Her eyes were the colour of faraway love . . .

She put the book down as Roberto came back in with some tea.

'How are you feeling?' he asked and she nodded, although she was still feeling both dizzy and alienated from her surroundings.

'It was the train,' she said.

'The train?'

She explained about the children on the miniature railway and the evening that she had spent with her father at Francisco Miranda's house in London, the Wimpy bar afterwards, then the journey home through the darkening countryside. If Roberto was confused by this association, then he was polite enough not to show it.

'It's so long ago,' Fresia said.

And perhaps that was the source of the sadness. She could never be that child again, nor even be sure if she *was* that child, what their connection was, how she had got from there to here. She could remember the exact colour of the sky that day, the smell of the station in the evening, the doors of the train slamming, the fuzzy texture of the seats, falling asleep under his arm. The sorrow was not just for her father's death but for her parents and the times they lived in, for that lost time, that other era of her childhood and all the things that surrounded it, things that could never return, not for them, not for her.

. . . Her lips moved soundlessly in the coral light . . .

Roberto said, 'I'm glad you came back here. I didn't know whether you would.'

'Thank you for inviting me. Although I don't really know what I'm doing here. I suddenly felt so lonely. I don't mean to be rude . . .'

'Oh don't worry,' he said. 'I understand what you mean. It is strange, isn't it? We've only just met after all. I want you to feel that this place is here for you if you need it.'

'It is lovely up here. But don't you feel isolated sometimes?'

'Isolated?' he laughed. 'Sometimes I could do with a bit more isolation. I always have visitors, not all of them welcome. And I'm not a complete recluse. I do go down to the city sometimes.'

'Oh yes, Valentina said that you teach . . . are you preparing a lesson?' She gestured towards the desk.

'That? No, it's just a short article.'

'And who's that in the photograph?'

'My son, Ariel. He's about four years younger than you, I guess.'

'Does he live in Santiago?'

'No, he lives in Paris at the moment.'

'Studying?'

'Well, that was the original idea.'

'What about his mother?'

'We're not together any longer.'

'Oh right. Sorry.'

'Why?'

Fresia laughed. 'I don't know, it's just the kind of thing you say, I suppose. Maybe you couldn't stand the sight of each other any more.'

'Oh no, not at all, it wasn't that bad.'

'That's good. Anyway, I wasn't trying to pry into your private life. What is your article about?'

'Neruda and death.'

'Do you think that is what the poem is about? The mermaid dying?'

Fresia knew that with this question she was admitting that she had been snooping at his desk but she did not care.

'Well, partly,' Roberto said. 'But it's an ambiguous ending. She is also cleansed and reborn. I think that it's a very mysterious poem, which is why I like it. In fact I would say that it's my favourite Neruda poem. What about you? Do you have a favourite?'

'I like the epitaph he wrote for Tina Modotti. About her heart listening to the roses.'

And suddenly, Fresia could feel tears welling up in her eyes again. This was so ridiculous and quite unlike her. She would look like some kind of emotional incontinent or, worse, somebody pretending to be so deep that they could be moved to tears by some fragments of poetry. *Pull yourself together, you idiot*, she told herself sternly.

. . . *Swimming toward never again, toward her death.*

A little girl in her favourite cheesecloth shirt sleeping happily under her father's arm after a day out in London while he stares at the darkening countryside. The echoing laughter of children as a miniature train disappears into a tunnel, a last wave from its smiling driver, a girl with plaits playing with a plastic dolphin. *Is England a long way away? Yes, it's a very long way away.* A grey London sky, a house of exiles with a blue plaque, caged animals, a depressed condor that had made her father angry, the funny-shaped frankfurter in her burger, swinging her feet on the red plastic chair, eyes the colour of faraway love, eyes that would never see again, a room by a roof terrace, an old treasured photograph, swimming toward never again.

'Are you sure . . .' Roberto said, '. . . that your preference for that poem isn't just professional solidarity?'

'I haven't taken any photos for ages,' she said.

'Well, you haven't been here for very long. Just let things happen in their own time.'

The tears rolled down her face and Roberto silently handed her a handkerchief.

'I don't know what's the matter with me today,' she said. 'I'm never normally like this.'

He stood up and put his hand lightly on her head.

'Go and lie down for a bit in there. Come back to us when you're ready,' he said and left her.

She went into the room he indicated. It was his bedroom and smelled faintly of aftershave. The windows were open and a light breeze came through; she could hear the sound of somebody somewhere playing a cello. She lay down on sheets which were soft and white and smelled so deliciously clean that she slipped quickly into sleep.

She woke up after half an hour, remembered their conversation, the feel of his hand on her head, and was suddenly filled with an aching, almost agonising desire that the fading light only accentuated. She lay for a moment listening to the river below them and then she got up, washed her face and returned to the veranda.

'Is everything OK?' Barbara asked. 'Roberto said you were feeling a little poorly from the sun.'

'I think I underestimated it,' Fresia said. 'It made me go all weird. Tearful.'

She smiled apologetically at Roberto.

'It can do that,' Barbara nodded. 'It's my fault. I should have warned you but there I was wittering away about my feckless ex-husband. Remember that there's a bloody great big hole in the ozone layer around this part of the world.'

Dusk embraced darkness and moths started to flutter around the light from the kitchen. Valentina yawned several times. She had all the glamour of a tulip at exactly the point before its real decline, the curly hair falling across a face showing just a few lines of age, the crow's-feet around her eyes, the slight downturn of the mouth.

'I should take you home,' Barbara touched her arm. 'Do you want to stay with us, Fresia, or save yourself the walk and trust Roberto? I'm sure you'll be safe with him.'

'And more comfortable,' Valentina said. 'That camp-bed is horrible. Besides, if the sun has affected you then you're better off just staying here.'

'Although I'm sure Tulio would put you up,' Barbara said and they laughed and imitated the little eyebrow movements that Tulio had made to Fresia.

'Did you see that?' Fresia asked.

'Oh, he does it to everybody. The worst thing is it often works. I've seen some very pretty girls disappear with him.'

'There's no accounting for taste,' Valentina got up. She looked at Fresia and then at Roberto and there was something odd in her look – not hostile or unpleasant but still vaguely unsettling.

'Well?' Barbara said to Fresia. 'We'll see you in the morning maybe?'

'The fewer times I have to cross that bridge the better,' Fresia said, trying not to blush. She sounded foolish.

'Well, if you want a lift to Santiago tomorrow, be at the house at ten,' Valentina said.

'I'll take you down to the bridge,' Roberto said to them. 'Fresia, why don't you collect some *cedrón* from the garden and we'll have some tea when I get back. Although there is more wine and whisky if you would prefer that.'

'Tea will be fine,' Fresia said.

When Roberto had gone, she wandered out into the darkened garden. She suddenly realised that she had no idea what she was looking for and poked about a little among the herbs, smelling mint and lavender and basil but not the lemon verbena with which Roberto made the fragrant tea. It was still quite hot and she wandered over to the pool, took her flip-flops off and sat on the edge. She dipped her feet in, made little splashes which sent the abandoned plastic dolphin bobbing to the other side of the pool.

She sat in silence for a moment. The river flowing through the dark mountain valley. A sudden disturbance of wings in the branches of a cherry tree. The sky cluttered with stars.

'Is there a lost mermaid in my garden?' Roberto had returned from the river and came and sat beside her, kicked off his espadrilles and dipped his own feet in the pool.

'I couldn't find the *cedrón*,' Fresia said.

'I hope you're not going to start crying about it,' he said.

'Don't be so cheeky. I'm fine now. It was just an excess of sun. The sleep sorted me out.'

70

'That's good.'

His foot touched hers in the pool. She looked down at it, did not move her foot away. Then she looked up at the sky.

'There's no man-in-the-moon in Chile,' she said.

'Hadn't you noticed?' His toe had started the tiniest of caresses. 'You're on the other side of the world now.'

Impaled

Sharks and rays began to swim across the screen of Joe's laptop as he stared out from his window to the low hills covered with eucalyptus and pine on the darkening horizon.

The war in the Arauco region against the Mapuches became increasingly savage after the death of Pedro de Valdivia. For a time it seemed as if Lautaro might succeed in driving the Spanish out of Chile but then he was betrayed and captured as he advanced towards Santiago. After the battle of Peteroa, his head was displayed on a stake in the capital. The violence of the campaign against the Mapuches increased, distressing even some members of the Spanish court. The warrior Galvarino was dragged before the Governor and his hands cut off. Galvarino departed cursing the Indians in the service of the Spaniards and swearing revenge. Meanwhile, the fierce Caupolicán was also captured and horribly executed in the city of Cañete. The story goes that his wife Fresia . . .

She was coming tomorrow; perhaps now her face would be pressed to the window of a bus or a train, staring out at the passing countryside. Joe had called her a couple of times during the week at Guillermo's but she had not been there. Then she had called on Thursday and told him that she would arrive at the weekend.

'Where will you stay?' Joe had asked.

He was staying in a room in the house of Oscar Ramirez, a good-natured history professor from the University of Concepción with garlic-white hair and patches of vitiligo which had appeared a few months after the coup. Oscar had spent many years in exile in Canada – his wife was currently visiting their children in Toronto. He lived now in a suburb across the river from Concepción and helped run an Internet group which sought to protect the environment around the Bío-Bío and stop the construction of hydroelectric dams in its upper reaches.

'Don't worry,' Fresia had said. 'I've booked a room at a hotel. I'll call you from there.'

'I'll come and meet you.'

'There's no need. Besides, I'll probably want to sleep for a bit.'

'How are you coming? On the bus or the train?'

'I haven't made my mind up yet.'

Oscar had raised his eyebrows when Joe had told him the name of Fresia's hotel.

'I wonder what her father would have made of that. That's one of the most expensive hotels in the city.'

'Did you know him then?'

'Oh yes. A very difficult man. He had many enemies, not all of them from the right wing. Is there something between you and this girl, his daughter?'

'Why do you ask that?'

'The way you bring the conversation back to her always. You like saying her name.'

And Joe had smiled, allowing Oscar to think that there was something between them, pleased with the idea. Perhaps, after all, there *was* something between them – she was coming to see him and they would be alone together.

'Bring her round if you like,' Oscar said. 'I'll be interested to see how Ricardo's daughter has turned out.'

. . . dashed their infant child to the ground in fury at his capture. The poet Alonso de Ercilla recounted this story (along with legends such as Caupolicán's trial of strength) in his epic work La Araucania. It is a work in which the Spanish poet is unable to conceal his admiration for the bravery of the Mapuche resistance because, in spite of all the atrocities, the invaders were unable to subdue the indigenous people. Concepción was destroyed on numerous occasions and finally the Bío-Bío river became a frontier between the two societies, with only Valdivia and the island of Chiloé to the south under Spanish control. Both enclaves were supplied by sea until Chile's independence in the nineteenth century, when the Chilean government acted with considerable brutality to assert its authority over the south and 'pacify' the Arauco region . . .

Joe always joked that he had no religious, spiritual or mystical leanings, that he was a die-hard historical materialist. In general this was true – he had inherited his grandfather's dislike of organised religion and he also had no time for weak-minded mysticism. Nevertheless, he was susceptible to the poetic energy of this place, the river curling up through dark forests, the necklace of city lights at the point where its waters collided with the ocean, the narrow peninsula of the *desembocadura*. Bío-Bío, it also sounded like bird-song, the wide frontier separating the bearded invaders from the angry glittering eyes of those they could not conquer.

He closed his eyes as the soft night breeze teased his papers.

'It's strange to think that my dad taught here once,' Fresia said as they sat beneath an intense blue sky watching black-necked swans drifting slowly across the lake.

She had called Joe from her hotel at lunch-time and they had agreed to meet at the famous white arch of the School of Medicine – the gateway into the green campus of the university. Joe had been worried that she might not find it and had offered to pick her up but Fresia had refused, saying that it was not far and that she would attempt to be adventurous.

She had not been sleepy or needed much recovery time from the journey because, rather than bus or train, she had caught a plane from Santiago that morning. She had dismissed Joe's disappointment and told him that there had been no turbulence, it had been a beautiful morning, and that sometimes you could see both of Chile's boundaries – the line of mountains on one side, and, on the other, the sea stretching away to the horizon.

Still Joe *was* disappointed, especially as it disturbed his imaginings of Fresia travelling through the night towards him. He said he thought that it was an unromantic way to travel, that her first trip to the south should have been by night-train. Fresia just shrugged.

'Oh, it was romantic enough for me. And it got me here in forty-five minutes instead of ten hours. Why do you think these swans have black necks?'

'I don't know,' Joe said. 'Some mystery of evolution I suppose.'

During the afternoon, they wandered about Concepción, passing the cathedral steps where, during Pinochet's rule, Sebastian Acevedo had doused himself in petrol and turned himself into a flaming torch in protest at the detention of his children. In the Plaza de Armas they sat by a fountain where mermaids blew water from pipes, little stone hybrids with bare chests and elaborate fishy tails. Then they took a bus from the town centre across the bridge to Oscar's house.

'But the river's so low,' Fresia exclaimed.

It was true. The Bío-Bío was wide but shallow – the river-bed exposed in places like bald patches, gulls pecking in the mud.

'Why?' Fresia turned to Joe in disappointment.

'Well, partly because of the weather,' Joe said. 'And then there are the dams higher up.'

'That's a crime,' Fresia said.

'Talk to Oscar about it,' Joe said. 'His whole life is dedicated to this river.'

Oscar had made a big bowl of punch with fresh peaches in it and a *pastel de choclo* was baking in the oven. They sat and drank punch and laughed at the participants on Chilean *Family Fortunes* who were dumber even than their British counterparts. The Gonzalez family from Puerto Montt could not even manage to name four ingredients you might find in an *empanada*.

Fresia padded about the living room like an inquisitive cat.

'Are those your children, Oscar?' She gestured to a family photograph.

'Yes,' Oscar said. 'But they'll never come back here now.'

'Well, I can understand why they might not,' Fresia replied. 'What do they do?'

'My son? God knows. He says that he's an artist but the only art form he appears to have perfected is finding people gullible enough to sponge off. My daughter is a fashion designer, she does OK for herself. It's not just that they won't come back, it's that they are so lazy and contemptuous about it and they are always telling me what it is like here, which I wouldn't mind if they knew anything about it. My son is the worst. "Chileans are this and Chileans are that." How can you generalise about a country or a people like that? Especially when he's spent the grand total of three weeks here. If a Canadian person said that, they would quite rightly be called a racist.'

Fresia laughed, clearly able to imagine the scenario and remember her own outrage when she first returned.

'Well, don't be too hard on them,' she said.

'Too hard on them! They're adults now. They should grow up and get on with things, stop blaming everybody else for their problems. I didn't *choose* to lose my house and job and country just to make their lives more complicated.'

'I'm sure they know that really,' Fresia said.

Oscar poured them more of the punch, which was surprisingly strong.

'I think it's weird,' Joe said. 'They have the chance of a second country.'

'It's different for them than it is for you,' Fresia said with a sudden sharpness that surprised Joe.

They went out on to the patio to eat their *pastel de choclo*. Fresia took a piece of lemon verbena and held it to her nose while Oscar brought out some glasses and a huge flagon of home-made *aguardiente* with cherries. They sat and drank the strong sweet spirit while he told them about the battle for the Bío-Bío, about how they had once believed that they could change the world and now could only aim at saving a river.

Oscar's words suddenly reminded Joe of a scene from the book he was reading – a group of young men in the Balkans smoking and hotly debating on the bridge over the Drina river just at the outbreak of the First World War. Every generation, according to the author, believes that it is witnessing either the dawn of a new civilisation or the ultimate catastrophe of humanity but – and the phrase had stuck in Joe's mind – *it all depends on your place and angle of view*.

It grew late and Fresia yawned and asked Joe if he would take her to the bus stop so that she could return to her hotel.

'But you can stay here,' Oscar said.

'Thank you,' Fresia replied. 'I hope you don't think this is rude but I was quite looking forward to a couple of nights in a hotel and I've already paid. So . . .'

'Well it *is* a good hotel,' Oscar said. 'You'll be more comfortable there than on the sofa. What about tomorrow? Do you want to borrow the car? You could go to the beach or something.'

'I'm at your disposal,' Fresia smiled at Joe.

'I thought we might go to Cañete,' Joe said. 'The place where they impaled your husband on a stake.'

'If you go there,' Oscar said, 'then make sure that you also go to one of the lakes near by or to the beach at Laraqueta or something. I hate to tell you this, Joe, but the town of Cañete is actually rather boring.'

Joe walked Fresia to the bus stop. He asked her if she wanted him to accompany her into town but she just laughed and said she would be fine. They stood waiting for the bus watching gulls drift across a pale moon.

'Thanks for today,' Fresia kissed him goodbye as the bus turned the corner. 'It's been lovely.'

Joe watched the bus go and then wandered back to the house

where Oscar was rinsing the earthenware bowls and scraping away at the rim of encrusted sweetcorn.

'*Simpatica,*' said Oscar. 'And very attractive. Quite like her father in some ways but not in others. He certainly wasn't attractive. Even when he was young he looked like a bad-tempered, undernourished owl. Everybody always wondered what a beautiful, talented, high-class girl like Rebecca Morganstein was doing with Ricardo Castillo. In those days of course everybody wanted to hang out with a revolutionary . . .'

Joe lay awake in the silent darkness thinking about Fresia's father and the reasons that had led him to take his life in such a terrible way. What conclusion had he reached as he sat in his study with his hand on his finished manuscript? Even the Bío-Bío – the great frontier – was drying up, the Pehuenche people removed to make way for dams in which leading politicians had shares. The white-haired historian downstairs made punch with fruit from his garden, he talked with Joe in the evenings, he sat late in the evenings sending his protests down a telephone line. *We used to think that we could change the world, now we just want to save a river.* What if, staring from the window one dark and lonely night, you realised that it was not even possible to do that?

Oscar was right about Cañete. It was a smallish dusty town about two and a half hours south of Concepción, hemmed in by the nearby mountains of the Cordillera de Nahuelbuta. They drove south past Coronel, Lota, Carampangue, San José, Curanilahue, Tres Pinos. This was the militant coal-producing region which had once made the Pacific waves black with coal dust. But now the mines were closed and their car crawled behind the lorries of the great forestry companies laden with smooth logs from the imported fast-growing pines that had replaced the native monkey-puzzle trees.

'*Close your eyes as you enter Cañete,*' Fresia read from the rather flowery brochure which Oscar had given them, '*you who are the product of the two races that both spilled their blood here. Close your eyes and you will see the glorious deeds out of which our nation was forged.*'

'If I close my eyes we'll crash,' Joe said. 'I don't think we should add to the blood that has been spilled here. Anyway, you're the Chilean so you should close your eyes.'

'No way,' Fresia tossed the brochure aside. 'And as you know, I don't believe in all that bullshit about race and blood anyway. The only thing I'm going to see if I close my eyes is my lunch.'

They parked the car and wandered about for a while, inspecting the square where Caupolicán had met his terrible end, the fort where Pedro de Valdivia had been ambushed by Lautaro's forces, the tree which supposedly marked the spot where he had died (drinking molten gold? struck suddenly from behind?).

'Do you want to go to the Mapuche museum?' Joe asked doubtfully. They glanced at the brochure which showed a few examples of cooking implements, musical instruments and a reconstructed Mapuche house which looked like a large shredded wheat.

Fresia tucked the brochure inside her book. 'No. I'm not very comfortable with the concept of a Mapuche museum. Anyway, I'm starving. Let's get something to eat, and then I want to go to one of those lakes or to the beach or something.'

They sat in a small restaurant in the hard dry heat. The table wobbled; the place smelled of floor wax and insect repellent and the waiter treated them as if they had just stepped off a spaceship from Mars. Joe ordered a beer and Fresia a bottle of Fanta.

'You should take advantage of the fact that I'm driving,' Joe said to her.

'I hate drinking in the daytime.'

Joe told Fresia about his work: how he was fast-forwarding from the conquest to the early nineteenth century and the wars of independence against the Spanish. He recounted stories about Bernardo O'Higgins the liberator, Manuel Rodríguez the guerrilla, the noble demented Carrera family. As he talked, he realised that he was quite looking forward to returning to the university libraries of Santiago. It was not as laid-back and stylish as Concepción but it was still the capital, the place where everything happened. He missed his balcony, the red Metro signs, the view out over the city at night.

'What about you?' Joe asked Fresia. 'When is your return flight?'

'I didn't get one. I'm not really sure what I'm doing next. I might go further south for a bit.'

Joe was surprised. 'On your own?'

'I don't mind being on my own.'

'But you'll come back soon to Santiago?'

'Why, will you miss me?' she joked.

'Yes.'

'Oh well, you've got Magdalena. And go and see Guillermo, he gets really lonely sometimes and he loves chatting to you about history and politics.'

'And what are you going to do down there?'

She mimed a camera.

'Right,' Joe said, feeling uncomfortable. He had invested Fresia's visit with far too much significance. If she had been interested in him she would have stayed at Oscar's last night or asked him to accompany her to her hotel. She would never have said, *Oh well, you've got Magdalena* in that casual way. Here he was semi-consciously deploying all the things that were attractive about him; she *liked* him for it and that was it. Did he expect that Pedro de Valdivia or Caupolicán might suddenly step out and give him manly advice as Humphrey Bogart did for Woody Allen in *Play It Again, Sam?* He suddenly felt sick of himself, a sad weariness filled him; he could use all the charm at his disposal and it would still make no difference.

'Hey,' Fresia put her hand on his wrist. 'It won't be for that long. I know that I'm irreplaceable really but I'll be back soon and we'll go out again. There's no need to look so heartbroken.'

He looked down at her wrist with its silver charm bracelet – a clog, a heart, a ship, a space rocket, a Cornish pasty. He laughed.

'A Cornish pasty?'

'I bought that in St Ives once,' she shook her hand and smiled. 'It's my favourite.'

And once again he felt helpless and dizzy and hopeful.

They drove to a nearby lake where they lay by the shore and read their books. At one point, Joe looked up to see that Fresia was no longer reading but her hand was on the open page and she was staring out over the lake.

They followed a path around the lake, which led into some woods. The trees were tall and thin as Giacometti statues, trembling slightly in the warm breeze. They stumbled upon a small clearing where there was a wooden stage and a little amphitheatre. Eucalyptus kernels were scattered about and Fresia picked one up, scratched it and held it to Joe's nose. They sat down looking at the empty stage.

'What an odd little place,' Fresia said, brushing one of the seats and sitting down.

'It looks like they have concerts here,' Joe said, sitting down beside her.

A shaft of sunlight broke through the forest canopy and fell upon the empty stage. They sat without speaking for a while as if awaiting the appearance of an important actor, the only sound made by eucalyptus kernels falling from the trees, the breeze in the branches. Joe felt as if every nerve in his body were exposed; he longed to reach out and touch her, to take her hand. But he could not do it, he had no idea what she was thinking and he was far too scared of rejection.

Later, as they drove back through the pine-covered hills, Fresia chattered to Joe to stop him from growing tired. She told him about growing up in Oxford, how she had been teased about her name at school because it resembled a breed of cow and how she had longed to be called Emma or Sophie or Sarah.

'That's stupid,' Joe said. 'Fresia's a great name.'

'Yes, well . . .' Fresia scratched her leg where she had been bitten, '. . . I didn't think so at the time, I hated my parents for it. The kids in my school didn't have your understanding of my historical significance, they just used to make mooing noises at me. It was only when I got to college that I became exotic.'

'Well, you do have quite an exotic mixture,' Joe said.

'I've told you . . .' Fresia scratched frantically at her ankle, '. . . it's all bullshit. You are what you are. You shouldn't romanticise people too much, you'll only be disappointed.'

'I shouldn't or one shouldn't?'

Fresia laughed. 'Both.'

It was dark by the time they could see the lights of the city along the banks of the Bío-Bío. They stopped at Oscar's and he made them *onces* – avocado, slices of cheese, pâté, fresh bread, tea infused with cinnamon.

'I must be going,' Fresia said when they had finished eating.

'I'll drive you.'

'No, it's a lovely evening. The bus only takes a few minutes.'

When Joe returned from escorting Fresia to the bus stop, Oscar held up the book that she had been reading. It was an old anthology of Neruda poems called *Extravagario*.

'She forgot this.'

Joe took the book and opened it to where one of the page edges had been folded over.

. . . She was a mermaid who had lost her way. . . .

'Can I borrow the car?'

'Sure . . . but it could wait until the morning, couldn't it?'

Joe looked at him and Oscar laughed.

'Oh well, good luck.'

Joe drove fast across the river into the centre of Concepción. It was still busy for a Saturday night, couples and families strolling about eating ice-creams. He didn't really think about what he was doing as he made his way to the Hotel Carrera, he just knew that he could not leave things as they were. He walked into the lobby where a group of Japanese with suitcases were standing at reception. In the background he could hear piped muzak – 'Take a Chance on Me.'

'Joe?'

He turned and saw Fresia. She had changed and was sitting in the lobby flicking at a paper.

'I brought you your book,' he held up the copy of *Extravagario*.

'Oh. Thank you. You didn't have to though . . .'

'I needed to see you. Can we get out of here?'

'Well . . .'

And at that point he felt that she was looking behind him and he turned to where the lift doors were opening.

'Hello, Joe,' Roberto Walker held out his hand to him. 'Fresia tells me that you've been on an historic tour.'

Joe stared at him for an instant and then turned back to Fresia with humiliation and bewilderment in his eyes. It was the timeless, eternal scene – the sudden revelation of sexual intrigue and he was the dumb gatecrasher. How could he have been so stupid not to have suspected something? To have thought that she might be here because of him?

'We were just going for a drink,' Roberto said, admirably playing out the role of the unflappable character who maintains the charade that there is nothing untoward in the meeting. 'Would you like to come?'

'No,' Joe said. 'I'm in the car. Here's your book.' He held it out to Fresia. 'I'll see you.'

He hurried out towards the car, heard Fresia calling his name, pretended not to have heard.

'Joe, wait, please, wait.'

He turned to her coldly. 'What is it?'

'I'm sorry I didn't tell you. That was stupid of me. It was just that I was a bit embarrassed. Roberto is down because of his missing nephew, he's been in Chillán with his sister.'

'And you're going to the south with him?'

'Probably, yes, I think so. Roberto has had some new information about . . .'

'Not on your own.'

'I didn't actually say that I was going on my own.'

'As good as.'

'Well, like I say, I didn't really know what to say to you.'

'It doesn't matter.'

'It obviously does. I deceived you and I'm sorry. I should have just told you. You're my friend.'

Joe gave a short and bitter laugh. Roberto appeared at the hotel entrance. He was holding the book and Joe knew that he had lent it to her. He hated them both and he especially hated Pablo fucking Neruda.

. . . Her eyes were the colour of faraway love . . .

'You'd better go.'

'Joe, I'm really sorry. Will I see you tomorrow?'

'Why? Do you need to kill some time while Roberto is away?'

Fresia flushed. 'It's not like that. Can't we meet up?'

'I don't know. Probably not – I've got a lot of work to catch up on. You'll have to rely on that adventurous side of yours.'

Fresia ignored the sarcasm.

'I *did* come here to see you. That's why I came to Concepción. If I just wanted to be with Roberto we could have stayed in Chillán.'

'Oh well,' Joe prepared the barb that would hurt him more than the recipient, leave him floundering like a bee without its stinger. 'Sorry that I've got work to do. Maybe you can read some poems.'

Fresia stared at him for a moment. 'OK,' she said. 'If that's the way you want it. I'm really sorry.'

She turned away from him and Joe watched her for a second before walking quickly to the street where the car was parked. Then he turned to walk back again and apologise but his pride got the better of him and he returned to the car.

Joe sat staring in quiet misery from the window, fighting the jealous and voyeuristic images that tormented him. It was one of the oldest miseries in the world, retracing the evidence of one's own gullibility. When had it started? Where? Both nights she had left him she would have returned to Roberto, they would have gone out to eat together, returned to their hotel room and . . . he almost groaned and clenched his fists angrily. Well, fuck her, the silly spoiled girl with her affectations and her dead dad – big deal, she wasn't the only one

82

to have suffered in this life. *Why can't you see all the things I could have been to you?* He would go back to Santiago, he would get on with things, he would read about Manuel Rodríguez, the legendary guerrilla leader who stayed to fight the Spanish after the re-conquest.

'I should have let them stab him,' Joe said out loud to the empty room.

What was she doing drifting about with this literary dilettante father-replacement figure? His family made money out of the privatisation of the banking system after the coup. There you go then – blood money. Did Fresia have no political conscience? Probably not. She was a bit of an intellectual lightweight and only got away with it because she was pretty and she wasn't even that pretty when you thought about it. But he could not stop himself from remembering other things: her low laugh; the way she had scratched her bare tanned leg; a silver Cornish pasty jiggling on a slender wrist. *She has chosen, she has chosen and she has not chosen you.* Outside the window, the moon hung heavy over the land – when he closed his eyes he felt as if he could almost hear the whispering of the eucalyptus trees by the empty stage in the forest clearing.

PART TWO

Oops

In the hotel restaurant, Fresia Castillo poured herself a glass of kiwi juice and put a couple of croissants, some butter and jam on her plate. She returned to the table where Roberto was already tucking into scrambled eggs and reading the paper. He smiled at her as she sat down.

'Is that all you're having?'

She nodded. 'And some coffee.'

Roberto signalled to the waitress who came over with her silver jug and filled Fresia's cup.

'Are you going to Gilda's this morning?' Fresia asked.

'Yes.'

'And in the afternoon we are going to go and look for this girl?'

Roberto wanted to try and talk to the girl who had been with Pablo on the night that he disappeared.

'I think so. You don't have to come to Gilda's if you don't want to.'

'Do you mind? I'd like to send some e-mails. Then we could go together.'

Fresia felt sorry for Gilda but had absolutely nothing in common with either her or her husband. And Gilda's suffering was too overwhelming, almost suffocating; it had squeezed out all the vitality the house had obviously once possessed. There was a terrible tension as the other children attempted to get on with their lives, moving about fearfully as if the smallest mistake could unleash yet further disaster. Gilda and her husband barely spoke to each other. Fresia was glad that Roberto had decided to stay on in their hotel rather than move to the large farm in the countryside just outside Chillán. There were acres of vines and tomatoes, a couple of horses in a paddock. Roberto told Fresia that Gilda had been a great one for horses; now she did not leave the house in case of a phone call.

Over the last few days, Roberto had gone to meetings and press conferences with his sister, consoling her after the stress of yet another corpse discovery which turned out not to be Pablo, which turned out to be . . . nobody. He had agreed to meet some of those claiming to have information because Gilda and her husband were exhausted by the false trails set by freaks and attention-seekers. They had been told that Pablo had been killed by drug-dealers, by the police, by jealous boyfriends (his own and those of the various girls he was supposed to be seeing), by the owner of the bar where he had last been seen, by his best friend, by organ-traffickers, by a spurned girlfriend, by business enemies of his father.

Fresia had seen the boy on a family video which Gilda watched compulsively. She knew his likes and dislikes from profiles which had been written about him – profiles which confirmed him as typical of his age, class and background. He studied agricultural sciences at a private university, his marks were average. He was popular with girls, enjoyed dancing, his favourite singers were Lenny Kravitz and Britney Spears. He had been known to smoke marijuana with his friends (his mother denied this), liked football, supported Colo Colo, wasn't so keen on reading, had been planning a trip to Patagonia when he vanished.

Fresia felt her own position bordered on the fraudulent because, although she felt sorry for Gilda, she had not known Pablo. She could hardly pretend to be emotionally affected by his dis-appearance although she found it unsettling. It seemed certain that he was dead but she did not discuss this with Roberto who was fond of both his sister and his missing nephew. Fresia still suspected that his recent decision to travel to Valdivia to interview somebody who claimed to have reliable information was also influenced by a desire to get away from the suffocating atmosphere in Chillán.

Fresia sat down in the Internet café, logged on to the computer and found one (1) message waiting for her.

To: FresTam@hotmail.com
Subject: Mi querida hija

How are you, my darling daughter? It is horrible weather here so I imagine it must be lovely where you are. There have been gales and floods everywhere. How is Guillermo? Send him my love. Have you been to see Aunty Ruth or Sara yet? I know that you think that the latter is a spiteful cow – as I do – but she is my sister and it would make things easier for me if you did not ignore her completely.

Alex and Lucy are talking about getting married – I'm sure he'll be in touch as I've given him your address. They came round last night and we watched videos. Have you seen 'The Sixth Sense'? Lucy spoiled it for everybody by guessing the twist after about ten minutes and telling us. And then apologising throughout the rest of the film. I thought it was overrated rubbish anyway and found the child who saw dead people very irritating.

A baby was stolen from my hospital yesterday which caused a great scandal but they've found it now.

Darling, I miss you terribly sometimes. Please answer this e-mail, I know you must be very busy but it would be nice to hear what you are up to. Somebody wrote a generous piece about your dad in one of the Latin American journals which I'll try and send you.

A thousand besos for you mi querida (y unica!) hija.

PS Are you taking any photographs?

Fresia felt a lump in her throat as she thought of her mum but couldn't help sniggering as she imagined her face of tense impatience as Lucy apologised for spoiling the ending of the film. She knew that her mother had reservations about pleasant, eager-to-please, utterly conventional Lucy who would ascend the ladder of academia by carefully following the rules. Lucy was not a big mouth, she did not get too drunk, say outrageous things, or see other men. She would no more cheat on Alex than she would cheat on her long and exhaustive bibliography – she had actually read all the references in her thesis. Before long, she and Alex would have children and Lucy would be a very good mother. She made you want to pick on her.

Fresia's fingers paused over the keyboard and then, instead of replying to her mother, she opened a new message.

To: Joe4@yahoo.com
Subject: Stop sulking!

Dear Joe4,

I am sorry that I did not get to see you again before you went back to Santiago and I am also sorry about what happened at the hotel. I can understand that it must have been awkward and that you felt annoyed that I hadn't told you. But as I tried to explain to you, it wasn't a matter of trust, it was just that I felt quite shy about it. Nevertheless, it was cowardly and I feel as if it was a bit babyish. Please stop ignoring me though as I don't have enough friends here to lose you. Especially not you. And I want to hear about your book – how is Manuel Rodriguez? According to the songs, he smiled as they led him to his death at Til-Til. Do you think that is true?

Well, the mystery of Roberto's nephew continues. He has been seen in every city from Arica in the north to Punta Arenas in the south. He is in Argentina, Bolivia, Cuba, Algeria, Equatorial Guinea. He is being held alive by kidnappers, has joined a religious cult or a terrorist organisation, been abducted by aliens on to their spaceship. His body has been chopped up, dissolved in acid, dumped out at sea, cremated, fed to pigs. Small wonder that his mother is losing her mind.

In a couple of days I go to the south.

Fresia paused, backspaced, deleted the 'I' and replaced it with 'we'.

first to Valdivia and then I hope to Chiloé. I don't know when I'll be back but I hope when I do return to Santiago we'll be able to meet up and have a drink. Joe, I really enjoyed the time that we spent together in Concepción and I have been very sad at the way things turned out that day, especially because we had had such a lovely day. I hope you are well, that you will have forgiven me by the time I return and that you will go and see Guillermo as he gets lonely.

All my love, Fresia

After paying the lemur-eyed boy at the till who was reading *Crime and Punishment*, Fresia wandered back to the centre of town. She missed Joe and felt terrible about the scene in the hotel when he had suddenly appeared with her book. She had phoned him a couple of times afterwards but he had been out. In the end, she had spoken to him and he had told her that he was returning to Santiago the next day. She had suggested meeting for a drink that evening but he had said that he was having dinner with Oscar and didn't invite her.

It was clear to Fresia that Joe's anger could only partially be explained by her deception and that jealousy must have played a part in it. She had known friends who could exhibit such jealousy towards a new partner but also knew that it was likely to be more than that in Joe's case. How much more than that she did not know, and did not want to know because she had not come here to become some obscure object of desire or to play adolescent love-triangles. Joe had come close to sabotaging things between them with his clumsy hostility, his anger. Only she could restore things now by obliterating it, by minimising it, by not choosing the obvious explanation. There was a sense in which she resented having been so apologetic in her e-mail but only by apologising in that way could she offer him an escape route.

And she *had* lied to him.

She sat down by the fountain where the stone mermaids were playing their trumpets and dipped her fingers in the water.

Is there a lost mermaid in my garden?

Roberto had touched her face with his hand and commented on the heat from the sun that lay trapped there. *Kiss me*, he had said quite simply, knowing that she would. And afterwards, lying still half-clothed by the pool, she had teased him.

Is that your ultimate fantasy then – a one-night stand with a mermaid?

Oh no, I want you to stay here for ever.

She had only returned to Guillermo's to pick up clothes, taking the *collectivo* back into the mountains which were now charged with promise, every bend in the road bringing her closer again. She would get out at the little grocery store where he sat waiting for her reading the newspaper, where they bought fresh bread rolls and cool watermelon, crossing the bridge over the flowing river with confidence now, evenings on the veranda under the apple tree. At night, she would sometimes look at Roberto as he slept, listen to the sound of dogs barking, the plangent, solitary cello played from somewhere near by. Often when she awoke, he would already be up and she would go swimming beneath the looming mountains while he set out coffee and rolls under the parasol. Was this not bliss? Was this not paradise? Could she not stay here for ever? And then travelling together for the first time, holding his hand on the plane, on one side the mountains and on the other the sea.

How could she tell Joe about all of this? But why had she lied to him in the first place? This was exactly the kind of tedious self-examination that she did not want to be burdened with. And yet she remembered laughing as Joe imitated Tulio or pointed out Chilean foibles, the way she would come into his flat and find him sitting with his hands above the keyboard staring out at the fading sun before they went out to drink in Bellavista or the Barrio Brazil, or to

91

see old art-house films at the Normandie Cinema. She wondered whether she might have been jealous if he had suddenly taken up with somebody else.

Fresia splashed water irritably in the face of one of the stone mermaids, got up and headed back to the hotel.

Claudia Sepúlveda lived in a middle-class suburb where women stood with hoses, seemingly watering the pavement, and dogs, half-crazed by lack of exercise, prowled front gardens.

'I think this is it,' Roberto said as he knocked on the door. A dog in the yard began to hurl itself at them but it was chained up so it kept getting yanked back.

'Be quiet, Fatán,' a voice shouted and a young girl appeared.

'Yes?'

She was a very pretty girl, around eighteen years old, wearing tight jeans and a sweatshirt which said *Catch the Sun*. For some reason, she appeared to have decided to sabotage her looks by backcombing her fringe into a ridiculous roll so that she looked like a character from a US teen-soap.

'Claudia Sepúlveda?'

'Yes.'

'My name is Roberto Walker. I am the uncle of Pablo Errazuriz.'

The girl's face flickered. 'I've got nothing to say.'

'Can't we . . .'

'I've said everything there is to say. Why can't you leave me alone.'

She glanced nervously around them as if looking for somebody in the street.

Fresia could see that Roberto was freaking the girl out.

'I'm sorry to hassle you,' she stepped forward, smiling. 'We've had quite a long journey and I would love a glass of water and to use the toilet. Please. We won't take up much of your time.'

The girl sighed and checked the street again.

'Come in.'

They passed into the living room. Claudia's parents were obviously very devout – a big Jesus with pumping scarlet heart and outstretched hands dominated the room. There were photographs of Claudia with her brothers and sisters, a drinks cabinet, a stack stereo system with elaborate ladders of green and red lights of dubious purpose. She was listening to Britney Spears – 'Oops I Did It Again'. The lights raced up with each 'Oops'.

'I've already told the police what I know,' the girl said, passing Fresia a glass of water as they sat down on the sofa.

'Which isn't very much,' Roberto said. 'You were seen leaving the bar together but you say that Pablo decided to go somewhere else without you?'

'Yes. He was totally drunk. He said he was going to a disco to find some friends, *cachai*?'

She had the speech and verbal mannerisms of the Chilean teenager that Fresia found annoying. Exile had deprived her of them because they had not been part of the vocabulary of her parents' generation. She found them ridiculous. *Cachai* as a ubiquitous 'Know what I mean' or *Malaonda* for something disagreeable.

'So you went home on your own?'

'That's right.'

'And you noticed nothing unusual in the bar while you were there? Nobody who might have a problem with Pablo?'

'No,' said the girl and looked down at her hands. Fresia knew that she was not telling the whole truth but also knew that she wouldn't while Roberto continued to speak like a policeman. Roberto sighed.

'Pablo didn't give any idea which disco he was going to?'

'No, but probably somewhere on the Pan-American Highway. Look, I haven't got anything else to say,' she said. 'I've already told the police.'

'It's just a little odd that Pablo didn't meet anybody after leaving you,' Roberto said.

The telephone rang and Claudia answered it. Her voice seemed to rise another octave.

'*Kiu, loquilla*. No, Enrique's not here. He's gone to Pucón with Esteban and Loreto. Really? *Ay que atroz. No te puedo creer*. We'll talk later. *Chaito*. A kiss to Diego.'

Roberto glanced at Fresia and raised his eyebrows.

'I like your rings,' the girl suddenly said to Fresia as she came to sit down again. 'They're really pretty. Where did you get them.'

'In England,' Fresia said. 'That's where I grew up.'

'Fantastic,' the girl's expression changed from guarded mistrust to interest. 'I would like to visit England. Have you ever been to Stonehenge?'

Fresia shook her head.

'Stonehenge, Buckingham Palace,' the girl mused. 'It's my dream to visit them one day.'

'Maybe you will.'

'My dad gave me some money on my eighteenth birthday and I had some savings as well. I could go to Europe or buy a car. I really did want to travel but . . . that's my car outside – the Peugeot. It's good to have a car.'

'It gives you independence?' Fresia smiled at her.

'Yes. I love my car.'

'And at least you've still got it while a holiday only lasts for a few weeks.'

'Yes,' the girl said almost excitedly. 'Yes, that's it.'

'Did you have the car with you that night?' Roberto asked.

'Which night?'

'The night Pablo disappeared.'

'Yes.'

'So how would Pablo get to the disco if you were using your car?'

The girl looked confused for a moment.

'I don't know. We had both been drinking. Maybe he went to another bar first and met up with some friends. He just went off, *cachai*? And I called my cousin Pamela on the mobile and then I went home.'

There was silence.

'How long were you going out with Pablo?' Fresia asked her.

'We weren't really going out. Just now and again. I liked him though. He was very handsome,' she smiled wistfully. 'I hope they find him. I want to help . . . I can't.'

'Look,' Fresia said. 'I'm going to give you my phone number. If anything comes into your head, if you remember anything, then give me a call. Please? It's horrible for his mother not knowing what happened.'

'*Malaonda*,' the girl murmured and turned to look at the dancing lights on the stereo.

A key turned in the front door and a middle-aged woman came in – obviously Claudia's mother. She looked questioningly at Roberto and Fresia; her expression turned to anger when the girl explained who they were.

'You must leave,' she said. 'You have no right to come round questioning my daughter. She's told the police everything she knows. She has nothing to do with any of this, nothing to do with it at all. How dare you! And you, Claudia, how could you be so stupid? Leave now please or I'll call the police.'

'I find your attitude very strange, Señora,' Roberto said. 'We're just trying to find out what happened to a missing boy.'

'Well my daughter knows nothing about it.'

'*Mami*, they're just . . .' the girl began but her mother cut her off.

'Enough! Get out of my house.'

Fresia and Roberto walked to the front door. Claudia followed them, her face tense with embarrassment. Fresia pressed her phone number into the girl's palm.

'Call me,' she said. 'If you remember anything.'

That night they sat down for dinner with the Errazuriz family. Gilda Errazuriz pushed her steak around her plate and drank wine from a long-stemmed glass. Her husband Gustavo, who was the head of a construction company, talked about cars and asked Roberto whether he found his Daewoo reliable. Roberto answered him politely and Gustavo said that he thought that a Peugeot might have been a better choice. The stem of the wineglass cracked in Gilda's hand.

'For Christ's sake,' she stared at her husband, 'what does it matter what make of car somebody has?'

He stared at her with hurt and anger in his face and also perhaps a tiny subconscious recognition that his marriage might not survive this tragedy.

'*Mami*, your hand is bleeding,' said Carolina, the youngest daughter, a sweet-natured girl who was about fourteen.

Gilda Errazuriz looked down at her hand, closed it around the bulb of the glass and squeezed. Gustavo and Roberto leapt up and Carolina screamed as the blood began to flow on to her mother's dinner plate.

Later, when Gilda's hand had been bandaged and Gustavo had driven her to a clinic in Chillán, Fresia and Roberto went for a walk.

'I think we should go to see this guy in Valdivia tomorrow,' Roberto said.

'If you're sure,' Fresia was relieved.

'I don't think that we're helping matters being here. Who knows, anyway, this guy might have some real information. Somebody out there knows something.'

And Fresia suddenly felt a shiver of apprehension; a strange anxiety gripped her. People went missing in Britain – usually children or young women – often meeting sad and cruel fates. She had watched the photos on the news while thinking that. *Somebody out there knows.* But it was different here, that unsettling feeling of an unstable surface, treacherous depths. What had happened to Pablo Errazuriz, the boy who had walked exactly where she was walking now, who had seen what she was seeing? *Something* had happened and *somebody* knew. Probably more than one person. And his mother clenched glass into her hand to alleviate the pain of this knowledge.

They stopped by a fence where Gilda's horse stood in the paddock.

'Poor old thing,' Roberto said. 'Nobody rides you any more.'

'Can you ride?' Fresia asked him.

He pulled a face at her. 'No way. I find horses terrifying. I'm not very sporty.'

'Even skiing? Barbara told me the skiing around here was simply wonderful.'

Roberto laughed. 'Barbara's terribly jolly hockey-sticks,' he said. 'But she's also generous and good-natured. No, I don't ski or raft or go bungee-jumping on horseback like Tulio and his family.'

She patted his stomach. 'You'll get fat and unfit.'

'And will you still love me if I do?'

'Who said I loved you?'

'Ah,' Roberto shaded his eyes and looked at her. 'I don't mean like that. You just don't strike me as one of those people who fears love in any of its many manifestations. I love many people in lots of different ways.'

'Oh really? Do you love Valentina?' Fresia grinned as she said this to let him know that he need not be afraid of his answer.

'Yes,' he said. 'I love her very much. But then I also love Pancho.'

Fresia punched his arm.

'God, you're such a bunch of hippies,' she said.

'I was born in a less cynical time than you,' he said and put his arm around her waist. They walked back to the house watching the strange dying light over the snow-covered mountains where they would never ski together.

'Tomorrow,' Roberto said, 'we shall take the unreliable Daewoo to Valdivia. *De acuerdo?*'

'Absolutely,' Fresia replied.

Funa!

1962 World Cup Group D: Estadio Braden, Rancagua.
(Final positions)

	P	W	D	L	GF	GA	PTS
HUNGARY	3	2	1	0	8	2	5
ENGLAND	3	1	1	1	4	3	3
ARGENTINA	3	1	1	1	2	3	3
BULGARIA	3	0	1	2	1	7	1

Joe sighed and stared at the computer screen. He had been doing some research on the battle of Rancagua and an Internet search had thrown up a World Cup statistics site which had distracted him for over an hour. Greaves, Armfield and Charlton must have strolled about the copper-mining town which lay just south of Santiago on the Cachapoal and Tinguiririca rivers.

What's it all about then, even the football team in this town named after a Paddy?

Perhaps they had had a beer in the Plaza de los Heroes where Bernardo O'Higgins and his men had fought with such desperation against the Spanish who had invaded from the south after Chile's declaration of independence. O'Higgins had finally fought his way out of the town (after a criminally inept decision by the Carrera brothers not to relieve him) and the Spanish had entered the town in a frenzy of vengeful rape, looting and murder of the wounded. Another heroic defeat, another procession of weary refugees heading across the mountains to Argentina as the Spanish went on to take Santiago and impose the conquerors' code.

Joe went to his e-mail where he found two (2) messages. One was from the college about changes to exam-marking procedure. The second was an advertisement promising to enlarge his penis by three inches. He remembered an old joke about twelve inches being enough for any man, deleted the penis offer, and then clicked on 'Compose'.

Thanks for your e-mail. I am also sorry about not seeing you again but it was actually true that I had a lot of work to catch up on. It was a bit of a shock seeing Roberto and – although it is none of my business of course – I was annoyed that we had spent all that time together and you hadn't mentioned that you were actually down with him. When things like that happen one tends to see the subterfuge as somehow malicious which I'm sure it wasn't. And, I probably over-reacted so let's just forget about it . . .

Joe certainly hoped that this would be possible. His anger and jealousy had been quickly replaced by a fear of not seeing Fresia again. She seemed to be offering a way out of this, an alternative explanation that involved the fiction that all he had cared about was her deception. He *had* cared about that but obviously it was not really enough to explain his fury and refusal to see her again in Concepción.

Everything's fine and hot here in Santiago. Our football team is on the brink of qualifying for a regional championship. Team selection depends more on criminal than playing form and the governing authorities do everything possible to make life difficult for us because of the bad reputation of the area the team is from. But I think we stand a good chance. Sadly, there also seem to be people within Villa Caupolicán itself who are plotting against Lalo.

I went to see Guillermo the other night to borrow a book of Goya prints. We sat on the balcony and denounced Roberto for taking you away from us. Actually, we talked about Bernardo O'Higgins and Manuel Rodriguez. Yes, I know the song about Manuel smiling as he went to his death. Did you know that the father of Bernardo O'Higgins was a Spanish viceroy called Ambrosio and was from County Meath in Ireland (as opposed to County Meath in Chile!). He was so ugly that he was known as the 'shrimp'. Manuel Rodriguez might have been the popular hero but Bernardo is mine. The aristocracy despised him which makes him OK in my book and he was a far better soldier than any of the Carrera brothers but he only has streets named after him and no songs.

Oh yes, that woman we met at Roberto's called me up and invited me for a drink. Valentina. I thought she was strictly of the Sapphic order but I can always hope.

Well, I had better go now. Hopefully, I'll see you when you get back.

Love,

Joe

He disconnected from the Internet and put on a CD he had bought from the Santa Lucia artisan market – songs about Manuel Rodríguez smiling as he was led to his death at Til-Til, the blue-blooded Carrera brothers and their hotheaded sister Javiera who danced the *refalosa* and dreamed of Independence night and day. There was no song, however, about the awkward and illegitimate Bernardo O'Higgins who had actually done most of the liberating along with the Argentinian General San Martin.

The telephone rang.

'Do you want to come and "Funa" somebody today?' Magdalena asked. It was her birthday.

'Funa?' Joe asked. 'Happy birthday by the way.'

'Expose a torturer to his work colleagues and neighbouring businesses . . . thanks.'

Magdalena had decided to celebrate her birthday by protesting outside the offices of Gonzalo Espinoza – businessman and ex-torturer.

'You haven't considered a drink or a party?' Joe said.

'We can go for a drink afterwards,' Magdalena said. 'But you should come to this. It will be educational for you.'

'So what's your thing with this Espinoza character?' Joe asked her when they met at the Pedro de Valdivia Metro station. 'Was he a member of the DINA?'

Magdalena shook her head.

'He started off as a civilian fascist carrying out terrorist actions against Allende. After the coup, he was linked to various assassinations and then he joined the Comando Conjunto which was set up by the air force as a rival of the DINA and was mainly responsible for attacking the Communist Party. Things got bad between the Comando Conjunto and the DINA, they even started assassinating each other's agents. Espinoza managed to stay out of that one and began setting up companies to channel the profits they made from their various illegal activities and finance foreign missions. Now he specialises in helping ex-agents find jobs in other cities. Chiefly, he employs security guards but he also owns some bars and motels.'

Magdalena gave Joe the name of a bar in the Barrio Brazil where they were to meet later in case they got separated.

A few of the workers in the office peered out of the window when the group of about fifty people arrived with placards and a banner saying: *A torturer works here.* The protesters were mostly young people, although there were a couple of older women carrying photos of dead or disappeared relatives. Joe waved to Vasily who was wearing a bandana and a *Red Hot Chili Peppers* T-shirt. Together with a couple of friends, he was making provocative comments to a pair of policemen who had arrived and were radioing for back-up.

A few of the staff from Espinoza's office came out and stared at the protesters; a couple of them made calls on mobiles. Some secretaries – who had clearly never contemplated the idea of restraint when it came to the application of make-up – stood watching and giggling. Other people emerged from neighbouring offices to see what all the fuss was about. A couple of journalists took some photos. It wasn't long before the police vans arrived and a bus containing riot police with helmets and shields pulled slowly round the corner.

Vasily and his friends began to jump up and down and sing a song from the football terraces about having their view obstructed by the same cops in green who had tortured people under Pinochet.

Es la policia verde, esa que no deja ver
Esa que nos torturaba
Mientras estaba Pinochet.

'Have you got your passport?' Magdalena asked Joe. He swallowed and nodded.

'Do you think Espinoza is in there?' Joe asked her.

She shrugged. 'Could be. Although he spends a lot of time in the south. He works with one of the forestry companies destroying the environment down there. He provides them with security to deal with Mapuche protesters.'

The commanding officer of the police walked over to stand in front of the group. This man was born with a toothbrush moustache and a swastika birth-mark. He stared at their banner for a moment. 'This is not an authorised gathering,' he said. Magdalena stepped forward. 'We're not supposed to be a dictatorship any more. This is a peaceful protest.' The officer stared at her as if he wished he could just draw his revolver and shoot her. Then he nodded to a couple of his men.

They came forward and began to tug at the banner.

'*Pacos culiados*,' Vasily yelled.

A girl trying to tug the banner back was hit across the face with a truncheon; a couple of people watching from the office giggled and applauded. A boy who remonstrated about her treatment was punched in the stomach and dragged towards the waiting police vans. Then the police moved in, truncheons swinging. Joe felt an agonising blow on his back and turned to stare into the emotionless face of a young cop. He wasn't one of the larger riot police; he was small and dark-skinned, with indigenous features, barely out of his teens. 'You fucking snidey little cunt,' Joe snarled. The cop might not have understood the words but the meaning was clear enough. He approached Joe with his truncheon raised again until, suddenly, he jerked forward as a flying kick in the back sent him to the ground.

'Run, *huevón*,' Vasily said. 'Otherwise you'll be spending the night in the station.'

They were sprinting up the street when a couple of cops on motorcycles turned the corner, glancing from side to side. Joe grabbed Vasily and pulled him behind a newspaper kiosk. The man in the kiosk looked down at them and Vasily put his finger to his lips and then made a mock-praying gesture. The kiosk owner grinned and gave them a clenched-fist salute. He indicated to them when the motorcyclists had passed.

'You coming out tonight?' Vasily asked as they moved quickly away from the area and then relaxed as they strolled past the ice-cream parlours and cafés of the Alameda. 'Magdalena wants to go to some stupid bar where they'll sit around singing "Gracias a la vida". I keep explaining that wanting to dance to something with a beat doesn't make you a fascist.'

'No it doesn't,' Joe agreed.

'What have we got to thank life for anyway? They killed my uncle after the coup and now they're saying they threw him in the sea and my aunt is supposed to be grateful to them for their honesty. We don't even know if it's true – they're only saying it to close the case.'

'Do you think Magdalena's been arrested?' Joe said.

Vasily laughed.

'You're joking. Any cop that busted her would be in big trouble. They know her really well. Would you want to be doing your night shift in a police station with her yapping in your ear about her human rights?'

'No,' Joe admitted.

'I think they actually kicked her out once, they got so bored of her lecturing them,' Vasily said. 'Although she should watch her back because if there's one thing that fascists hate it's a mouthy woman. And Magdalena is the queen of mouthy women.'

Vasily was right. Magdalena had not been arrested although one of her friends had. Magdalena had helped to try and sort this out and then gone shopping at the mall with her mum to buy some clothes for her birthday. They had met up again in a bar near to the Plaza Brazil. She was wearing the new outfit and Joe had felt a surge of affection for his friend when she arrived looking like a child still slightly bemused by her party frock.

He gave her a present which he had brought for her from England. It was a music box without the box, just the internal mechanism, a little spiky drum and metal teeth with a handle. When Magdalena turned the handle it tinkled out the melody of 'Imagine'. She squinted as she put it up to her ear and listened to it, trying to work out the tune. Then she broke into a big smile.

'I thought you didn't like that song,' she said.

'I don't,' Joe replied. 'But you do. And it's your birthday.'

More of Magdalena's friends waved from across the square. Joe groaned inwardly as he saw Patty among them. Patty hated Joe, had done so since their first meeting because he had sniggered when she had said that the best film ever made was *Dances with Wolves*. Since then, they had argued every time they had met: about the merits of faith healers; the intrinsic bond between indigenous people and the earth; the validity of palm-reading. Patty was an anthropologist, a cultural relativist, a stubborn opponent of what she called the hegemony of the Judaeo-Christian scientific tradition.

'Oh look, Talks-like-a-twat is coming,' Joe said to Magdalena, waving cheerfully at the advancing group.

'You should hear what she says about you.'

'What does she say?'

'Oh, that you're arrogant and rude. A typical gringo who comes to this country and thinks he knows all there is to know about it.'

'Not all there is to know but I know a lot more than her. That's what pisses her off. It's not my fault if she's ignorant of her own history.'

'Well, she's an anthropologist, not a historian.'

'She's an idiot. I wonder if she came by bus or flew in on an

102

empanada? There's no reason why we have to stick to Judaeo-Christian modes of transport, you know.'

Magdalena spat her beer back into her glass. 'Don't fight with her when you get drunk,' she spluttered.

'I'm not going to get drunk.'

Magdalena arched an eyebrow.

'Feliz Cumpleanos,' Patty said as she arrived, ignoring Joe completely. 'What are you laughing at, Magda?'

'Joe just told me a joke.'

'Really?' Patty regarded Joe coldly.

'A joke in the Judaeo-Christian tradition I'm afraid,' said Joe and Magdalena kicked him under the table.

Later in the evening, when everybody was drunk, they went to another bar where a long-haired girl with a guitar was singing a folk repertoire mingled with a few Beatles numbers in broken English. The bar was popular and among the clientele were blond-haired foreigners, some of them wearing environmentalist and pro-Mapuche T-shirts. They nodded happily at each other whenever they recognised a well-known song and mouthed the words ostentatiously in Spanish. Joe could see that Vasily – who was very drunk – was getting restless, especially when the singer began an anguished number about the death of Camilo Torres.

'Fucking masochists,' he said loudly.

A couple holding hands in front turned round and glared at them.

Vasily was undeterred. 'Something a bit more depressing please!' he yelled sarcastically at the request-taking singer, who did her best to ignore him.

A North American student demanded 'Gracias a la vida'. The singer smiled but had only played a few chords when Vasily began to bang his glass and shout that he wanted to hear an old song called 'Puerto Montt'.

'Sentado frente al mar . . .' he sang tunelessly, trying to get the rest of the bar to join in and banging his hands on the table. A couple of young waiters watching the tables tried not to laugh.

'Shhh,' said the North American who had requested the original song. He had a blond beard and was wearing a T-shirt with the Mapuche flag on it.

'Don't tell me to shut up, you bastard. Go home and protest about what's going on in your own country.'

The bar manager stared pointedly at Vasily as he dried a glass. Joe felt a not-so-sneaky admiration for Vasily's performance but put his finger to his lips and made a placatory gesture at the bar manager to suggest that he had him under control. Vasily winked theatrically at Joe and then turned round and gave a clenched-fist salute to the manager. The bar manager touched his eye and pointed to indicate that he was watching them and Vasily did the same before slumping back down on the table.

When the singer had finished 'Gracias a la vida', Patty called out for a song called 'Cambia todo cambia' – 'Everything Changes'.

Joe glanced nervously at Vasily who shot up again.

'Great idea,' he shouted. 'And change the singer as well before we all slit our wrists!'

Joe couldn't help sniggering. Patty gave them both a murderous stare.

'What are you looking at?' Vasily demanded. 'She's a lesbian,' he muttered loudly to Joe. 'Don't pay her any attention.'

And he began to sing again.

The singer put her guitar down and the bar manager called to one of the waiters who stopped laughing, straightened his face and nodded. Magdalena motioned Joe desperately to take Vasily outside.

'Come on, Vasily,' Joe said. 'Let's go and get some air.'

Joe led him out, sat him down and ordered a couple of beers.

'Let's go dancing,' Vasily said. 'I know a great place. Do you like techno parties?'

'Well . . .' Joe began.

'The girls in this place are fantastic, we'll pick a couple of them up. Last time, one of them did a striptease for me back at her flat in Las Condes and then we took cocaine and bam bam bam – we were fucking all night. She'll be there and she's got some nice friends as well.'

'I must admit that's quite a tempting offer, Vasily. Maybe another time though 'cause Magdalena's staying with me tonight.'

'The police are still beating us, thirty per cent of the dumb fucks in this country vote for the fascists and we're sitting about in bars singing "Gracias a la vida" and "Cambia todo cambia". Who are the idiots here? By the way, are you and Magdalena . . .'

'No.'

'Right. Didn't think so. Well if you want to stay here rather than come out, take drugs and dance with stupid but beautiful *cuicas*, that's your decision. You should come up to La Pincoya some time though.'

There was a round of applause from the bar as the singer began a version of 'Yesterday'.

'I'm out of here,' Vasily said. 'I'm going to search the bars and discos for Pablo Errazuriz. See you, José.' And he staggered off.

Joe sipped his beer and gave a hundred pesos to a kid selling gum. He was tired, had drunk too much and wanted to go home. Magdalena came out and sat beside him.

'Has Vasily gone?'

'Yes, he's gone to search for Pablo Errazuriz.'

'Let's go as well.'

As they left, Joe glanced into the bar and saw the long-haired singer putting her guitar away. The bar manager gave her a cup of coffee and she smiled wearily and brushed the hair away from her face, before hopping up on to one of the stools.

Back in his flat, Joe made tea and they ate some *churros* which Magdalena had bought from a van on the way home. She had argued about the size of the *churros* they had been given until the exasperated seller had taken an extra five and stuck them in the bag.

'Have these free,' he said. 'And get lost.'

Joe smiled to himself and remembered Vasily telling him that the cops didn't arrest her any more.

Magdalena was lying on the sofa eating her free *churros* and watching the programme about crime reconstructions. Today it was about a man who had an affair with a younger woman, lost all his money, killed his wife and child and then lived with the corpses before the smell alerted the neighbours.

Freeze-frame.

The presenter emerged into the family living room and put his hand on the shoulders of the motionless wife.

The terrible fate of Yolanda and little Claudia is now sealed. Pedro has stepped into the abyss of madness and there is no turning back . . .

Joe jumped as he realised that the actress playing the doomed wife was Valentina, whom he had arranged to meet in a bar at the weekend. She threw her arms up in stagey horror as the presenter withdrew, shaking his head sadly, and the axe descended on her own. Magdalena's eyes widened, her *churro* halfway to her mouth.

'Bastard,' she said. 'Typical man.'

'If he were that typical there wouldn't be many women left alive,' Joe said.

Magdalena licked sugar from her fingers and flicked through the book on Goya that Guillermo had lent to Joe, pausing momentarily to raise her eyebrows at the picture of Saturn devouring one of his children.

'What's this for?' she asked.

He took the book, turned to the paintings of the *Second* and *Third of May 1808* and then flicked between the two images. 'This was after Napoleon invaded Spain,' he said. 'He forced the abdication of the King and stuck his own brother Joseph on the throne. The Spanish got very pissed off about that. This is their uprising and this . . .' he turned the page '. . . is the aftermath.'

A blaze of light from a white shirt awaiting the crimson stain. A dark picket of bear-skinned, knapsacked grenadiers stretching into the distance, a pitiless fusillade. A fireship exploding from the dark sea-swell, a colossus stirring its limbs and rising to stride through a landscape of chaos.

Viva la patria!

The cry rose from the Spanish Americas as Spain itself was ripped apart, while a deaf painter paused before the scene which would be repeated again and again during the disasters of war that followed the proclamations of independence. Did it start there? With Napoleon pulling the rotting Bourbon tooth? With the shadow of the Inquisition or the torch of the Enlightenment? With the founding fathers or the swish-thump of the guillotine? With aristocrats or sans-culottes? With Miranda, Bolívar or San Martin? With a lonely young man learning mathematics in a house in Grafton Street? With an aristocratic young woman dancing the *refalosa* and urging her impetuous brothers to acts of glory? With an unlikely Governor from County Meath leading a young girl to his bed – the shudder in the loins of the 'shrimp' engendering the downfall of the empire he represented?

Magdalena took her glasses off and rubbed her eyes.

'You're weird,' she said.

After making Magdalena's bed and tidying up, Joe read for a while. He had forgiven Neruda for getting between him and Fresia and took down his copy of *Canto General*. Neruda was sympathetic to the Carrera brothers but he was also generous about O'Higgins.

'*You are Chile,*' he wrote of Bernardo. '*Close your eyes, sleep, dream a little.*'

Because of the stories of his grandfather? Because of rockets slamming into the presidential palace? Because 25F is next to 25E?

Because of air currents swirling over the ocean? Because one hand reaches for another in the midst of the turbulence?

How does anything really start?

From the next room he could hear the tiny strains of 'Imagine' as Magdalena turned the handle, holding her present to her ear in the darkness.

Human Rights

The River Calle-Calle patted the wooden hotel pier in the cool, green city of Valdivia. Fresia and Roberto were waiting for a man called Sergio Valenzuela who claimed to know something about the disappearance of Pablo.

They had driven south from Chillán through the Arauco region until they reached the lakes and volcanoes around Temuco, lingering for a day in Panguipulli – the city of roses. They had swum together in the waters of the ice-clear lake, the white peak of the Choshuenco volcano rising above them. At night, from their bed, Roberto pointed out the southern cross in a sky giddy with stars.

The following day, they had driven to Valdivia, checking into a decorous old-fashioned hotel with large rooms and tall windows that opened on to a garden leading down to the river.

'You should feel at home here,' Roberto said as they leaned together with their forearms on the window-sill and watched morning rain sheeting across the river. 'There was a terrible earthquake in 1960 followed by tidal waves. That's how Chile got the World Cup instead of Argentina in 1962. People felt sorry for us.'

'Do you like football?' Fresia was a little surprised.

'I'm not a fanatic but I still support Unión Española and I like to watch the national team. I was nine years old during that World Cup. My father took me to see England play Argentina in Rancagua. It was my first football game.'

'Who did you support?'

He looked at her as if she were mad.

'England, of course.'

'Oh yes, because of your mother's family.'

He laughed. 'And because I'm Chilean. It was Argentina, remember.'

Fresia did feel at home in watery Valdivia, watching the big clouds which sometimes rolled in from the sea, the sudden downpourings of rain. She loved the cafés in the centre of town that served cakes and coffee with whipped cream, the sounds of the dark river at night. They walked from the hotel to the fish market with its bass, conger and hake belly-up on the stalls, an exuberance of shellfish. There were prawns and mussels and clams, of course, but also *machas* and *erizos* and others whose names she did not even know in English – the mighty and endangered *loco,* the difficult-looking *picoroco* with its single claw emerging from a craggy shell. Roberto had taught her how to eat these, using the shell as a cup to drink the wine-rich soup in which they were cooked.

'Do you think this guy will have any information?' Fresia asked now as she sipped a cup of tea.

Roberto shook his head and looked at his watch. 'It'll probably just be another lunatic saying that Pablo's at the North Pole eating ice-cream with the Eskimos. He's late anyway.'

But then the waiter approached and told them that there was a man enquiring for them at reception.

'Show him over,' Roberto said.

Fresia's eyes widened as the man walked across the lawn towards them. His face was terribly burned down one side, the skin pulled pink and tight like a starfish. The other side was normal, as if reminding the observer what his face should really be like.

Roberto stood up. 'Can I get you something to drink?' he asked courteously, holding out his hand. The man extended an awkward left hand in return and Fresia noticed that his right hand was also burned, the flesh taut and livid.

'A beer.'

Roberto signalled to the waiter and the man sat down and turned to Fresia. Only one of his large olive eyes had survived whatever accident he had suffered.

'Who's she? I only said I'd meet you . . .' the man was nervous. 'If she's a reporter I'm not saying a word.'

'She's not a reporter,' Roberto said.

'I can go back to the room if you like.' Fresia half rose.

'It's OK,' Roberto detained her and turned to Sergio Valenzuela. 'Are you comfortable here? We can go somewhere more private if you prefer?'

The man looked around him and shrugged. He turned to Fresia again.

'Are you Chilean? You've got a strange accent.'

'I was born in Chile. But I've lived all of my life in England.'

He nodded; the information seemed to reassure him.

'So?' Roberto asked. 'You said you knew something about Pablo.'

'Yes,' Sergio said. 'I'm a security guard. Or rather I used to be a security guard until this happened . . .'

He indicated his burns.

'Were you in a fire?' Fresia asked.

'I was *set* on fire,' the man said. 'I was working as a security guard for a big forestry company near Temuco. The Indians were demanding their land back, saying that it had been stolen from them. Rubbish. You can't undo history. Winners and losers, that's what history is about.'

He looked at Fresia for confirmation and she made a noncommittal movement of her shoulders. A small power boat driven by wealthy teenagers zoomed past, sending wavelets thumping against the pier beneath their feet.

'Well, it's crazy down there. The Mapuches wanting their land back, the forestry company trying to do their business.'

'Were your injuries caused by the Mapuches?'

Sergio shook his head and smiled bitterly.

'That's what the public would think because everybody knows that there's nothing more dangerous than a Mapuche with a box of matches. One night we were patrolling and we were attacked by some hooded men. They poured petrol on me and set me on fire. But I know that they weren't Mapuches. They had been hired by the forestry company.'

'Did you report this?' Fresia asked.

'There was no point speaking to the cops. I spoke to my senator. And I told a newspaper what I thought. They'll make me pay for that one day. But nobody will care because nobody cares about anything in this shitty country apart from money. For all I know, the senator is a shareholder in the company.'

'Why did the forestry company burn you?' Roberto asked.

Sergio's laugh turned into a cough. He sipped at his beer.

'Why do you think?' he asked. 'They did exactly what one country does if it wants to start a war with its neighbour; they staged an incident. After that, they could blame the Mapuches who were giving them problems and arrest all their leaders.'

Fresia stared at the damaged hand, tried to imagine the agony that he must have felt.

'So . . .' Sergio set his beer down. 'I came back to my home town. But I still stay in touch with a few people.'

'And you know something about Pablo?'

Sergio looked around him and leaned forward.

'I won't make any public declarations. I just don't like seeing the Señora on the television. I would want my mother to know what had happened to me.'

'So what do you know?' Roberto asked.

'Where do you think most security guards come from?'

'Ex-cops?'

'That's right. And ex-secret police. The company that employed me was full of them. Some had moved from places where it had got too hot for them. There were a few guys from the north – they were really crazy. Anyway, the head of the company that employed me lives in Santiago, a guy called Gonzalo Espinoza. This is a guy who had his finger in more pies than anybody will ever know. He was high up in the secret police. He would help set up companies to finance missions abroad and to launder money. Travel agencies, import-export firms and, of course, security. He knew everybody – drug traffickers, arms traffickers, cops, judges, politicians, business-men. He had some motels in Chillán . . .'

He took out a pack of Lucky Strike and shook one clumsily into his undamaged hand.

'The night your nephew disappeared, Gonzalo Espinoza was in Chillán. I don't know all the details. The person you need to speak to is called Fernando Araya but everybody calls him El Trauco.'

Roberto raised his eyebrows. 'What a flattering nickname. What does he have to do with it?'

'He's worked for Espinoza and he knows people in Chillán. He's the one who told me that Gonzalo Espinoza was in a Chillán bar with one of his guys and two detectives the night your nephew disappeared. It was the bar that your nephew was last seen alive in. That's what he told me but then he clammed up.'

'Which is interesting but proves nothing.'

'Surprising that none of those guys have been interviewed, don't you think? That the bar owner who knows them pretty well has never admitted that they were in there.'

Roberto stroked his chin and studied the half-burned man.

'Where will I find this Fernando Araya?'

'He moves about a lot but he owns a restaurant on the island of Chiloé. It's in Ancud. That's where I think he is at the moment.'

'If we find him, won't he work out that you told us something?'

Sergio shrugged. 'That's the least of my problems at the moment. Besides, if you ever do get anything on Espinoza then I'll be glad. He must have known that one of his men was going to get burned and he didn't care. He might even have suggested me because I didn't have the connections that some of the others had.'

'You know,' Roberto said, 'my sister's family have been tortured by rumours and false trails. Some of the stories have been very convincing. Why should I believe you? You've obviously got a grudge against Espinoza. This might just be your way of getting your own back.'

Sergio Valenzuela exhaled a long stream of smoke.

'You don't have to believe me. I'm telling you what I know, what I was told. Maybe it isn't true, maybe El Trauco is just shooting his mouth off. It's worth a try though, isn't it? At least you might find out what really happened.'

'Find out what happened . . .' Roberto murmured. 'I think my sister would like a little more than that.'

Sergio raised his one eyebrow.

'Well, she shouldn't hold her breath. They might have got rid of Pinochet but he was just the head of a very long snake. Do you think what happened to him had anything to do with human rights? Cocaine and cluster bombs – mess about with those and see where it gets you. Even today.'

He suddenly turned to Fresia.

'I don't understand why you bothered to come back here. What is there for you in this place? My God, if I had the chance to live in England that's where I would be. I'd go tomorrow.'

'And if you did,' Fresia said, 'you might end up as a security guard. Or cleaning offices. It's not so different from here.'

'Oh yes? And is that what you did then? That's why you're sitting in the most expensive hotel in Valdivia?'

He gestured around at the green lawn, the waiters with trays, the expensively dressed woman by the pool who had shuddered slightly and raised her eyebrows at her husband when she had seen Sergio.

'I had never been in here in my life before today. Or is *Papi* here paying for it all? All these people going on about human rights! I had human rights and look at me now. Your nephew had human rights and where is he? A gun or a gold American Express card – they're what give you human rights.'

Sergio put another cigarette in his mouth. Roberto calmly lit it for him.

'What did you do before you became a security guard?' Roberto asked him.

'I was studying,' Sergio said. 'My mother worked her fingers to the bone and saved up so that I could study. I was doing accountancy. But then my dad's scrap-metal business went bust, the fees went up and I got thrown out.'

'And before that?'

'How old do you think I am?'

Roberto shook his head. 'In your thirties. Forty maybe?'

'Wrong. I'm twenty-three. Before I got kicked out of university I was at school. Anyway, if I were you I would look for El Trauco in Chiloé.'

And he got up and walked away without saying goodbye.

'Are you OK, Fresia?' Roberto asked her. 'You've been very quiet.'

Fresia was sitting on the bed drying her hair. She had showered while Roberto called Gilda to let her know what he had found out. The net curtains of their room billowed in the soft breeze, a faint river smell entered the room.

'I'm fine.'

'You would tell me if something was wrong.'

'I *said* I'm fine!'

Roberto shrugged calmly and turned back to his laptop, began scrolling through his article. But Fresia could tell he was only pretending to work.

'Sorry,' she said to his back. His fingers paused on the keyboard, waiting.

'I didn't like what that guy said.'

'About human rights?'

Fresia shook her head.

'He's probably right about that.'

'Then what . . .'

'I didn't like . . . I know you'll think it's stupid . . . I didn't like that he called you *Papi*.'

Roberto turned around and placed his chin on his hand.

'Ah . . .' he said. 'Well, you know, it is just a figure of speech really.'

'Yes but that's what some people might say, isn't it, some amateur

113

psychologist, because you're older than me and everything . . . what are you laughing at?'

'Well, I'm not sure why I'm not more offended. First, you never struck me as somebody who cared much what other people thought. And second, I'm not *that* old. I'm forty-seven. What difference does it make?'

'It doesn't. Not to me. I've never cared about age – I've always had friends of different ages, but I would hate it if . . .'

'If somebody thought you were seeking a father replacement in me?'

'When that guy said that . . .'

'Fresia, it was just a figure of speech. You know that. Partners often call each other *Mami and Papi*.'

'I know. It sounds horrible. Creepy.'

'Well, yes, and I'll never call you *Mamita*, I promise. But I think you've taken it a little to heart.'

He came and sat on the bed beside her, played with a strand of her hair.

'I don't feel old. I know I'm getting older, that I'm twenty years older than you but I don't feel very different from when I was your age. Twenty years is nothing. The only thing that terrifies me is that another twenty years passing will mean that I won't be looking at another twenty. I look at photos of myself when I was young and I know I've changed but I don't feel any different. Well, if anything, I feel younger now than I did then, more adventurous.'

She smiled at him. 'Were you a very serious young man?'

'I thought I was a poet. I struck a lot of poses and wrote poor imitations of Neruda. I wore a poncho.'

'You'll have to show me the photos.'

'There is a photo of me in Galway wearing a poncho. At Yeats' Tower. It was very cold, snowing, I remember a robin . . .' he broke off for a moment, lost in the memory. 'I'll show you the photos when we get back.'

'I miss your house,' she said.

'So do I. Although I like hotels too.'

He put his arms around her and kissed her forehead. She looked back solemnly at him.

'You don't know how beautiful you are,' he said.

'Yes I do.'

He laughed. 'I don't think you do. You would be far more

114

big-headed if you did. I'm starving, Fresia. Let's go and eat. I'll let you pay.'

'I hope you like pizza then.'

'What does El Trauco mean?' Fresia asked as they sat drinking wine and eating *machas* and *locos* at a restaurant near the fish market by the river-front. Pleasure boats advertised trips around the islands, to the old Spanish forts at Corral and Niebla.

'El Trauco is part of the mythology of the island of Chiloé,' Roberto said. 'A fairly typical beauty-and-the-beast fantasy figure. He is a monstrous character but capable of casting a spell over any woman and making her find him irresistible and succumb sexually to him. In the past, women who became pregnant would blame it on El Trauco.'

'How convenient,' Fresia said.

'Yes, it probably explains the durability of the myth. There are lots of mythical figures on Chiloé. La Pincoya for example.'

'I've heard of her. She's the mermaid, right?'

'Yes, she is a distant relative of yours, although not quite as domesticated. La Pincoya appears at certain times dancing on the beach. She provides an omen for fishermen. If she is staring out to sea, then the fish will be plentiful. If, however, she is looking towards the beach then there will be shortages.'

Fresia scraped the mayonnaise from her *loco.*

'What is it with Chileans and mayonnaise?' she murmured. 'Are we going to go to Chiloé and look for this guy?'

'What do you think? I think Gilda might like us to go. It might just be some boastful guy who thinks he knows the answer to everything. But you wanted to see Chiloé.'

'I do,' Fresia signalled for the bill and put her hand on Roberto's as he reached for his wallet.

They walked back towards the hotel and he put his arm around her, resting his hand lightly on her hip as they walked. And Fresia suddenly felt an intense feeling of liberty, of self-composure, as if some previously essential but now unnecessary load had fallen away. She was light but not insubstantial, as if she had suddenly left a familiar atmosphere to embark on a strange trajectory beyond the old trivialities of happiness or sorrow.

That night they sat out drinking piscos on the pier again as the dark water lapped around them. People came out of the hotel to watch a lunar eclipse: chattering guests, shivering chambermaids and laughing waiters alike stood outside and fell silent as the moon's light went out.

Claws

'You were great,' Joe said to Valentina as they sat in the Plaza Nuñoa with a group of actors from the play, drinking cold beers. 'Scary. Although you and Goneril were far too attractive.'

'Flatterer,' said the balding Gloucester.

'Which of us was the *most* attractive?' asked Goneril, fluttering her eyelashes mock-innocently.

'No way,' Joe said. 'I've seen the pair of you in action so I'm not answering that.'

Valentina laughed. 'An English diplomat.'

'I'm not English,' Joe retorted.

He was enjoying himself with the actors, who were a noisy, hard-drinking, irreverent group full of banter and loud jokes. There was a comfortable and stylish pluralism about the gathering. Goneril was sharing a private joke with silver-haired Lear, Edmund and Cordelia were holding hands under the table, Kent and Edgar were arguing loudly and placing bets on the forthcoming match between Colo Colo and Universidad de Chile.

Somebody mentioned a party and when Joe and Valentina declined to carry on with them they were teased mercilessly and Joe was pleased to see that Valentina smiled at rather than rejected their innuendo. The actors departed, warning Joe to be careful of Valentina's sharp claws. He felt a pang as he watched them leave, their laughter fading as they exited waving goodbye.

'So what about you?' Valentina asked as their waiter brought them some more drinks.

'What about me?'

'Tell me something.'

'Like what?'

'I hear you play for a football team in La Pintana?'

So Joe told her about the team, about Lalo and his many-sided battle to keep the club going.

'You should bring him up to the Cajon del Maípo with you some time,' Valentina said.

'Yeah,' Joe said. 'Maybe Roberto will let his kids swim in the pool.'

Valentina looked at Joe mischievously from under her dark curls.

'Would you be so critical of Roberto if he hadn't run off with your friend?'

'Run off with?' Joe looked back at her. 'He's just acquired her as an accessory to his elegant lifestyle.'

Valentina shook her head vehemently.

'No, no . . .' she said seriously. 'You've got him completely wrong. I'm surprised at somebody as clever as you making that mistake. Roberto doesn't want that at all.'

'Do you know when they're coming back?' Joe asked.

Valentina shook her head.

'I thought *you* might. You miss her, don't you?'

Joe nodded.

'Well, I miss Roberto as well. There was a time in my life . . . I was pretty messed up. Roberto helped me a lot. I might not have got through it if it hadn't been for him. He is kind . . .' She laughed. 'And that's not such a common quality these days.'

Joe considered this. What would Fresia make of her relationship with Roberto? What would she do? His jealousy had not subsided but he also thought that an elegant mountain retreat was exactly what Fresia did not need at the moment. A bit of sightseeing under the excuse of looking for the nephew was one thing but he hoped she was not going to return and hide behind Roberto in the Cajon del Maípo.

'Do you want another drink?' Joe asked Valentina.

'No,' she said. 'I want to go home.'

'Oh right. OK.'

She put her hand on his wrist. 'Do you want to come with me?'

'Yes.'

She held up her hand for their waiter but he could not see them so she went inside to pay.

Joe watched her as she stood at the bar laughing with the man behind the till. He was still holding the theatre programme tightly in his hand. He unrolled it and looked at the cover; it showed a helicopter which had whirled through the north of Chile after the coup – stopping in La Serena and Copiapó and Antofogasta and Calama, murdering prisoners who were supposedly awaiting trial.

The page also featured the post-mortem report on one young detainee, which showed that – among other cruelties – his eyes had been gouged out with a service dagger.

'You smoke too much,' Valentina said as she poured them more brandy and Joe sat on the sofa in her small living room. The flat proclaimed a comfortable but well-guarded independence. There was a guitar in the corner, photos of her in different productions. There were also some family pictures. One showed a young Valentina with her parents and a boy who must be her brother, a more recent one of a laughing young man that he was sure he had seen somewhere before.

Outside the window, a display of neon pink, blue and green stockinged legs cancanned in a circle. A yellow Monarch Lingerie sign in the centre lit up and flashed every few seconds, filling the room with light and shadow.

'Really,' she said, handing him his drink, 'I hate to think what it is doing to you.'

'I know,' he said, watching the legs behind her head like a rotating neon halo. 'I either don't smoke at all or I chain-smoke.'

'It doesn't suit you. It makes you look too anxious.'

'It is a nervous thing, actually. I don't like cigarettes but it's as if I want to light the next one before the one I'm smoking is actually out.'

'And why should you be nervous?'

'Why should I be nervous? I don't know really. It's my nature I suppose.'

'And yet you seem so confident in other ways.'

'Did you bring me back here for a counselling session?'

She laughed. 'No I didn't.'

'Wouldn't you be nervous if you were alone with somebody who gouges eyes out and stabs people in the back?'

'Well, all that unpleasantness could have been avoided if my priggish little sister had just been prepared to compromise a little.'

'Yeah, it's never a good idea to interfere with the carving up of a kingdom.'

There was silence for a moment and then she leaned forward and kissed him on the lips, her mouth tasting of brandy. He felt her soft curls on his cheek, could smell the shampoo in her hair and the soft insistent pulse in her neck.

She flexed her hand like a cat. 'See. No claws really.'

Joe looked into her large eyes. He splayed his fingers through the soft hair as they kissed. Then she stood up and held her hands out to him.

'Let's go to bed,' she said.

Joe opened his eyes and groaned as the bus hit another pothole in the Avenida Santa Rosa on the way to Villa Caupolicán. He was hung-over and exhausted from the night before and the last thing he wanted to do was play football. It was, however, the penultimate game and they could theoretically win the championship that day if they won and Nueva Estrella lost their game. This was not very likely as Nueva Estrella were playing the team at the bottom of the table. Caupolicán were playing a mid-table team but Joe knew that this meant nothing – on a good day they could beat anybody, on a bad day they could lose to a team of one-legged blind men.

He had woken that morning in a strange bed, wondering where he was. Then he heard Valentina singing cheerfully from the kitchen where she was making them a breakfast of coffee and hot rolls with apricot jam. *Los pollitos dicen pio pio pio, cuando tienen hambre cuando tienen frio.* Cheep, cheep, cheep, say the chicks when they are hungry and cold. They had eaten a companionable breakfast with no analysis of what had happened and parted with no word about when they might meet again. 'Enjoy your game,' Valentina had said as she kissed him goodbye at the door.

A sudden memory from the night before clawed at his consciousness, making him open his eyes. They had moved from the living room to the bedroom and were undressing each other and as their movements grew faster and more urgent he had been whispering in her ear. She had suddenly stopped responding to him and he had realised something was wrong. 'Please don't say things to me,' she said, staring at the ceiling. He had been humiliated. She had misinterpreted his shame as irritation. 'Don't be angry,' she said. 'It's not your fault. You weren't to know.' There was a long silence. 'Maybe if you had been speaking in English . . .' she said, and then almost desperately, 'I can't . . . I don't like being commented on.' They had lost all the momentum and it was only later in the night, when they seemed to both wake simultaneously and she had taken his hands in the silent darkness, that they had recovered it.

'Where were you last night?' Magdalena said in the bus on the way to the game. 'I was trying to call you.'

'I was out,' Joe said.

'Are you all right?' Lalo asked suspiciously. 'You don't look too good.'

'Raw egg,' said Lalo's toothless next-door neighbour who was slurping red wine mixed with Coca-Cola from a plastic bottle. 'Raw egg with salt and lemon and a tiny bit of beer. That'll get you back on your legs.'

'Sounds delicious,' Joe's stomach turned over. 'I haven't got a hangover though.'

Lalo snorted contemptuously.

A couple of the kids running up and down the bus had long pink plastic horns like rigid elephant trunks and were blowing them noisily and incessantly. Joe closed his eyes and wished he could strangle the noisy little bastards.

Any hopes that Caupolicán might be handed the title by default evaporated as they watched Nueva Estrella thrash their opposition 7–0. The victory took Nueva Estrella a point ahead of Caupolicán with a superior goal difference. If Caupolicán did not win, then they would have to beat Nueva Estrella in the last game of the championship.

'They're good,' Lalo had said to Joe as he watched the game, chin in hand. 'Especially the number seven. They're disciplined, hard-working.'

As he said this, he had glanced at his own team with their colour-run green and white shirts (a nod to Joe's team of preference), sitting around laughing and smoking before the game, chatting up the sisters and girlfriends of the Nueva Estrella players who were trying not to allow themselves to be distracted by this. Caupolicán were without two important players – José, the central defender, was working on a construction site up in the *barrio alto* while Lenin, the pacy midfielder, had been arrested for trying to hold up a lottery kiosk in San Miguel. Lenin's parents had been eccentric in their choice of names. His other brothers were called Washington and Bismarck. Both Washington and Bismarck Jimenez were in and out of prison and it looked as if Lenin Jimenez was following in their footsteps.

And judging from the red eyes and yawning, it also seemed that several of the players were in the same condition as Joe.

This might be one of Caupolicán's bad days.

By half-time, Caupolicán were 2–0 down – having also conceded an own goal – and the players from Nueva Estrella, now seated with their girlfriends, raised a derisory cheer whenever their rivals managed to string two passes together.

'There's nothing to say,' Lalo said at half-time. 'You're a fucking disgrace the whole lot of you.'

At the beginning of the second half, a ball punted aimlessly from the halfway line dropped in front of Nacho the goalkeeper. He leapt for it – more sumo wrestler than salmon – completely mistiming his jump so that the ball bounced over his head and trickled into the net. 'Well played, fatty!' the Nueva Estrella players shouted from the touch-line. It took a few minutes to restart because even the Caupolicán players and the referee were doubled up with laughter. In fact, Lalo was the only person not laughing; he was staring at Nacho with arms folded and a just-you-wait look on his face.

There were a few minutes to go when the ball was pulled back for Joe on the edge of the six-yard box. Joe had made a decent enough run but it had exhausted him and, with the whole goal in front of him, he leaned back and sent it about a mile over the bar. He could hear groans and mockery from the stands as he stood, hands on hips, trying not to throw up. From the resulting goal kick, the Caupolicán defence all backed off as the opposition centre forward burst through and tapped it past a flailing Nacho to make it 4–0.

'Can't wait to play you,' one of the Nueva Estrella players said to Joe as they trooped off to get changed.

On the bus, the players at the back amused themselves by doing impressions of Nacho leaping in vain for the ball and then legging it to Chelo's car at the final whistle before Lalo could get to him.

'He ran even faster than the time they were trying to shoot him.'

'They must have heard the ground shaking in Valparaíso.'

'I would rather have been shot than face Lalo.'

The laughter stopped, however, when Lalo got on. Normally, he gave them a post-match talk even when they had lost but this time he just took his daughter on his lap and sat staring from the window. Joe felt the silent disapproval as Lalo sat in front of him with America; he knew that Lalo was disappointed with him in particular, that he had expected more from him. Normally, Lalo would have turned around and discussed the game or the national championship or the political situation; now he radiated anger and betrayal. And Joe began to feel – instead of remorse – a growing irritation with the sulking back in front of him. He felt like saying,

I'm sorry, Lalo, I understand how important this is to you but it's actually not the whole of my life and I'm not going to pretend that it is.

'You were terrible today,' Magdalena said to Joe.

'Thanks,' Joe said.

'Everybody was surprised. You're normally really good. What were you up to last night?'

'Mind your own business.'

'Lalo's pissed off.'

'Yeah, I can see that. Somebody should tell him it's only a game.'

'Is that what you think this is then?'

Before they got off the bus, Lalo did stand up to address them.

'I'm not going to tell you how bad you were, you all know that. I'm not going to tell you how shameful that was, you should feel shame for yourselves and if you don't, well there's nothing to be done. I expected more from some of you.' He glanced at Joe. 'It comes down to this: we have to beat Nueva Estrella. At the moment that looks as likely as snow in the Atacama. I hope that you will all think about what happened today and come into that match with a different attitude. At least you've got some time to think about it. That's all.'

'Are you going to come back to my house?' Magdalena asked.

'Thanks,' Joe said. 'But I need to get back to the flat.'

'Get some clean clothes?' she said pointedly.

'Sort my work out. I'm going to get a cab. I'll drop you if you want.'

'A cab all the way to Providencia? It's so far. It will be really expensive.'

'I don't care. I'm tired and I want a shower and I've got stuff to do.'

'But it's such a waste of money.'

Joe restrained several hostile retorts.

'It'll cost the same as a short cab journey in London. Look, I'm not going to argue about it – it's my fucking money anyway. Are you coming or not?'

'I'll get the bus.'

'Suit yourself.'

Lalo called his cabbie cousin from the house and they sat waiting for him in uneasy silence. Through the flimsy wall of the house next door, they could hear loud *cumbia*, a woman swearing at a child. Lalo went outside to chat to somebody from the club committee

123

about dividing up the money they had collected from the attendance at the match. After a while, he called to Joe that the cab had arrived.

When Joe got home, he shook a packet of powdered pineapple squash into a jug, added water, filled it with ice and drank several glasses. Then he lay down on the sofa, staring at the city lights stretching out into the distance, listening to the sound of the buses changing gears down below in Providencia. He could still feel his hangover, still smell the woman he had slept with the night before, still hear Lalo's angry words. Magdalena was right though: for him it was much more than a game, it was a battle for survival. He would phone Lalo tomorrow and apologise; he was too tired now.

You are Chile. Close your eyes, sleep, dream a little.

He looked up from the sofa at the picture of Bernardo O'Higgins that he had hung on the wall. It was certainly more possible to feel sorry for him than for Pedro de Valdivia. Ugly Bernardo, the bastard child abandoned by his father and detested by the aristocracy who had got rid of him after Independence. For all his faults, O'Higgins was a man without blood-lust and he had departed for exile in Peru with his mother and two adopted Mapuche daughters, neglecting – in a strange repetition of the sins of the father – his own illegitimate son. There were songs for his enemies the Carrera brothers (for whom Joe had no sympathy) and for Manuel Rodríguez (for whom he did) but there were no songs for plain old Bernardo, who was blamed (wrongly, in Joe's opinion) for the deaths of his fellow liberators. And this was the man who had fought his way wounded from the ruins of Rancagua, who had organised the Army of the Andes and embraced San Martin on the battlefield of Maipu.

Far from his homeland, O'Higgins waited for news that his exile had been lifted. But on the day he was due to return he suffered a massive heart attack and died without ever seeing again the country he had helped to liberate.

La Pincoya

Salt spray in her face, the smell of diesel from the launch, wind-blown hair, fat seals tangling with seaweed in the swell, the sullen outline of the mainland, low dark clouds, the screech of gulls.

The passengers had been allowed to descend from their buses for the short journey across the Chacao channel and they had climbed up metal steps on to a narrow platform on the side of the launch, looking into the water for seals and porpoises.

'That smell of diesel's giving me a terrible headache,' Roberto complained.

'Poor delicate thing,' Fresia pulled him towards her and kissed his forehead.

In her childhood, Fresia had learned songs from the island of Chiloé: songs about shipwrecked men sleeping in the depths of the sea, mermaids sighing with love for long-gone sailors, fierce pirates, old fishermen, wise women. She knew that she was travelling now to a strange and different place, looked down into the dark sea where the round face of a whiskered seal blinked up at her.

The coast of Chiloé approached and Roberto touched her shoulder lightly.

'We have to get back on the bus,' he said. 'We're nearly there.'

Fresia felt odd on the bus, they had spent so long alone in the car together. Cocooned, nobody had been able to hear their intimate conversations, they had control of everything. They had stopped in different places: fading truck-stop cafés, little restaurants, petrol stations. She had stocked up with cakes, ice-creams, newspapers and fizzy drinks – buying less out of necessity than for the cosy feeling that loading the car with supplies gave her, feeding Roberto as he drove. They had found out a lot about each other. Now they were back in this public domain – babies crying, children fighting with their siblings, the fat bus driver joking with the luggage-handler. They had picked up a bus which had come overnight from Santiago – it smelled of orange peel and was stale like unbrushed teeth.

As they headed towards Ancud, Roberto browsed through a newspaper which they had bought in Puerto Montt. Suddenly, he drew in his breath and began to read more intently.

'Look at this,' he said to Fresia, passing her the paper.

Arson victim killed in street robbery

A second tragedy took the life of Sergio Valenzuela R. last night when he was attacked by two young criminals in Valdivia. Not content with stealing the wallet of the victim, they also stabbed him twice in the heart during a savage assault which cost the life of the young man. Previously, Valenzuela had been the victim of an horrific arson attack while working as a security guard near to Temuco.

Grieving mother

The tearful mother of the victim Mrs Eliana Valenzuela stated that her son had been working as a security guard because he had lacked the financial resources to continue his studies. She also claimed that her son was living in fear of his life because he had questioned the role of the forestry company in the previous arson attack.

Terrorism

Twenty-three-year-old Sergio Valenzuela had suffered horrifying burns in the attack which was believed to have been carried out by Mapuche extremists demanding the return of their land from the forestry company in the area. This conflict has already led to violent clashes and the detention of several Mapuche leaders. It is alleged to have been exacerbated by the presence of foreigners working under the cover of NGOs and extremists who were once members of terrorist groups such as the Manuel Rodríguez Front. Local landowners have established armed self-defence groups and have complained at government inactivity in the face of provocation by extremists.

Crime wave

In spite of his mother's allegations, the police are satisfied that the primary motive of the assault which cost the life of Sergio Valenzuela was robbery. It would appear that the wave of crime which threatens to overcome the country has claimed yet another victim.

'He had the air,' Roberto said, 'of somebody who knew that something was going to happen to him.'

'It's so strange to think that just a few days ago we were talking to him,' Fresia said.

She remembered the way in which he had shaken a Lucky Strike from its packet, his one remaining long-lashed eye, his contempt.

'Maybe it *was* just a street robbery,' Roberto said, as if this were what he wanted to believe. He folded the paper away and stared from the window.

They arrived at the bus station in Ancud and took a cab to a *pensione* above a little café on a hill, which Roberto knew from a previous visit. The owner of the *pensione* showed them to their room, which smelled of new paint and wood varnish. The owner demonstrated the shower and they all nodded and smiled. Fresia opened the window and looked out at the bay.

'What do you want to do?' Roberto asked. 'I don't want to try and find this guy until tomorrow.'

'Fine with me,' Fresia said. 'Let's go and have a look around.'

'Why don't you take your camera?' Roberto held it out to her.

She looked at it for a moment. Behind him, through the window, the sea sparkled in the bay.

'OK,' she said, taking it from him.

It was a short walk down to the harbour where the fishing fleet was moored and rubber-suited fishermen with hard alcohol-and-weather-beaten faces stood around on the street corner as if waiting for work. An old radio balanced on a low wall was playing Latino ragga and a floppy-limbed drunk was trying to dance to it before dropping as if his bones had suddenly melted, a collapsed puppet sniffed at by a three-legged dog. It was a warm day but out over the sea, there were low dark clouds. They wandered past the harbour wall and Fresia noted, to her surprise, a sign outside a house advertising Internet services.

'Let's go in,' she said. 'I can check my e-mail.'

They knocked on the front door, which was opened by an elderly woman. The house smelled of baking bread. Fresia pointed to the sign.

'Can I use the computer?' she asked.

The woman wiped her hands on a tea towel.

'Tomás?' she called and a glass door across the patio opened. A young man with an anxious expression like a jittery deer poked his head out.

'Oh, do you want to use the Internet? Come through.'

The room was covered in papers and books and an elderly man

was sitting drinking coffee. There were old maps of the island on the wall. The younger man gestured to Fresia to go ahead, moving maps and charts out of the way so that she could sit down.

'Where are you from?' the elderly man asked Fresia as she waited for the connection to be made. His eyes were blocked by cataracts.

'Well, I was born here but I was brought up in England.'

'Did you go and visit that old bastard when he was there?'

Fresia laughed. 'He was the reason I grew up in England.'

'So many children,' the old man said, 'so many children scattered across the globe.'

'Dad . . .' the younger man said, looking half apologetically at Fresia.

The old man suddenly grabbed Fresia's hand from where it had been moving the mouse gently to and fro.

'Come with me.'

'Dad, let her send her messages.'

'Come with me,' he insisted.

Fresia nodded at the son. She stood up.

'Give me your hand,' the old man said to her. 'I can only see shadows.'

Fresia led him to the door and they stepped out on to the patio. There was an old blue Fiat with a Greenpeace sticker in the rear window, which obviously belonged to Tomás.

'Tell me what you see,' the old man instructed her, holding tightly to her arm, pointing out to the bay. 'Tell me what you see in my garden.'

'I can see the ocean,' Fresia said. 'And the hills in the distance and gulls over the harbour. On the other side of the bay, there are houses on the hillside. There were clouds earlier but they've cleared away now and the sky is very blue although it's yellower, more hazy over the top of the hill. There is a small boat heading out to sea.'

'I used to be able to see all of that, I used to watch the fishing boats. This is still your country, you know.'

He reached for her arm and touched her camera case.

'You're a photographer,' he said.

'Yes.'

'Well, if you're a photographer then you must take pictures. Take a picture of my garden.'

'OK.' Fresia took her camera out. She felt it in her hand, the familiar satisfying weight, the fat round lens.

'What are you waiting for?'

Instead of looking out to sea, Fresia turned the camera on the old man, his hand on the wall, staring blindly out to sea. *Click.* It was the first photograph she had taken since arriving in Chile.

'I can't see the fishing boats any longer,' the old man said. He shivered.

'Would you like to go back in now?' Fresia said.

'Yes. Take me back in, *mi hija.*'

Fresia blinked at his use of the word 'daughter' and led him back into the small office where Roberto and Tomás were chatting about cartography. The old man sat down and blew on his coffee. Fresia sent quick messages to her mum and to Joe.

'How much is that?' she asked the young man.

'Seven hundred and fifty pesos, please.'

'No, no,' the old man said. 'You can't make her pay. You are very welcome in your country, it is good that you have returned. The children are coming back. Didn't I tell you, Tomás, that they would come back? You have been away far too long, *mi hija.*'

To Fresia's horror, hot tears sprang to her eyes and began to spill down her face. She brushed anxiously at them and made a gasping noise that was half sob, half hiccup.

The old man turned towards her at the sound and put his hand almost wonderingly to her cheek. Then he wiped her tears with his thumb.

'But you mustn't weep,' he said. 'Don't weep. You can still see, you will see such beautiful things in your lifetime. You are so lucky.'

And he took his hand, wet with Fresia's tears, and rubbed his own sightless eyes.

As they left, Tomás took Fresia's arm.

'I'm sorry you were upset, ' he said. 'My dad gets quite emotional and confused sometimes.'

'Don't worry,' Fresia said. 'I got a bit emotional as well. Here, let me give you the money now.'

Tomás laughed. 'No, he was right,' he said. 'A gift to welcome you to Chiloé.'

They wandered hand-in-hand back along the harbour wall, passing stalls selling a variety of folk kitsch as well as ponchos, woollen socks, shawls, hats, and jumpers. All the stalls seemed to have the same stuff. Fresia found these markets oddly depressing.

'Shall we eat something?' Roberto asked.

'Maybe we'll end up in Fernando Araya's restaurant. What's it called?'

'El Pato, I think. Let's leave that for now. We'll have to ask for it. What about this one?'

'Come in, come in,' said the waiter on the door, gesturing extravagantly into the empty restaurant. 'I have crab, delicious crab, lovely crab for the Señorita, just come this way, *mi reina . . .* '

They took a table upstairs overlooking the sea, ordering bottles of Fanta and spreading warm bread rolls with bright red chilli sauce. Fresia's heart sank when a young man came to their table and began to strum his guitar. But then she was transfixed by the first gentle chords of his song as he began to sing in a clear, true voice.

La sirena está llorando a las orillas del mar
Por el amor de un marino que no la vino a buscar . . .

A mermaid weeping by the shore, eyes the colour of faraway love.

When he had finished, they applauded and he took a leaflet from his shoulder-bag.

'There's a festival of Chilote folklore tonight. Down on the beach.'

Roberto took the leaflet and gave him some money. The singer reached in his bag again and handed something to Fresia. It was the roughly carved stone figure of a mermaid.

'It's La Pincoya,' he explained.

'Ah, that's what you were telling me about . . .' Fresia said to Roberto. 'The one who looks out to sea.'

'Or not, as the case may be,' Roberto said.

'I hope she brings you luck,' the singer said.

When he had gone, Fresia put the stone mermaid on the table in front of her.

'My second present of the day,' she said.

The mermaid stared back at her.

'Chiloé is strange,' Fresia said as they made the sharp descent to the beach that evening. She could hear the waves splashing on the shore, voices from the PA system, the sound of accordions. Below them, the crowds moved towards the festival, children riding on their fathers' backs.

'It is strange,' Roberto agreed. 'It was completely isolated during Spanish rule so it kind of developed its own culture.'

'It's not like anywhere in Britain. Well maybe the Scilly Isles, a little.'

On the stage, in front of the cliff they had just descended, a group of women were dancing. Their shining black hair was adorned with red and white blossoms, their white dresses printed with red bell-shaped *copihue* flowers, their slender waists pulled in with a red sash and tied with a white ribbon. They were tapping out the half-moons of the *cueca*, circled by elegant *huasos* wearing knee-length boots and spurs.

Some of the other musicians who were to play that night lounged with their guitars and accordions, drinking and flirting. Smoke drifted up from barbecues. Fresia and Roberto bought a bottle of red wine, a paper plate of hot *empanadas* and sat watching the dancers. Participants had come from all over the country to the festival – guests from Copiapó and Ovalle in the north, Concepción and Osorno in the south. There were the groups from Chiloé itself – from Ancud, Castro, Chonchi, Dalcahue and Quellón. Fresia put her head on Roberto's shoulder and stared beyond the singers, dancers and spectators, out to where the black night sea fell hissing on the sand.

A group from Concepción began to perform. They were younger and more raucous than the rest, sometimes playing with the audience and dragging them up to dance. Fresia laughed as a young woman with a fantastic figure but dressed ludicrously with white socks, painted freckles, pigtails and holding a rag doll, stamped out an obscene *cueca* with a tatty young man who had a fake moustache and a pink heart stitched on his arse. They danced with a sexy, careless, playful, knowing expertise that made her suddenly envious. She watched them flash smiles as they circled each other, playing games of acceptance and rejection, pursuit and retreat, these children of the theatre, of the circus.

Later, when Roberto had gone in search of some more drinks, Fresia noticed the woman again. She was still holding the rag doll but also smoking a cigarette.

'I liked your dance,' Fresia said.

'Thanks,' the woman replied. She was slightly older than Fresia had first guessed – in her early thirties. She offered Fresia her hand. 'I'm Paola.'

'Are you from Concepción?' Fresia asked.

'The group is. I'm from Santiago. What about you?'

'I was brought up in England,' Fresia was beginning to grow very weary of this phrase.

'Exiles?'

Fresia nodded.

'I miss the dictatorship sometimes,' Paola said, coolly exhaling a stream of cigarette smoke. 'We knew our enemy, we used to have some ideals, we performed theatre in shantytowns, we thought we were making a difference. Nobody cares about that any more.'

'Things are better now though,' Fresia said.

'Are they?' Paola swung her rag doll viciously against the wall. 'I don't know. I'm off to Europe soon anyway. A friend from the theatre company moved to Berlin. Do you know Berlin?'

Fresia shook her head.

'It sounds great,' Paola said.

The peasant with the heart on his arse walked over. He jerked his head at the stage where the women in the *copihue* dresses were dancing elegantly again, holding their dresses as they made polite little movements.

'Bullshit,' he said as he took the cigarette from Paola. 'Dumb *Pinochetista* snobs.'

He flicked his handkerchief at her and they began to imitate the women on the stage with exaggerated dainty steps and fixed smiles. Fresia laughed.

'You wouldn't say no to any of them though,' Paola took her cigarette back.

'Of course not. Especially the cute one on the end. I may have to give her a private lesson, explain to her that the *cueca* . . . ' he shifted back into his raucous, lecherous dance, circling Paola who continued to simper behind her handkerchief '. . . is not about drinking tea with your posh friends, but about the ultimate submission of the hen . . .' he went down on one knee '. . . to the cock.'

Paola looked at him and then stretched out a leg and pushed him over.

'Not this hen, *huevón*,' she said.

Fresia watched them walk away, smiling as they twirled round each other, sometimes grabbing a startled member of the audience. She looked around for Roberto and suddenly found herself staring into the face of a man who had occupied the place where Paola had been standing. He was wearing a hooded sweatshirt. He leaned forward, took a strand of her hair and stared straight into her eyes.

'What is it you are really looking for, *cariño*?' he asked, his face close to hers. 'The revolution? You're too late, I'm afraid.'

Fresia was speechless, dizzy. She stared back at him. The man stroked her cheek, laughed, let go of her hair and walked away into the crowds.

'Probably just a drunk,' Roberto said when he returned with the drinks. 'What did he look like?'

'I can't remember,' Fresia said. 'He had a hood on and he was in the shadows. It was as if he knew me, as if he had been waiting for me.'

'Well, that's not very likely,' Roberto said. 'Unfortunately, you get a lot of drunken idiots at these things. He was just trying to scare you.'

'He succeeded,' Fresia said and shivered.

That night she dreamed that she was crossing a bridge to the mainland but the bridge was sinking into the sea. Soon she was up to her waist, then she had to swim, then she could no longer see the shore, had no sense of direction. She woke with a start and looked out of the window. Sky and sea were indistinguishable now, there was no man-in-the-moon, she was on the other side of the world. She remembered Roberto's story about the island's isolation, how it had been cut off for hundreds of years from the rest of the country, how its settlers had pleaded with the Spanish in Peru to be allowed to leave, how it had been attacked by Dutch pirates. Suddenly, it no longer seemed like an enchanted island of music and mermaids dancing on the shore, but a dark and terrifying place where nobody was safe and where strangers snarled out of the shadows. She felt a terrible panic. A disappeared boy, a young man burned and then bleeding his life away. What was she doing here with this man she had known for so short a time, searching for a lost boy she had never met in her life? Even the sheets smelled strange and threatening, the creaking wood of the building filled with menace.

'Roberto,' she nudged his shoulders with her head. 'Roberto, I had a bad dream.'

He turned and took her in his arms and kissed her forehead.

'Shhh,' he said gently. 'Everything's OK. *Hace tuto, ya.*'

'I don't like it here. I want to go back to Santiago. I want to go home. I hate this. I hate Chile. I want my mum.'

He laughed. 'Let's talk about it over breakfast. Everything is different at night. Don't worry, I won't go back to sleep until you do.'

And he stroked her head until her eyes fluttered and closed again.

Roberto was right about waiting until morning and she felt guilty for

133

her harsh thoughts towards him when she woke and saw that he had showered and was working on a book review.

The sun was shining through the window, everything seemed normal, she could hear somebody whistling downstairs.

'Hey,' Roberto smiled at her when he saw that she was awake. 'No more bad dreams?'

'No, I'm fine now. Sorry I woke you up.'

'Oh that's OK. I'm a light sleeper anyway. Shall we go out and get some coffee and eggs?'

She nodded. 'And El Trauco?'

'The woman on reception has given me instructions on how to get to the restaurant. We'll go at lunch-time.'

The woman serving in the El Pato restaurant looked as if she should have been working in some out-of-the-way diner in the United States, waiting for the travelling loner who would awaken her slumbering sexuality. She was attractive, hard-faced, gum-chewing and appraised Roberto with lazy approval as she brought them cold drinks. Fresia was not hungry but Roberto ordered a bowl of clams. When the woman came back with the clams, he asked her for Fernando Araya.

'My husband?' she said, surprised. 'He's not here.'

'Do you know when he'll be back?'

She shrugged and was about to say something when the door of the restaurant opened and a man walked in.

'He's here now,' she said.

The man was dark-skinned, long-legged, and had an agreeable round face, a scar on his cheek. He was in his early forties, wearing a leather jacket and jeans. He had an air of efficient purpose about him as he opened the till, a sense that he was aware of the reason for his every movement. It appeared to mesmerise the small group at the table and they all stared at him for a moment as he counted out some notes and slipped them into his pocket. His wife was the first to break the spell.

'Fernando,' the woman called. 'These people would like to speak to you.'

'Yes?' he said.

Roberto explained why they were there and the man sighed.

'I thought that this might happen but I'm afraid you've had a wasted journey. Sergio Valenzuela went a little crazy after the Mapuches burned him. He said a lot of things that weren't true.'

'He says that it wasn't the Mapuches who burned him,' Fresia said.

The man looked at her, his smile suggested weary amusement.

'Well, that's a good example of how crazy he was. Shall I sit down with you? I can wait until you're finished, of course.'

Roberto motioned to the empty chair and Araya asked his wife to bring him a drink. She fetched him a carafe of white wine and a glass. Araya inspected the glass, rubbed a smudge from the rim. He had a single gold ring on his finger.

'Sergio's dead now,' Roberto said.

'Yes I know. You expect such things to happen in Santiago but not in Valdivia. That's the problem with this government. Soft on criminals.'

'You preferred the dictatorship's approach?' Fresia said.

Araya laughed. 'Well, sometimes, you know, there's no alternative to the *mano dura*. The criminals understand that as well. But I'm glad we have a democracy now. Things are more stable and you need stability for a strong economy.'

His tone was calm and affable; he had the oddly fascinating quality that salesmen sometimes possess – soft, mesmeric certainties, hands together underneath his chin. He could have been explaining the benefits of insurance policies or vacuum cleaners, he knew how to caress with his voice.

'Sergio became obsessed with your nephew, he kept going on about the mother having a right to know what had happened to him. I don't know whether he told you but he was very close to his own mother. He got it into his head that the chief of the security company had something to do with it . . . . more bread, Alejandra.'

He said it without turning his head.

'Gonzalo Espinoza?'

'That's right. Now, things are getting serious down there, the government will have a Chiapas on its hands soon if it's not careful. But let me ask you something. How many Mapuches have died so far? None. They will soon, though, if they carry on burning private property. The landowners down there have spent years protecting themselves – from the agrarian reform onwards. They'll deal with them pretty soon.'

'Well they should be careful,' Roberto said. 'They wouldn't be the first to make the mistake of using force to "pacify" the Araucania.'

'Ah yes, but things have changed a bit since Pedro de Valdivia. I'm sorry, would either of you like some wine?'

They both shook their heads.

'And Gonzalo Espinoza?' Roberto asked.

'He's no angel, his methods aren't always orthodox, but why would he have anything to do with your nephew?'

'Sergio said that it was *you* that told him that Espinoza was involved. That Espinoza was in the bar in Chillán the night that Pablo disappeared.'

Araya laughed and tapped his head with his finger.

'You see. I would never say that without proof. Even then I would be pretty careful.'

'Was Espinoza in Chillán that night?'

'How would I know? But it isn't an offence to be in the same city on the night a crime happens. Listen, there have been twenty million stories about your nephew, I've heard a lot of them. I'm sorry to tell you that this is just another one. Still, it did bring you to the most beautiful place in the world.'

He turned to Fresia. 'Is this your first time in Chiloé?'

She nodded.

'And you've only seen Ancud so far?'

'Yes, we've only been here a couple of days.'

'Ah, but you must see other places. Castro, of course, and the National Park. Near by there are some beautiful places. The penguin colonies at Pumillahue. The only place in the world I think where two different types of penguin nest together.'

'Well, we may not have much time for sightseeing,' Roberto said. 'Now that we've come to a dead end here, I shall have to get back to Santiago. I'm glad that's all sorted out although I suspected as much. As you say, there have been lots of stories of this type. Perhaps you might bring us the bill now.'

'Please. You are insulting me. Would you like some coffee?'

'Thank you but I think we've taken up enough of your time.'

'So what now?' Fresia said when they were back in their room.

'Dead end. He's not going to say anything. He was a very cool character. Either Espinoza had nothing to do with it or Araya is a very good liar.'

'What about Espinoza?'

'We'll look him up in Santiago, I suppose. Just see what he's got to say although I don't hold out much hope of anything useful. I'll just pass this information on to Gilda and the magistrate.' Roberto grimaced.

136

'Are you OK?' Fresia asked.

'I feel a little sick, that's all. Listen, I'm sorry we can't stay longer and explore Chiloé but I would quite like to get home. I was thinking of leaving tomorrow. Aren't you looking forward to getting back to the mountains?'

Fresia glanced at him. During their time together they had not discussed what might happen when they returned. They had spent the journey getting to know each other, talking about the past rather than the future. Fresia suspected that Roberto wished her to stay with him in his house but had been too delicate to raise the matter. *I want you to stay here for ever.* She remembered him saying that the first time they had slept together. The problem was that the more she liked Roberto, the more sure she was that she could not take such a step, that it would be a disaster for her. She knew that she had issues to resolve but she was certainly not going to become the aristocrat's bride, the decorative mermaid in the pool. Roberto suited his life-style but she was not foolish enough to think that such elegant captivity would satisfy her. It would be a lazy choice and Fresia had not come to Chile to make lazy choices. She was about to say something when she saw Roberto wince again and decided to bide her time.

That night it was Fresia's turn to stay awake as Roberto spent the night vomiting in the small bathroom. She could tell that he was distressed at her seeing him like this, all the degrading smells and noises of illness within the confines of a small room. She remembered him clean and relaxed walking across the bridge to meet them the first time they had visited his house in the Cajon del Maípo. His face now was drawn from the exertions of vomiting, the indignities of illness. She patted his head as he groaned miserably, she wiped his mouth and brought him glasses of water. Fresia was not particularly squeamish and found his shame more irritating than the illness. Neither was she made to be a nurse, however, and she developed strong yearnings to get out into the fresh air.

'Poor thing,' she said, feeling a guilty relief that she had turned down the raw clams that he had offered her in the restaurant.

In the morning, Roberto was even worse. Fresia suggested a doctor but he shook his head weakly.

'They're so stupid here, they'll give me antibiotics or something. I'll just have to wait until it's gone, starve it out. Could you tell the woman that we won't be leaving today after all. I'm really sorry.'

'You've nothing to be sorry for,' Fresia said. 'I'll tell the woman and I'm going to go out for a bit and get some peppermint tea for you and something to eat for myself. Don't worry about it – we're in no hurry.'

After Roberto had fallen asleep, Fresia went out to buy peppermint tea. The evening was warm and so she wandered along the seafront, stopping for a moment to sit on the harbour wall. Suddenly, she was filled with the acute sensation that she was being watched. She looked around but could see nobody. Still, she felt as if a pair of eyes was burning into her and she was about to walk back to the hotel when somebody tapped her shoulder. She jumped but it was only Tomás from the house with the Internet.

'Come and have tea,' he said to her. 'My father would like to see you again.'

'OK.'

They walked along beside the calm sea watching the seagulls soar and plunge until they arrived at the house. The old blind man was standing looking out at the sea but turned when he heard them approach.

'Ah good,' he said. 'You have brought our visitor.'

Up for Grabs

'Over here. Wilson! Pass it, pass it.'

There were only a few minutes to go in the final match of the season and the score stood at 1–1. Nueva Estrella had scored first but then Joe had equalised for Caupolicán at the beginning of the second half. If it stayed like that, it would still be Nueva Estrella rather than Caupolicán who won the championship and qualified for the regional cup.

It seemed that Nueva Estrella would not be satisfied with taking the championship with a draw and had been putting pressure on the Caupolicán goal in an irritatingly cocky way, emphasising their technical superiority by spraying the ball about – clever flicks, little touches; they wanted to pass the ball into the Caupolicán net. When one of their moves suddenly broke down, however, a long punt upfield was knocked on to Wilson, who had come on as a substitute for the injured Chelo, and there was a two on one on the Nueva Estrella goal. Joe knew that if Wilson tried to take the last defender on he would lose possession. He also knew that Wilson had endured a lot of teasing because of losing his regular place to Joe. Another defender was powering back and would – if Wilson did not release the ball soon – be able to cut off the pass.

'Wilson! Come on! Now! Now!'

Wilson looked up and saw Joe. He had an understandable grudge against him and hesitated.

'Give me the ball!'

Wilson flicked the ball to Joe who returned the pass quickly as the defender moved across. Now the goalkeeper was coming out. Surely Wilson had taken too long, surely the goalkeeper would smother the ball. Then, in a moment which seemed to last for ever, Wilson flicked the ball over the advancing keeper and into the net.

2–1.

He wheeled away and turned a somersault before the rest of the team fell upon him. The referee ordered them back. A fight broke out in the stands between the supporters.

When play started again, the number seven from Nueva Estrella skipped past several Caupolicán players and into the penalty area where he was brought down. He began to writhe and roll about as if he had just been shot, but there was no need.

Penalty. No question. On the touch-line, Lalo fell to his knees with his head in his hands. Joy to Despair, Ecstasy to Agony, etc.

They were now in injury time.

Nacho the fat goalie spat on his gloves and pulled his shirt down. He was not the strongest link in the Caupolicán team. Joe felt the vinegar of imminent defeat in his mouth, the irritating pinprick of hope against the odds. Nueva Estrella's number seven – recovered from his fall now – stepped up to take the penalty himself.

He sent the ball to Nacho's left. Nacho had obviously decided on a fifty-fifty gamble and hurled himself, arm outstretched, in the same direction.

None the less, the penalty was well struck towards the far corner of the goal.

Nacho hit the ground with such force that drowsy seismologists across the world must have jolted awake as their needles swung off the graph. He also managed to touch the ball with his hand so that it grazed the post and went away for a corner.

Which was taken and headed away as the whistle blew.

Lalo was running across the pitch, Nacho was being hauled – with some difficulty – on to many shoulders.

The Nueva Estrella number seven squatted on the penalty spot with his head in his hands.

He would always remember the moment, it would come back to niggle him at the strangest times; lying in bed at night just before he closed his eyes, he would remember the day he missed a penalty and lost his team the championship.

Lalo's toothless neighbour handed Joe a plastic bottle of cheap red wine mixed with coke which Joe drank before he and Wilson were also hauled aloft and carried around the pitch. He saw Magdalena jumping up and down and waving at him from the stands.

When the bus finally set off back to Villa Caupolicán, the team sat in the back singing, smoking and drinking litre bottles of beer. Happiness and energy lit up the faces of young men some of whom were little more than children. Miguel and Danny and Alex: teenagers who did not even really remember the Pinochet years although they had all grown up in his shadow.

Joe and Magdalena sat with Lalo at the front of the bus. Mothers caressed the heads of sleeping babies, children played in the aisles, people swapped food and coffee. A little girl came up to Joe and shyly offered him a ham and avocado sandwich which her mum had sent for him. Joe patted the kid on the head and turned to wave thanks at the mum.

'What are you going to do about a celebration?' Joe asked Lalo.

'We'll organise something properly. We'll also be able to make some money for the team out of it. But hang around and have a beer tonight.'

'Sure,' Joe said. He turned to Magdalena. 'Shall I stay at yours tonight?'

'Maybe I'll come up and stay with you. I have to be up early tomorrow and go to the centre to do some *tramités.*'

Joe grinned. He was always teasing Magdalena about the Chilean love of basic paperwork. Whole mornings would be set aside for standing in different queues to pay bills, photocopy bits of paper and argue with clerks. It was as integral to the national tradition as red wine, *empanadas,* dancing the *cueca.*

'Don't you start,' Magdalena said when she saw his grin. 'They're important things I have to do.'

'I'm not saying anything,' Joe said. 'But if we're going back to Providencia tonight then we're getting a cab. I'm not messing about on buses if we're staying for a drink and I don't want you going on about how expensive it is.'

Magdalena sighed. 'I suppose I could make an exception this time.'

'That's very gracious of you.'

Lalo and Joe sat out on the porch drinking a beer.

'That's some feat,' Joe said. 'Building a team from virtually nothing and winning the championship in its second season.'

'Yes,' Lalo said. He seemed a little subdued.

'Are you OK?' Joe asked.

'Sure.'

'The players were so happy. You've really given them something.'

Lalo looked down at his bottle of beer.

141

'It doesn't really mean anything though. I can remember times when I felt so alive, when I knew that what I was doing was important.'

'Well,' Joe said carefully, 'there are always different types of moment.'

'I had friends who died, special people. Is this all we have now? A football team? There has to be something more than this.'

'Perhaps there will be,' Joe said. 'But enjoy it in the meantime. Sure, it's only a small victory but that doesn't make it irrelevant.'

Ximena came out on to the porch with Magdalena. She stroked her husband's hair.

'Are you worrying again?' she said softly. 'You'll tire yourself out.'

'I am tired,' Lalo said. 'I'm really tired.'

'Poor thing,' Ximena said.

A woman came to the door and asked Ximena if she was going to the town hall the next day. They had been granted an audience with the mayor because the bus drivers were refusing to come to the neighbourhood. The drivers claimed frequency of assaults as a reason for their reluctance to pass through Villa Caupolicán's dusty streets but, as a result of their action, a woman had been raped walking from the bus stop on Santa Rosa.

A couple of players wandered past with their girlfriends, laughing and waving on their way to a party. Loud music started to blast from the house of Lalo's neighbour.

Joe stood in the shower letting the hot water wash over his aching muscles. He had prepared some food for them – scrambled eggs, avocado, tomato salad.

'Can you manage to toast some bread?' he had asked Magdalena before jumping into the shower.

Now, he smiled as he heard her singing, struggling with the lyrics of 'Imagine'.

'I've never heard the Serbo-Croat version before,' he said as he came out of the shower wrapped in his towel. The evening was warm, the balcony door open to all the light and sound of the city.

Joe put on a T-shirt and tracksuit bottoms and checked out his e-mails as they waited for the kettle to boil. There was one (1) message in his in-box.

Subject: Trapped in Chiloé!

Hi Joe,

Hope you and your book are both well. Guillermo tells me that you have become very attached to Bernardo O'Higgins. He may not have many songs but he does have the biggest avenue in Santiago named after him.

I'm sitting – believe it or not – in an Internet café by the seafront in Chiloé. Actually, it's not a café as such, it's a house which belongs to an old blind man. We have become quite good friends since Roberto got ill here and I take a break from mopping his fevered brow. We sit and put the world to rights.

Tomorrow, I'm going to see a penguin colony! It is one of the only places in the world where different types of penguin nest together I'm told. How exciting is that? That's far more interesting than Pedro de Valdivia and Bernardo O'Higgins. Chiloé is beautiful but I am quite looking forward to coming back. What are you doing at New Year? Roberto has talked about having a party. It would be nice up there I think, so try and keep it free and bring some friends if you want.

Anyway, we did come down here for a reason. Somebody in Valdivia told us about a guy here who knew something about Pablo's disappearance (linked to an ex-secret policeman called Gonzalo Espinoza in Santiago). But the contact he gave us here isn't saying a word and our original guy died (rather suspiciously) in a street robbery the other day. So that looks like another dead end although we may check out this Espinoza character when we get back to Santiago and find out whether he was in Chillán when Pablo disappeared.

I'm glad you are still seeing Guillermo – have you had your date with Valentina?

Send my regards to everybody there.

All my love, F.

'What was the name of the guy whose office we were picketing?' Joe called to Magdalena.

'Gonzalo Espinoza. Why?'

He told her what Fresia had said in her message.

'That's pretty interesting,' Magdalena said thoughtfully. 'I might try and find out whether he was in Chillán when the boy disappeared.'

'But why would he be involved with that?'

'No idea. But he's certainly the kind of guy who knows how to make a body disappear. You know, I've always thought there was something odd about the girl that the kid was with. She must know something.'

'Then why wouldn't she say?' Joe wiped a smear of avocado from his T-shirt.

'Maybe she's frightened. If Espinoza is involved, then she would have good reason to be. He has friends everywhere . . . here, you're just making that worse.'

She took a wet cloth and wiped his shirt for him.

'Take it off. You need to wash it.'

As Joe was taking his T-shirt off he suddenly felt Magdalena trace a line with her finger on his stomach. He recoiled in surprise.

Her face was flushed.

'What's the matter? I was only looking at your scar.'

He looked down at his appendix scar.

'Nothing's the matter, it's just that your hands were cold.'

At that moment the telephone rang. It was Valentina.

'How are you?'

'I'm fine. Tired. I've been playing football.'

Magdalena went over and stood by the window and lit a cigarette.

'I've spoken to Roberto. They're in Chiloé; he's been ill but he's getting better. They're coming back soon.'

'Yes I know, I just got an e-mail from Fresia.'

'Oh well, I thought I'd let you know. How's your book? The war for independence?'

'It's OK. I didn't know that so many of the soldiers in the Army of the Andes were black men. That's one in the eye for the Chilean racist mentality. Liberated by an army of black men led by an Argentinian and an Irishman.'

Valentina laughed. 'Like a typical man, you're forgetting about O'Higgins' mother Isabel Riquelme. He was only half-Irish. Anyway, what are you doing later?'

'I've got a friend round.'

'OK, well give me a call some time. It would be nice to see you again.'

'Sure.'

Joe put the phone down. He liked Valentina's relaxed approach.

They both knew that nothing of any great significance was going to happen between them, they might not even sleep together again. There was a kind of mutual shrug between them but it was a friendly shrug.

'Who was that?' Magdalena asked.

'Just a friend.'

'Are British people not racist?'

'What?'

'Well you talked about the Chilean racist mentality. As if British people weren't racist.'

'Are you starting an argument?'

'No. I just want to know why you think you have the right to call us racists.'

'Right, you *are* starting an argument.'

'I think it's a bit arrogant for an Englishman to call us racists.'

'I'm not English.'

'Whatever,' Magdalena said.

Joe frowned and shook his head. He hated arguments but Magdalena had lit her own blue touch-paper and was in no mood to retire. She glared at him.

'You love showing off how much you know about Chile but there's lots you don't know, you're not such an expert.'

'Fair enough,' Joe said stiffly.

'In fact it's quite embarrassing sometimes hearing you go on about it. Trying to be more Chilean than anybody else. Showing off.'

'I'm sorry if I've done that,' Joe said.

'Yeah you do, you can't keep quiet about it. What if a Chilean person came over to your country and started going on about the figures that you learned about in school, singing the songs you knew when you were a child. What right have you got to tell people who they should know about, like you're here educating the savages?'

'I don't know,' Joe said, helpless under this sudden assault.

Magdalena stared at him for a moment and then turned away to the window. She took her glasses off and rubbed her eyes but did not turn round again. Joe went into the other room.

He lay awake thinking about what Magdalena had said to him. He knew that she had a vile temper at times but her assault had drawn blood. A big-mouth? A show-off? She was right. What if a Chilean came over and started boring everybody about Oliver Cromwell or Robert the Bruce and speaking in rhyming slang? He remembered drunken arguments with Chileans about dates and places. On the whole he had been correct but did that warrant his loud insistence like some pedantic trainspotter? What would he think about a Chilean who started pulling him up because he didn't know the date of Gladstone's first Home Rule bill or the exact number of Spitfires shot down in the Second World War? Who started singing 'Flower of Scotland' or 'D'ye ken John Peel' every time he got drunk?

He rubbed his eyes in the dark. A loud-mouth, a show-off, a bore.

There was a tap on the door.

'Yes?'

Magdalena stood at the door; he could see the enlarged shadow of her hair on the wall.

'I'm sorry,' she said.

'Why? You were right.'

'No,' she said. 'Don't ever think that. Well, it's true you can be a bit over the top sometimes but I shouldn't have said what I did. The way you get excited about things is really nice. And people don't laugh at you – well they do, but not like the way I said. I'm really sorry.'

'That's OK.' Joe was taken aback. Magdalena making an apology was not something he was likely to hear twice in a lifetime.

'And I didn't actually know that most of the men in the Army of the Andes were black. They didn't teach us that in school.'

'Well, I think it was about half of them actually. About a tenth were Chilean exiles, so the rest . . .'

Magdalena sniggered. 'Goodnight, Joe,' she said.

Her shadow vanished from the wall.

Joe slept for a few hours but woke up and could not return to sleep. He lay awake thinking about the football that day, about the goal he had scored which had helped to win the championship. He got up and walked to the window, the city still working out there, in full swing at 3 a.m.: people dancing, talking, drinking, taking drugs, having sex. Prostitutes on street corners, taxi drivers looking for fares, plans made, conspiracies hatched, deals struck, fights starting, eyes meeting, hands touching, roulette wheels spinning, a helicopter buzzing across the skyline, heading up towards the far north-east of the city, the scattered lights of extreme wealth in the foothills.

A typical gringo who thinks he knows all there is to know about this country.

Magdalena's friend Patty had said that about him and maybe it was true. But then Patty also thought that *Dances with Wolves* was the best film ever made so it might not be too wise to trust her judgement on anything. Yet Joe suddenly felt a terrible wave of *People don't like me and they are right not to* washing over him. He had thought that Fresia had liked him, that she had come to Concepción to see him when, in fact, nothing was further from her mind. Now she was down in the south with her lover while he worried away in Santiago about the connections between historical figures and different types of political violence. And Magdalena, his oldest friend, he had never questioned their relationship. Yet she had turned on him suddenly like that and, in spite of her apology, she must have thought those things to say them; there must be some dislike for him behind their friendship.

Joe suddenly felt immensely tired and depressed. He fell asleep and dreamed that he was lying with Lalo on a hillside on some kind of ambush. But suddenly he noticed that there were soldiers on the other side of the valley, a whole army of green ants just looking for him and Lalo. Together they were forced to leap into a fast-swirling river which quickly carried them away, although Joe kept bumping up against Japanese lanterns and wreaths of flowers also swept along by the current. Lalo vanished and out of the corner of his eye Joe could see a stretch of water which was so fierce and fast that he would surely drown but he was being drawn inexorably towards it. *I am dreaming*, he told himself, *this is just a dream*. But he could not get out of the dream; it held him like the current; he was trapped in the dream. He thought that he had woken up but this was still part of the dream. He was dreaming his resistance to the dream and he had to get his eyes open but they would not do so. He awoke suddenly, terrified that he was still dreaming, and was relieved to see the familiar outline of the room, his book and a glass of water, the grey dawn of real life outside the window.

Penguins

'This is where you want to get off,' the driver leaned on his steering wheel and spoke to Fresia, who was one of the few people left on the bus.

'Here?' Fresia had expected a village or a settlement at least. There was no sign of human habitation and she felt a sudden flash of anxiety.

'Walk down that track there. It will take you about half an hour. The buses pass by here every hour on the way back. I go to the end of the road and turn round so if you get here when the bus is going in the other direction it will come back about ten minutes later to take you to Ancud.'

Fresia hopped down and stood in the warm sun, watching the bus disappear. She took a sip from her water bottle and put on her sunglasses. Sure enough, at the entrance to the track which led from the main road there was a handmade sign with an arrow and a picture of a penguin.

Fresia had left Roberto behind in the *pensione*. He was recovering from his food poisoning but was still weak and not in a fit state to make an excursion. They had decided to attempt the return journey on the following day and so Fresia had chosen to spend the last day on the island visiting the nearby penguin colonies. Roberto stayed behind reading her copy of *Mrs Dalloway*. She had just started it but he had finished all of his books and was growing impatient and bored.

Tomás from the Internet café had given her instructions about buses from Ancud to Pumillahue. She had drunk a cup of sweet black coffee early in the morning at the terminal and felt a sudden pleasure at sculling out on her own. The paper she bought for the bus lay unread by her side as she stared from the window at the sea, the wild Pacific waves rolling on to long beaches.

The track curved round, dipped and rose, until she wondered

whether she would ever find the beach. Sometimes it was quite enclosed and claustrophobic. A large horsefly followed her, buzzing aggressively, impervious to her attempts to flap it away from her hair. She vaguely remembered that they were attracted to black and finally she untied her white sweatshirt from around her waist and tied it Babushka-like around her head, glad that there was nobody about to see her. The fly buzzed around for a bit longer and then there was silence, as if an alarm had finally stopped. At last she rounded a corner and saw below her a long, broad sandy beach, a green headland, the turquoise ocean, fishing boats bobbing around small islands.

Fresia watched her footprints in the sand behind her as she crossed the beach to a solitary, modern building. A couple of young, dark-skinned shell fishermen in tight rubber suits suddenly emerged from the sea, nodded courteously to her and said *Buenas tardes* as they passed. She smiled to herself and turned to sneak a glance at their sleek, rubber-clad bodies as they padded up the beach – two sets of flippered footprints in the opposite direction from those made by her own sandals.

The penguin colonies were supported by an international environmental agency and administered by a German university. Two German female students were responsible for welcoming the visitors and selling them a ticket for a boat trip around the islands. Both were blonde, had very bad acne and were either extremely stoned or extremely stupid or both. The local fishermen and the stray kids seemed to find the two spotty German girls as fascinating and entertaining as a whole colony of penguins, nudging each other and giggling whenever they moved or spoke. Fresia bought a ticket and sat outside waiting for the man who was going to take them out in the boat, flicking the arm of her sweatshirt to fend off a squadron of giant horseflies which buzzed insistently around her head.

A kid came up to Fresia.

'Do you want to see something?' he asked.

'Sure,' Fresia said.

He led her round to a shed where a couple of fishermen were fixing a yellow fishing boat. In the back of the shed, lying on an old Colo Colo T-shirt, was an injured penguin.

'It's broken its wing,' the kid explained.

'Oh dear,' Fresia said. The penguin blinked mournfully up at her. 'What are you going to do with it?'

'Eat it,' the kid said firmly and the older men laughed and glanced at Fresia to see how she took this.

'Is penguin good to eat?' Fresia asked.

'Delicious,' the kid said. 'Especially the breast.'

'I don't believe you,' Fresia said. 'I think you're going to make it better and return it to its home.'

''*stai loca*,' the kid said and gave the penguin a gentle kick in the stomach. 'That penguin's for the pot.'

'Don't kick the penguin, Carlitos,' one of the fisherman said as if this were a routine reproach. His curly hair emerged over the edge of the boat and he glanced at Fresia.

'Where are you from?'

'Well I'm Chilean but I lived all of my life in Britain.'

'In Britain!' The fisherman stood up feigning awe and Fresia knew that she was being teased but not maliciously.

'Isn't Britain near Germany?' he said and they collapsed into laughter – Germany was obviously an unfailing comic trigger.

'What are they doing now?' And they all poked their heads simultaneously round the door like cartoon bank robbers to snigger at the two students.

'Do you want to see a dead rat?' the kid asked Fresia.

'No thanks.'

'Beat it, Carlitos,' said the curly-haired fisherman. 'So . . . did you go on one of Pinochet's special holidays to Britain?' he asked Fresia.

'Yeah, he made my parents an offer they couldn't refuse.'

'Did your parents come back with you?'

'No.'

'Ah well,' he turned and smiled at her. 'That's Chileans for you. *Pattiperros* and *trotamundos*. I've got a cousin in Australia. He's a miner. There's no corner of the globe where you won't find a Chilean. Even Germany.'

'That Pinochet was a motherfucker,' the kid piped up. 'My grand-dad says the only good president we ever had was Allende.'

'And that's about the only thing that old drunk has ever got right,' the fisherman muttered. 'So, you want to go and see some penguins, *mi 'jita*? Let's go then. *Ya po'*, Carlitos.' He clapped his hands at the boy. Go and tell the Fräuleins that I'm ready now.'

Carlitos scuttled away.

'Don't worry about the penguin,' the fisherman said to Fresia, handing her a pink life-jacket. 'Carlitos is quite gentle with it really.

150

Which is surprising because the only thing *he* gets at home is kicks and punches. Now, who have we got here?'

The boat party included a honeymooning couple from Antofagasta whose hands were superglued together, a Swiss tourist and – to Fresia's initial dismay – a British couple called Gary and Natalie from Brentwood. Gary was a chunky man wearing shorts and a T-shirt with *Never Trust a Hippy* on it. He introduced himself to everybody as he struggled to fit into his life-jacket.

'I feel like a giant prawn, Nat,' he grumbled to his slender girlfriend.

'Don't be silly,' she said. 'You look fine.'

'Why does that kid keep pointing at me and sniggering then?'

It was true. Carlitos had been given the job of pushing the dinghy out and was puffing loudly and speculating as to whether the boat might sink with the fat gringo in it.

'First I get attacked by giant flies then some lairy kid decides it's Red Nose Day. I'm not coming here again.'

Fresia laughed.

'*Ese guatón es aleman?*' the fisherman asked Fresia as he steered the boat away from the beach, bouncing in the incoming surf. He pointed at the couple. 'You Deutsch?' he repeated in pidgin English.

'Certainly not,' Gary said. 'Tell him I've never been so insulted in my life.'

'They're English,' Fresia said.

'What does *guatón* mean?' Gary asked suspiciously. 'I keep hearing that.'

'Well, I suppose a literal translation is "big gut",' Fresia said.

Natalie laughed. 'You'll have to lay off them pasties for a bit, Gal.'

'They're called *empanadas*, actually,' Gary said. 'And I'll eat what I like when I'm on holiday.'

'Oh right. Not like at home then?'

'It's usually said affectionately,' Fresia pointed out. 'More a description than an insult. Like they might call Natalie *Flaca* or Skinny. The fisherman might be *Crespo* because he's got curly hair.'

'What would those two dozy German birds be?' Natalie asked. 'I wanted a glass of water not the crown jewels.'

'Actually, I like that a lot,' the man patted his stomach. '*Yo soy guatón, compadre,*' he said cheerfully to the fisherman. 'And it's all paid for, mate.'

'*Que dice?*' the fisherman asked.

'He says his stomach's all paid for.'

'It must have cost a fortune then.'

'What did he say?' Gary asked.

Fresia explained and Gary laughed. 'He's lucky he's driving the boat . . . Fuck me, Nat, look at that! That's a fucking sea otter. I ain't joking. A sea otter! My life.'

'All right, all right, it's a sea otter,' Natalie rolled her eyes at Fresia. 'Don't fall out of the boat.'

'And would you look at that cormorant. And pelicans! This place is brilliant. Bring on the penguins.'

The fisherman grinned at Gary, pleased with his enthusiasm.

'Tell the fat pirate to stay and have a beer afterwards,' he said to Fresia. 'But not that one . . .' he jerked his head at the Swiss tourist who had not spoken or smiled the whole time. 'He's more boring than a Mormon at an orgy.'

The boat swung around the island and Gary jumped up as they sighted their first penguins, hunched up on the rocks like ninepins.

'Gary! You'll capsize us,' Natalie shrieked and even the fisherman looked concerned.

'I love penguins,' Gary said happily as he sat down. 'They don't do anybody any harm, they don't pick on other animals.'

'Apart from fish,' Natalie said.

'Fish don't count. When it's cold they all huddle together and keep each other warm. And they take it in turns to be on the outside and get a cold arse, they don't just push the weakest one out there.'

'They don't do much,' Natalie observed.

Gary stared at her.

'You might think so but at night it goes mental on this island. They get on their mobiles, invite some podium-dancing seals round, rack out the fish and wave their flippers in the air like they just don't care . . . Course they don't do much, they're wild penguins not fucking circus animals. Here Fresh . . .' he handed Fresia his camera. 'Take a photo of us. Try and get a few penguins in the background doing cartwheels for Nat. And leave Swiss Tony out.'

'Gary, he might speak English. Don't be horrible.'

He moved to sit next to her and put his head on her shoulder. The redistribution of weight made the boat lurch alarmingly.

'Cuddle up, my little penguin. Watch the birdie. Say *empanada*.'

'Blinding,' Gary said as he hopped out of the boat. '*Fantastico*,' he shook hands with the fisherman.

'He says to stay and have a beer,' Fresia said.

'Great idea.'

The fishermen distributed bottles of cold beer and they clinked them together. They sat around drinking, watching the sea birds over the islands. Gary was teaching Carlitos a song in English, they were both giggling.

'He's found his level,' Natalie said.

She told Fresia that she worked with young offenders and that Gary promoted DJs. 'That's why we come here,' she said. 'Mouthy little crims and caners with one brain cell between them – it can do your head in after a while. We thought about Australia but we'll do that next year.'

'Sounds perfect,' Fresia said. 'Have you been together a long time?'

Natalie held up a balled fist and showed her a diamond ring.

'Twelve years we've been married. We met at one of those parties in the nineteen-eighties. We were hardcore, scary when I remember how we used to go for it. But now we're older and wiser . . .' she laughed. 'Keep our arses warm like the penguins.'

'Gary's great,' Fresia said watching him as he pretended to be a penguin for Carlitos.

'Gary? Oh he's my soul mate. I couldn't live without him.'

'Do you have children?'

Natalie shook her head. 'I've got nothing against them, I love my little nieces and nephews. But I'm happy with how things are, I don't need anything else to make my life complete. And Gary doesn't want one.'

'He seems to like children though.'

'Oh yeah, that's the problem. You might not guess it but Gary's quite a thinker. He thinks it would be wrong to bring a child into the world because he can't see a future for it. He's always going on about how we'll be destroyed by technology, how there'll be a war over water and stuff like that, how we're stuck with this system and this system is going to kill us. We're all doooomed.'

Fresia remembered her father. *Capitalism will destroy us but there is no alternative to capitalism* had been one of his cheerier predictions. She watched Gary playing with Carlitos and took some photos of them. The kid struck poses for the camera and the fishermen smiled at each other.

'What about you, Fresia? Do you think you'll go back to Britain?' Natalie asked.

'I don't know,' Fresia said. 'Sure, to visit, see my mum and brother. I haven't made any decisions about the long term.'

'Lucky you. I'd love to stay here for a bit longer.'

The fishermen decided to make a *curanto* – a fish and meat stew traditionally cooked in the ground, which Fresia knew would take hours.

'I have to go,' she said.

'Come on, Fresh, stay and have some stew,' Gary said. 'We'll get a lift to Ancud later.'

Fresia did not want to be dependent upon a lift at night, especially since a bottle of pisco had now been produced.

'I should go.' She wrote her number and passed it to Natalie. 'Call me when you get back to Santiago.'

Natalie wrote her number in Britain down.

'Come out for some wild nights in Essex,' she said. 'If you ever come back. Good luck whatever you do.'

'Take the other path,' the fisherman said to her. 'It's about quarter of an hour longer but it's not as steep and you get better views. Goodbye, *mi 'jita*. Take care of yourself. Come back and see us some time.'

As she passed the reception area, she saw the two German girls sharing a joint and staring in utter bewilderment at Carlitos who was swinging a dead rat by the tail and singing 'Two World Wars and One World Cup' at them, glancing back at Gary for approval.

The unpaved road was wider and more open than the path by which Fresia had descended to the beach; her feet scrunched on the loose gravel, her new sandals were grey with dust. Tiny yellow flowers grew by the side of the road, fields and hills stretched inland. It was agricultural land, the road fenced with strands of barbed wire, the occasional glimpse of a remote farm with a dog in the yard. On the other side, beneath her, was the ocean.

In spite of the fact that this alternative route was less steep, the walk was still tiring and the afternoon sun was hot. She stumbled at one point and twisted her ankle; not badly but it niggled. Fortunately, she was nearing the point where the buses arrived. She had arrived early and stopped where the road curved at almost 90 degrees and ran up to the bus stop. The point at which the road turned offered a little space where she could sit down unobserved to inspect her ankle, look out to sea and rest for a while.

The sea was very blue, a fleet of fishing boats bobbed like invasion barges in the channels between the islands. Further away was the dark shape of the coast, fingernails of white surf breaking in the distance. She took a couple of photos of the islands, happy with the feeling of having her camera in her hand again. Just when she was contemplating moving up to the road to wait for the bus, she heard footsteps on the gravel and turned to see a figure coming out of the sun.

'I thought I might find you here.'

It was Fernando Araya – El Trauco. He was carrying a stick and she had to put her hand to her forehead to see him properly in the glare of the sun.

'Why did you think that?'

'My wife told me that she had seen you get on the bus this morning.'

'And what are you doing here?'

'I came to look for you,' he said. 'Do you mind if I sit down with you for a moment?'

Fresia watched him from under her palm. His presence was strange but she was not particularly alarmed by it. 'Sure,' she said and he stepped out of the sun and squatted beside her. He was wearing a New York Yankees T-shirt and Reebok trainers. He began spinning his stick between his palms as if trying to make fire.

'Keep still,' he said, suddenly moving with his hand towards her face. She froze and he took something from her hair. It was one of the large, ugly horseflies and he held it trapped by the wings.

'When we were kids we used to do a trick by putting them on the end of a blade of grass,' he said, inspecting the trapped insect.

'They're disgusting,' Fresia said. 'Do they bite?'

'Yes but they're slow and stupid. You always see them coming.' He sighed. 'I would really be careful about asking too many questions about Gonzalo Espinoza,' he said.

'Why do you say that?' Fresia asked.

Araya inspected the fly and then threw it into the air. It buzzed slowly away.

'He's never reacted well to people interfering in his business. That's what I came to tell you.'

'Nobody is interfering in his business,' Fresia said. 'If he has something to do with the disappearance of a teenager then he has to answer questions. These people seem to think they are above the law still.'

Araya raised his eyebrows and laughed, looking out to sea where a pelican suddenly flapped out of the waves and took flight.

'He's a very powerful man.'

'And what is your connection with him?' Fresia asked.

'I no longer have one. I just run my restaurant.'

'But you did.'

He shrugged. 'You know what they say. You can choose your friends but not your family. The same is true of your work colleagues.'

'I'm not sure about that,' Fresia said. 'Given Espinoza's line of work, I would have thought that you could choose rather easily whether to be involved with him or not.'

He turned away from the sea and looked her straight in the eyes.

'I like that directness you have – it's obvious that you weren't brought up here. But remember that Espinoza has many quite legitimate lines of work.'

'And which were you involved with?'

'Let's say that I was involved in the more administrative side of his import-export business. It's not important though, there aren't many people in this country who can claim to have an entirely clear conscience.'

'Maybe not,' Fresia said. 'But there is still a difference between people who are not one hundred per cent pure and those who have no conscience at all.'

'That's true,' Araya said. 'Espinoza is not a sadist, he's not one of those who particularly enjoys the sound of screaming. But he has no conscience.'

'Was he in Chillán that night?'

'He might have been.'

He turned to look out to sea again, a flight of sea birds taking off from one of the islands into the clear hot sky.

'So Sergio Valenzuela wasn't lying, he wasn't crazy?'

Araya shrugged. 'He was crazy all right. And now he's dead.'

There was silence for a moment.

'There's nothing that can be done about it now,' Araya said. 'OK, I'll be honest with you because I like you. This is what I think *might* have happened. Let's say there was some kind of an argument in a bar and some people decided to teach the boy a lesson. Maybe they went further than they wanted to, maybe they only wanted to give him a beating to teach him some manners . . .'

'Is that what happened?'

156

He was silent for a moment.

'I would say that the main uncertainty is whether they meant to kill him or not. But if that is what happened, and if Espinoza was involved, then two things are certain. They'll never find the body and Espinoza will never face charges.'

'He was just a little kid,' Fresia said.

'Yes, it's sad,' Araya said. 'But if you ask too many questions about Espinoza, then you'll find out his true character. And believe me, you don't want to see that.'

'And what does it matter to you?'

'I like you. You're not like Chilean girls.'

She laughed. 'I hope not.'

They sat for a while looking out to sea.

'How did you get your scar?' Fresia asked him eventually.

'*Problemas de faldas*,' he grinned at her. 'Skirt problems. Fighting over a girl.'

'It's never worth it,' she said.

'This one was,' he answered.

She rolled her eyes and shifted a little, wincing as she transferred weight to her sore ankle.

'What's up?' he said.

'I twisted my ankle earlier. It's nothing.'

He put his finger lightly on her ankle.

'It's just a bit bruised,' he said, tracing a delicate spiral around the contusion. Fresia felt a tightening in her throat as he moved the strap of her sandal slightly to inspect the skin underneath. The touch was suggestive, a tiny caress, exploratory. She could put a stop to it, should put a stop to it.

But the touch was also agreeable.

In the distance the unmistakable throb of a bus changing gears as it climbed the hill.

'That's my bus,' she murmured, moving her foot away.

'It's coming the other way,' he said. 'It has to turn around. It will come back in ten minutes.'

This was true. She remembered the bus driver telling her this.

'Besides . . .' his hand alighted again just above her ankle. 'They come every hour.'

He stared at her, half smiling, waiting calmly for her reaction. And all that Fresia had to do was not react, all she had to do was not shrug his hand off to show acceptance, she only had to transmit that simple message, to do nothing. And the temptation to do nothing is sometimes very strong, the temptation to use inactivity to signal *OK, yes, why not?* Fresia certainly felt that temptation now, the temptation to turn her head to sea, to accept the audacious invitation, to take control of and enjoy her deviancy. She could close her eyes, she could allow the tanned hand with the gold ring, the hand that had gently moved the strap of her sandal and touched the soft skin underneath, she could allow that hand to wander, to touch other places. An hour, a lost hour between one bus and another, all her senses already stimulated by the sweet warm air, here on this strange island, on this isolated outcrop overlooking the sea, the pelican in a tumbling dive for the fish beneath the surface, the sea otter sliding from the rock into the surf.

He smiled and moved closer to her, encouraged by the absence of recoil or rejection. They both looked down at his hand. It began trailing up her leg to her hip, the other moving down from her shoulder to her breast, closing gently around it. She exhaled and closed her eyes, shifted her position a little, her head turned skywards until finally the hand received a different, less passive signal – confirmation of the effect its explorations had had on her. Did he smile knowingly, triumphantly? She did not open her eyes to find out. He moved even closer, shifted again, the hand more purposeful now, pushing, rearranging.

She could hear the gulls crying out over the ocean. Somebody might come, somebody might see them. Not as long as she kept her eyes closed, and so she kept them closed.

Grass and gravel scrunched under her palms.

He took a strand of her hair and wound it around his finger.

'I liked you from the moment I saw you,' he murmured and stroked her cheek.

What is it you are really looking for, cariño? *The revolution? You're too late, I'm afraid.*

She snapped back and opened her eyes wide.

'It was you! At the festival by the sea. It was you!'

He looked startled.

'What are you talking about?' He tried to pull her to him again by the wrist but the spell was broken. She stood up quickly, pulled her skirt down.

'It was you!' she said angrily.

Walking across the sea waist-high on a sinking bridge. El Trauco the hunchback with his axe, waiting to jump into the dreams of tender maidens.

But she was no tender maiden; she had let him, she had wanted his hands to touch her, she had blanked out the other man reading Virginia Woolf, looking at his watch, anxious for her return. Now she had given something to this man whose past was at best dubious; not something huge in itself but something she could never take back.

'I don't know what you're talking about. What are you talking about?' He shook his head.

She kicked aside the stick that he had been twirling and began walking up towards the road. He got up and followed her.

'Calm down,' he said. 'Come back please.'

'Leave me alone,' she said, pain throbbing through her ankle. In the distance she could hear the bus making its return towards Ancud. She began to half-jog.

'Please,' he said, sounding genuinely distraught. 'I didn't mean to upset you.'

She reached the road and held out her arm for the bus. She thought for a moment that he might try and get on as well but he just stood watching her. The driver looked at her lazily over the steering wheel, his hand on the gear stick with a bleeding-heart Jesus set in the perspex bulb. He glanced at the watching Araya and when he saw that he was not going to get on the bus, he drove off.

'Lovers' tiff?' he asked sympathetically.

Fresia walked down the bus and took a seat by the window. She was numb, had not yet begun the process of dealing with what had just happened. But she would, of course, simply because she had to, because Fresia Tamara Castillo Morganstein was no tender maid, not even a tender mermaid, but an ordinary person, a mere mortal. She did not have a glimmering silver tail but normal (shaved) legs which could be unlocked by a hand in the sunshine, and the evidence of her very mortal desire was still uncomfortably apparent to her.

She looked out at the calm shining sea and wrapped the arms of her sweatshirt around her nose and mouth.

But she would deal with it, she would deal with this because these things are always dealt with in one way or another; they are packaged, marked and sent to the basement (or attic) of guilty secrets and unspoken memories. There they remain hidden but never absent, quiet but never completely tamed. They will burst from time to time into dreams or fantasies – bringing both shame and pleasure – the sudden disturbance of wings triggered by a faraway noise, the startled ricochet and truncated flight of caged birds.

PART THREE

I Like Pisco

'Ah, Joe,' Guillermo beamed at him as he opened the door. 'You have dropped by at a very opportune moment. There is an old acquaintance here I want you to meet. Come up, come up. Perhaps you could bring a bottle of beer from the fridge?'

It was a hot, smoggy Friday evening. The mountains were completely obscured from view, the white statue at the top of the San Cristóbal hill was fuzzy. Joe was at a loose end and had dropped by to see if Guillermo was there for a chat and a drink. He went to the fridge and took out a cold litre bottle of Royal, trudged up the stairs to the roof terrace.

'Hey, stranger.' Fresia was sitting with her feet up on a chair, drinking a glass of beer and dipping into a big bag of crisps.

Poor Joe. In Fresia's absence he had immersed himself in the war of independence, worried about the lack of songs dedicated to Bernardo O'Higgins, played in a championship-winning football team, and slept with one of King Lear's daughters. He had convinced himself that he did not really care about Fresia, she was just somebody he had met on the plane, a childish crush. But when he saw her sitting there in the sun, her hair tied back, the silver charm bracelet on her arm, he felt as if his heart had suddenly stopped, the terrible sickness gripped him again with all its previous force.

'Why didn't you tell me that you were coming back?'

'Technical problems on Ancud's only public computer I'm afraid. And I thought I'd surprise you.'

She got up to give him a kiss and Joe noticed that she was limping.

'What happened to your foot?'

Fresia laughed. 'Nothing. I sprained it a little but Guillermo is acting like I've broken my leg.'

'You're really brown.'

'Yeah, I got out in the sun a lot. We were lucky with the weather.'

Joe nodded. 'And how were the penguins?'

'What? Oh yes, the penguins. Rather a non-event actually, they just sat on their island and stared back at us. But I met some great fishermen.'

'And how long are you staying for?'

Fresia frowned at him.

'What are you talking about?'

'Well, when are you going up to the Cajon del Maípo?'

'I'm not sure. What a strange question.'

'Oh I just thought . . .'

'That because I went away with Roberto I would be moving in with him? I'm not quite ready to retire to the countryside yet.'

'But you're still . . . together?'

'No, he's up at his house.'

'You know what I mean. You're still seeing each other.'

'Yes, we're still seeing each other. Whatever that means.'

She was becoming irritated and Joe sensed that they were on the brink of another argument.

'Yes, Joe, stop being such an academic,' Guillermo surprisingly waded in on Fresia's side. 'Sometimes it is more convenient not to define one's terms, don't you think?'

Joe lit a cigarette and resisted the impulse to tell his host to fuck off and mind his own business.

Fresia picked up the camera that was on the table beside her.

'Say cheese,' she said, pointing it at Joe and taking a picture.

'Listen . . .' Joe said, 'I hope you won't see my next question as an intolerable attempt to invade your privacy or pin you down to dreary old specifics but what are you doing tomorrow?'

'Well, I was thinking of getting married but I could postpone that. Do you have a suggestion?'

'As a matter of fact I do. The team from Villa Caupolicán – against all the odds and assisted by my own modest efforts – won the championship.'

'Congratulations.'

'Thanks. Tomorrow there is a big barbecue to celebrate. Lalo wanted some photos of the team so I thought you might want to come and help out. Also, you mentioned Gonzalo Espinoza in your e-mail?'

'Yes. Have you heard of him?'

'I got hit with a baton outside his office the other day. Magdalena knows all about him, she's been chasing him for ages. She wants to talk to you.'

'I'll pick you up from your flat tomorrow.'

'Good.'

Downstairs the telephone rang. Guillermo looked at Fresia.

'I suspect that's for you,' he said. Fresia got up and limped to the stairs. Guillermo looked at Joe.

'What's he like, this Roberto Walker?'

Joe shrugged. 'Handsome, literate, rich, hospitable.'

'Ah. Well, I can see why somebody might be attracted to him.'

'He thinks *Love in the Time of Cholera* is the best book ever written.'

'Really? That's rather an extravagant claim.'

'I think so too,' Joe said.

'Well,' Guillermo poured them both another glass of beer. 'If I had been Fresia I would still have chosen you.'

Joe was surprised. He had never seen Guillermo as somebody who either observed a great deal outside his research or who possessed their own sexuality.

'I doubt if she felt that she was making a choice,' Joe said. 'We're just friends.'

'Yes of course,' Guillermo said, passing Joe the bag of crisps.

'Me, me, take a photo of me for the girls in England.'

'Why, you don't want to scare them off. Take a photo of me. I am Latin lover.'

'*Saaale, huevón.*'

The football team bounced exuberantly in front of Fresia's camera like a litter of puppies. The party was being held in the street, across which green and white bunting had been stretched and long tables set up for food. The courtyard of one of the corner houses had been turned into an improvised dance-floor; music began to thump out of large speakers. Smoke from barbecues curled into the warm air and small teams of women and kids were buttering rolls, slicing tomatoes and dicing avocado. A couple of older men were already legless and making idiots of themselves, to the great amusement of the kids.

'Hey, give her a break.' Lalo held up a hot dog and a beer and motioned for Fresia to come and sit down.

'I feel a bit out of date anyway,' Fresia gestured to Chelo who was walking around with an expensive-looking digicam but not receiving nearly as much attention.

Magdalena watched Fresia dispassionately as she ate. Joe hoped that she wouldn't start being aggressive, partly because he knew that Fresia could be equally acid-tongued.

But all Magdalena said was, 'She's got very brown.'

After the food had been eaten, Lalo made a speech about the importance of their victory and the need to build on what they had achieved. Ximena gave a report on the meeting that the women had had with the mayor, who had promised to talk to the bus company about restoring service to the area. Awards were then given out for outstanding contribution (Marcos), top goal scorer (Marcos) and best overseas player (Joe). As a gift, Joe received a bottle of pisco and an oven glove in the colours of the Chilean flag, which said *I ♡ Chile*. The boys whistled and made jokes about how they hoped that his cooking was better than his ability to beat the offside trap.

'So, let's talk about Gonzalo Espinoza,' Magdalena said to Fresia.

Joe left them to it and went back to Lalo's house to hide his bottle of pisco and oven glove before he started drinking and lost them, like so many other gifts he had received on special occasions. He particularly liked the oven glove which would go well in his kitchen in Finsbury Park. As he turned the corner, he almost bumped into the woman with dyed blonde hair who had come round to abuse Lalo after the first game he had played here. She did not appear to have a problem with the whole of Lalo's family because she was standing with his son Lucho and another man. The man was short and stocky and reminded Joe of an amateur boxer. He said something quietly to the woman, who laughed. Lucho looked uncomfortable.

'Are you OK, Lucho?' Joe asked.

'Why shouldn't he be?' the woman said.

'He's fine,' the man said. He was red-eyed and slightly wired. 'Tell the gringo, Luchito.'

'I'm fine,' Lucho said, staring at the ground and then scowling at Joe. 'What are you doing?'

'Dropping these off in your house.' He held up the oven glove and the pisco.

The man sneered and the woman laughed and said in pidgin English, 'You like pisco?'

They fell about laughing.

'You like pisco?' the man repeated and they screamed with laughter again.

Joe tried to be good-natured and show that he was not uptight.

'Yes, I like pisco,' he said slowly in English, sending himself up.

At this, though, they nearly collapsed in hysterical laughter. Lucho stared at the ground again.

'I too like pisco,' the man said pointing to himself. 'I like pisco. *A mi tambien me gusta el pisco, huevón.* God save your queen.'

And he supported himself on the woman's shoulder as they nearly hyperventilated at this piece of high comedy.

'Yeah, well, don't give yourself a heart attack over it,' Joe said in English with the same false smile and then turned away from them and went into the house, where he left his gifts on the kitchen table. When he came out of the house, they had gone and so he returned to the party where everybody was dancing. At the end of the dance, he sat down with Magdalena and Fresia who were laughing and panting after having been whirled around the dance floor.

'So?' he said. 'What about Gonzalo Espinoza?'

'I think we've got enough to run an article at least suggesting the possibility that he was involved in the disappearance of Pablo Errazuriz. I'll check out this guy from Chiloé as well.'

'He said that he was just involved in the administrative side of things,' Fresia said.

'Yeah he would. We'll see what we can find out about him anyway.'

'What do you think happened?'

'Somehow, somewhere, Pablo Errazuriz got mixed up with Espinoza and his men. That girl knows what really happened.'

'But she's too frightened to say,' Fresia added as she bent down to rub her ankle. 'My bloody foot's killing me after all that dancing.'

Magdalena suggested that they return to her house.

'Are we getting the bus?' Fresia asked.

'I wouldn't recommend it,' Magdalena said. 'Standing around in Santa Rosa at this time with a big camera is not the most sensible of ideas. If you don't mind sleeping in my room with me, Fresia, then Joe can have the sofa.'

'Sounds fine.'

'How will we get there?' Joe asked.

'Lalo's said he'll drive us.'

They looked at Lalo who was drinking what looked like a pint of pisco.

'He'll be OK,' Magdalena said in the face of Joe and Fresia's expressions. 'I've seen him much worse than this. Give him a coffee and he'll be fine.'

But before they could make Lalo a coffee, his next-door neighbour appeared and shouted to Lalo to come quickly as his house had been broken into. They all made their way swiftly back to the purple house on the corner, stepping over the front door which had been nearly smashed in two.

'They haven't taken anything,' Ximena said, frowning. 'Look, the TV and the stereo are still there. Why would they break in and not steal anything?'

'They've taken my bottle of pisco,' Joe said. 'I left it on the table. The bastards leave your TV and take my present.'

'At least they left your oven glove,' Fresia said, picking it up and putting it on like a puppet.

'Didn't you hear anything?' Ximena demanded from the neighbour. 'You must have heard something.'

He looked uncomfortable. 'Sorry, I had the music on loud.'

Lalo came out of the bedroom and stood for a moment with his head in his hands. Then he looked up.

'They've taken the team kit,' he said. 'And all the membership stuff. And they've taken the championship money we won that we were going to buy new kit with.'

'Nobody knew where that money was,' Ximena said. 'Nobody could have just walked in and found it like that. Are you sure, Lalo? Check again.'

'It's gone,' Lalo said.

Ximena turned as Lucho came through the gates into the front yard.

'What's going on?' he asked.

'We've been burgled,' his mother said, putting her arm around him. 'They've taken the team's kit and the money.'

Joe stared hard at Lucho but the boy would not meet his eyes.

They went out into the yard while Lalo and Ximena went through the house checking things. Across the road, he saw the man from earlier although the woman was nowhere to be seen. The man recognised Joe.

'I like pisco,' he said, but this time his eyes narrowed and he did not laugh.

New Year's Eve

The afternoon sun was warming the white tiles of the kitchen floor as Fresia stood barefoot in Roberto's kitchen chopping lettuce and avocado for a salad, drinking a glass of lemon soda and listening to a Cassandra Wilson CD. Beyond the shade of the apple tree, the heat was dry, hard and intense, a sharp cut of blue sky beyond the ridge of the mountains.

On their return from Chiloé, Roberto had made more or less the same assumption as Joe – that she would be staying up in the mountains with him. He had been surprised when she had got up one morning, collected her stuff together and announced that she was going home and would call him in a couple of days.

'This can be your home . . . if you like,' he said.

She shook her head. 'No it can't.'

If Roberto was hurt or irritated, he was clever enough not to show it.

'OK,' he had said calmly. 'But come and see me soon. I've got used to having you around.'

'Of course I will.'

After leaving Roberto's, she spent a few days with Guillermo who had given her a temporary job in the research institute. It wasn't very exciting work – some translations, inputting research findings – but she liked being with people, the liberal office atmosphere, the jokes. Vasily showed her funny websites and asked her about dark drum and bass. The office had a little garden and they would sit out in the evenings as the breezes cooled the city, drinking coke from paper cups and chatting about politics or music or football. Sometimes Joe would drop by to use the small library or to photocopy documents. He had increased his work tempo and Fresia both admired and slightly envied the sense of intellectual purpose about him. It also saddened her because she knew that it meant he was aware that he would be leaving soon.

'Hello?' Valentina appeared on the veranda with a salad which she had prepared for the evening cradled in her arms.

Fresia poured her a glass of juice.

'So, Joe's coming up tonight?' Valentina asked.

'Yes, with his friend Magdalena. Have you met her?'

Valentina shook her head.

'Well, she's coming. And another friend called Vasily.'

Valentina nodded. 'And how's everything with you?' she asked.

'Fine,' Fresia said. 'Good.'

She looked down at the grooves on the chopping board.

'Joe really missed you while you were away.'

'Oh yeah, you two went out for a drink together, didn't you?'

'Yes.'

Fresia nodded vaguely and prised the stone of an avocado away from the flesh, slid her finger under the skin.

'And how was Chiloé?' Valentina asked.

'Great. Do you like Chiloé?'

Valentina smiled at her. 'It's some time since I've been there,' she said. 'Did it rain?'

'No, it was hot.'

Roberto appeared carrying bags of steaks and chicken. He had been shopping in San José de Maípo.

'I hope you're not talking about me,' he said.

'We're not so short of conversational topics,' Valentina poured some more juice.'

'I'm going for a swim,' Fresia said.

Magdalena, Vasily and Joe came up fairly early and they sat around the pool drinking beers. Joe had been down to see Lalo who had been hauled in by the police, slapped about and accused of stealing the money himself. This accusation was also doing the rounds in Villa Caupolicán and Joe told Fresia that he knew who would have started that rumour and that the people responsible were almost certainly the ones who had stolen the money.

'And I think Lucho was in on it.'

'Have you told Lalo that?'

'No. I've got no proof. How do I say that I think his son was involved in robbing his own father? Not without real evidence. I told him about those other two hanging about outside but what can he do?'

'Lucho's messed up,' Magdalena said.

'Well he must have told them. Lalo had hidden the money where they used to keep guns when he was in the Frente. Nobody else knew where it was.'

'It won't be long before Lalo puts two and two together. He's not stupid.'

'No, but I think that it's a conclusion he doesn't want to draw.'

'It's fucked up,' Vasily said. 'The UDI are all over the *poblaciones* at the moment.'

'How much was it?' Fresia asked.

'About a thousand dollars. Lalo never asks me for money but he did this time. The only problem is that I don't have it at the moment.'

Vasily laughed. 'Nobody will believe that,' he said. 'Gringos always have money.'

It was nearly midnight, the embers of the barbecue were still glowing. People were standing around talking in small groups. Valentina was playing the guitar almost absent-mindedly, Barbara was sitting beside her.

'It'll be time for me to go back soon,' Joe said to Fresia.

Neither of them said anything for a moment.

'What about you?' he said. 'Travelling seems to have done you good. You seem . . . different.'

She laughed and twisted her wineglass in her hand.

'Different? Not really. But you're right that it was good because it sort of closed a period. I had time to think about things and I don't feel as if I've still got my suitcase half packed.'

They watched Valentina, who had started to sing.

'Singing to the sun like a cicada . . .'

'She's very beautiful, my rival,' Fresia half joked.

'Your rival?' Joe seemed taken aback.

'I think there's still something going on between her and Roberto.'

'Oh right, yes, I see . . . Really? Does it bother you?'

She shrugged. 'I don't know. It's something that doesn't seem to have much to do with me. So not really. You know that I think she and Roberto . . . I think that Ariel is her son.'

Joe suddenly remembered a photograph in Valentina's flat – the same smiling young man that he had seen on Roberto's desk. He did not say anything about it.

'In the hour of shipwreck and darkness, somebody will save you . . .'

Vasily wandered over with Magdalena, swigging pisco straight from a bottle he had picked up.

'I'm never coming here again,' he said. 'I mean she's got a great voice and I would definitely invite her round for a late-night game of cards but it's New Year's Eve. Don't intellectuals ever dance?'

'I've asked her to do "Gracias a la vida" for you at midnight,' Joe said.

Roberto wandered over, holding the hand of a little girl in plaits. It was the child with whom Fresia had played in the pool on the first day she arrived.

'She wants to say Happy New Year to you,' he said.

Fresia bent down and kissed her.

The girl put her arms around Fresia's neck and whispered in her ear. 'You're not a mermaid.'

Fresia laughed. 'How do you know?'

'Because mermaids have tails and they live in the water. They *can* walk but if they walk it hurts them, it hurts them like they're walking on broken glass.'

'Oh I see.'

'So you're not a mermaid really?'

'I guess not,' Fresia said.

'How did you get here from England then? I've seen it now. My mummy showed it to me on a map.'

'I came on a plane,' Fresia said. 'Just like everybody else. Look, it's nearly midnight.'

The little girl ran off to get some ice-cream and everybody began embracing.

'Happy New Year,' Roberto murmured but then he was being called.

'It's Ariel,' Pancho called. 'He's phoning from Paris to wish you a Happy New Year.'

And at that moment Fresia caught the glance which Roberto exchanged with Valentina. He squeezed her arm and went into the house. When Fresia looked up again, Valentina had disappeared from the garden. She went to look for Joe and Magdalena.

A couple of days after the party, Fresia sat on the roof terrace at Guillermo's reading a dossier which Magdalena had given to her. It contained a recent photograph of Gonzalo Espinoza outside his house walking an Alsatian dog. He looked like an ageing British gangster. There were a few photocopied statements and some press cuttings.

Declaration of Francisco Castañeda (in Costa Rica, 1982)

. . . I was also involved in the detention and disappearance of Miguel Figueroa, member of the Communist Party, in 1976.

The subject was picked up by a team which included myself and various others who used nicknames. There was an ex-soldier called El Lobo and there was a civilian whose name was Gonzalo Espinoza.

Figueroa got off the bus at the corner of Avenida Vicuña Mackenna and Avenida Matta. At some point he realised that he was being followed and began to call out his name and tried to run. People were scared when he began to shout that the DINA were about to kidnap him and nobody intervened. Then a carabinero appeared but we got rid of him and put Figueroa into the car and took him to a place called "The Firm".

. . . I remember that we were angry that he had tried to escape and so we all took turns to beat him. He was very scared and he defecated, for which he was abused even more and forced to eat his own faeces. We beat him pretty badly just for the sake of it and one person who I knew as El Negro wanted to carry on but Espinoza prevented him from doing this because he was in such a bad way that we worried that he might die and the subject had still not been properly interrogated. Espinoza told me to throw a bucket of cold water over him.

During his detention, he was beaten again, subjected to electric shocks in his mouth and on his genitals, his head was submerged in water containing excrement and he was hung from the ceiling by his feet. I only saw him one more time and I noticed that his hands were hanging oddly from his wrists because they had cut the tendons. I am not sure as to the whereabouts of his remains but I know that when he was completely broken he was taken out at night and driven somewhere outside Santiago – possibly to the Cajon del Maípo – where he was shot.

There were some other documents: accounts of Espinoza's various business activities; an indignant denial that he had ever tortured anybody as this would go against his firmly held Catholic beliefs; a statement from the wife of Miguel Figueroa who had seen all her attempts to take Espinoza to court frustrated by the justice system. She talked about eating lunch with her husband before he left the house for the last time, how he had studied architecture, his love for his small daughter.

Guillermo came upstairs with the cordless phone, handed it to her.

'Hello?'

'You don't know me, I'm afraid, but I have some information about the disappearance of Pablo Errazuriz.'

'Why are you phoning me? How did you get this number?'

'I can't tell you that. I want to meet you but it cannot be for another week. I'll call you then and give you a meeting place.'

'Yes but . . .'

The phone went dead.

Fresia put the phone on the table and sat for a while staring at the mountains, unsettled by both the phone call and by what she had just read. *At the corner of Avenida Vicuña Mackenna and Avenida Matta.* It was a busy intersection, she had passed it several times sitting on the bus. She sighed, looked at the photo of the young man who had run crying out his name to passers-by. What could they do after all? What might she have done? She thought about Miguel Figueroa, about Pablo Errazuriz, neither of whom she had much knowledge of apart from their faces in photographs, neither of whom she would have had any knowledge of were it not for their misfortune. They had learned to walk, to speak, to read. They had celebrated birthdays, fallen in love and out again, argued with relatives and friends. And for what? To meet cruel, violent and agonising ends. They had lived their whole lives without ever imagining that they might suffer such a fate, but anybody could suffer such a fate. And she suddenly thought of her father, working late into the night in his study, staring out into the darkness where the river moved slowly beneath the window.

Isla Negra

A friend of Guillermo's had offered Fresia a cabin by the beach near to San Antonio for the weekend.

'Let's go,' Fresia said to Joe. 'We can visit Pablo Neruda's house at Isla Negra. I've never been there.'

'What about Roberto?' Joe asked.

'He's going down to see his sister for the weekend. He's said we can take the car though because he's going to fly down to the south. All he wants us to do is drop him at the airport which is on the way to the coast anyway.'

'I've got lots of work on,' Joe said.

It was the conclusion, the grand finale to his work, he was on a roll now. The rest of the supporting cast had retreated into the shadows of the past; he had reached the part that had always fascinated him the most. Enter, stage left, a man of his time: Salvador Allende, the veteran socialist parliamentarian and elected President; a man who knew that violence was coming but dreaded its consequences. And then, from stage right, General (promoted to that position by the man he would overthrow) Augusto Pinochet, who would usher in a new era and who would bring more scars and solitude to the country than Pedro de Valdivia could have ever dreamed of.

'It's only a weekend. Please come. We can invite some others. Apparently, the cabin is quite big, there's lots of space. We can ask Magdalena and Vasily.'

'OK,' Joe said. He had never really seriously considered not going.

'There's only one thing. Can you drive?'

'Yeah.'

'Good, because I can't.'

Joe lay in the darkness with his eyes wide open. He had been reading until late a book about the last hours of Allende and his small band of supporters in La Moneda, a ridiculously unequal battle laden with poignant symbolism, a battle preceded – as in all tragedies – by a speech of great valedictory lyricism, a speech whose words could still bring tears to Joe's eyes, here in the dark, in a flat high above the city where all of these events had taken place.

Probably Radio Magallenes will be silenced and the calm metal of my voice will not reach you. It does not matter . . .

September 11th 1541. The city burning. Inés de Suarez strides across the square with her hand on the hilt of her sword. Seven hostages are approaching the last hours of their lives; their lifeless heads will soon be swung at those who hoped to rescue them.

September 11th 1973. The General waits in his command post. He has decided to defend and not debate the privileges of those who have appointed him. The palace in flames, a white flag in the gutter, a row of men lying in the street guarded by a tank. They are captured on camera but most of them will be dead in a few days' time.

It depends on your place and your angle of view.

Gazing into the determined face of a black-haired woman drawing her sword. Squatting in the dust beside the useless carapace of a dead *conquistador*. Last messages of love from a building filling with smoke and flames.

They say that Allende killed himself but that's a lie made up by the fascists who murdered him. He died still firing at them.

Joe's grandfather had insisted on this and Joe in turn had always believed it, but Joe's grandfather had been wrong because Allende had seen the footage of the beaten and pistol-whipped Patrice Lumumba in the Congo and made it very public that he would never leave La Moneda alive. *The President of Chile does not flee in a plane,* he said contemptuously to General Van Showen when the untrustworthy offer of leaving the country was made to him.

Joe had stared for a long time at the photograph of the men lying in the street after their capture. You could just see their backs, their hands behind their heads, the shoes that they had put on that morning before going to work. Impossible to link any of them to the individual photographs taken before they ended up lying in the street under the tracks of a tank. (In these other photographs they wear suits and ties and a couple sport the big moustache much favoured at the time.) One of the men in the street is Jaime Barrios, the president of the Central Bank, another is Eduardo Paredes who had once been head of Chile Films. Perhaps somewhere in the middle is Claudio Jimeno, a sociologist who studied during the 1960s at the LSE, and beside him Enrique Paris who entered La

Moneda that morning carrying a book by Roger Garaudy called *The Turning Point for Socialism* and made a wry joke about it.

The men captured in La Moneda spent a couple of nights tied with barbed wire in an old stable of the Tacna Regiment before being taken to the military base at Peldehue where they were killed. At some point, Enrique Paris was separated from the rest, told he was to be shot and asked if he wished to make a confession. *I have nothing to confess,* he replied. His was one of the bodies found later in Patio 29, along with Eduardo Paredes who had tried in vain to save the Declaration of Independence which was signed by Bernardo O'Higgins in 1818. Among other things, the post-mortem on Paredes confirmed that his captors had not left a single bone in his body unbroken.

. . . Close your eyes, sleep, dream a little.

But Joe cannot sleep; he is thinking about the photographs, about post-mortem reports, about violence and vengeance, people putting on their shoes in the morning, choking on the smoke from burning buildings.

History is ours, said Allende defiantly to the sound of crashing masonry and the shriek of Hawker Hunters. It sounds good but is it true? *History is ours and it is made by the people.* Do we really believe this any longer? *The great avenues will once more open through which free men will pass to build a better society.*

Up in his command post at Penalolen, the General heard the news of Allende's death. *Throw him in a box,* said Pinochet of the President around whom he had once fawned. *Throw him in a box and send him to Cuba. This one even had problems dying!*

You will continue to hear me, Allende said, *I will always be beside you.*

And this part at least was true. Joe lay in the dark – as he had once lain dreaming in an old miner's house in Cowdenbeath – thinking about the man with his trademark thick spectacles, the palace filling with smoke and flames and gas, the cries of the soldiers as they entered the palace, and Salvador Allende sitting down on the sofa in the small *salon*. Perhaps he spent a moment contemplating the events that had brought him to this grey and bitter moment, felt again the rush of fear for his supporters that was so obvious in his final speech, a fear which was all too justified.

His toe curled around the trigger.

Streets in Mexico, Leningrad, Paris and Madrid would be named after him, seminars dedicated to the lessons of his overthrow. And an old man who had once paraded before La Pasionara in Barcelona would stroke the head of his frightened and lonely grandson and tell him a story which, like most stories, was not entirely true to the facts, but which would, nevertheless, change his life completely.

His chin resting on the barrel.

The man who had done everything in his power to avoid a violent confrontation, now confronting not only his own death but the fact that a great storm of violence was about to break over the country in whose destiny he still claimed to have faith.

I am sure that my sacrifice will not be in vain, I am sure that it will at least be a moral lesson . . .

Bang! Bang! His body lifted from the sofa by the force of the bullets, his head destroyed.

The great avenues, the great tree-lined avenues will open, and free men will pass through them to build a better society.

But men are as their time is and to be tender-minded does not become a sword.

. . . I am sure that it will at least be a moral lesson which will punish felony, cowardice and treason . . .

Joe lies wide-eyed staring at the ceiling. He cannot sleep, he cannot dream.

Fresia and Roberto were sitting out on the veranda laughing at some shared joke when Joe arrived. They both had their bags ready. Roberto had put on a suit for the journey, she was straightening his tie. Joe had to admit that there was something agreeable and relaxed about them as a couple, they complemented each other well. They didn't bicker or interrupt each other continually or engage in ostentatious displays of physical affection. How much easier it would be if he could just hate him. Joe had wanted to believe that behind Roberto's elegant exterior there was a sadist or an angry control freak but he knew in his heart that there wasn't.

'How is your research going, Joe?' Roberto asked him.

'It's more difficult now with the contemporary stuff, it keeps me awake at night.'

'Ah well, that's another thing we have in common,' Roberto said. 'We're both insomniacs.'

'If there's one kind of person that I envy,' Joe said, 'it's the one who can fall asleep anywhere and who sleeps for hours.'

Fresia put her hand up.

Roberto might have murmured fond, explicit assent, he could

have used a tiny gesture to draw an exclusion zone around them, emphasised their status as lovers. Instead he said,

'Well, I think people who sleep too well probably lack imagination. It's like people who aren't afraid – there's something wrong with them.'

Fresia laughed in mock offence.

'Thanks very much,' she said. 'An alternative explanation is that people who can't sleep are just self-obsessed neurotics.'

'Perhaps both explanations are true,' Joe said.

Roberto told Joe that he should drive to get used to the car and so they set off down the curving mountain road towards the city and the airport where they would deposit Roberto before heading west towards the coast. Joe told them about the club's stolen shirts which had been left burning on pylons as a taunt to the team and to Lalo.

'They've got no kit for the first game in the regional championship,' he said.

Roberto leaned forward from the back. 'Fresia was telling me about this,' he said. 'Look, Joe, I hope you won't mind me suggesting this but I can give them the money that was stolen.'

Fresia glanced at Joe who narrowed his eyes at the road ahead.

'Give them the money?'

'Yes. That money is a lot in Villa Caupolicán but it's not that much for me at the moment. I don't want to seem paternalistic but it's a fact.'

Joe nodded slowly.

'I don't know La Pintana at all and I never could get to know it in the way that you have. That's just the way it is. But I can support a worthy cause and this seems to be one. It would help them out.'

'Yes it would,' Joe said.

'There's only one thing I would like in return.'

'What's that?' Joe said suspiciously.

'I'd like you to say that the money comes from you.'

'Why?'

'Well, it just makes things easier I think.'

'You don't want them pestering you for more afterwards?'

'I wouldn't put it quite so harshly. But that's part of it. Especially as I would also like to come and watch you play some time. It would just complicate things.'

'Do you like football then?'

'He supports Unión Española,' Fresia said.

'So no then,' Joe said and Roberto laughed and patted his shoulder.

They dropped Roberto off at the airport and watched him as he made his way into the departures lounge, carrying a new briefcase. He turned and waved and smiled and Joe sighed faintly.

Night was falling as they made the two-hour drive to the coast at San Antonio. They passed Melipilla and Joe told Fresia about the time when Manuel Rodríguez, together with a tiny guerrilla force, had surprised the Spanish garrison there. Finally, they arrived in a little place called El Tabito where Fresia registered for the key to their cabin. Near by, Joe could hear the ocean, the soft splash of waves on the beach at night.

The cabin was large with several beds downstairs and a double room upstairs with two single beds. Steps led from the sandy path to a wooden veranda with table and chairs which looked out towards the dunes and the ocean.

'This is great,' Fresia said. 'Shall we sleep upstairs since we were the first to arrive? I want the bed by the window.'

'Sure,' Joe said, imagining what Magdalena would say about this. She and Vasily had decided to catch the bus after work and would be arriving later. Joe had also invited Lalo and Ximena. At first, Lalo had said no but then Ximena had overruled him, saying that he needed to get away from the claustrophobic atmosphere of rumour and accusation and so they were bringing their kids down the following day in Lalo's cousin's taxi.

Joe watched Fresia unpack the food that she had brought with her: spaghetti and tomatoes and avocados and tinned seafood and packets of biscuits and crisps. Lalo was bringing up meat the next day so that they could have a barbecue on the beach. Fresia took out a bottle of wine and waved it at Joe.

They sat out on the veranda drinking the wine, eating mussels and a tomato and avocado salad and listening to the waves in the distance. Other people sat outside their cabins, children returned from the beach. It wasn't long before they could hear the sound of Magdalena and Vasily squabbling about the route to the cabin and Fresia called out to them while Joe went to get more glasses.

Magdalena and Vasily dumped their stuff inside. Vasily had bought a CD player with him. 'The only rule is no Silvio Rodríguez or Violeta Parra,' he said as he checked through the CDs that Fresia had brought for her Discman. He pulled a face and tossed aside both

Mercedes Sosa and some traditional folklore which she had bought on Chiloé, put on the Kruder and Dorfmeister sessions.

To Joe's surprise, Magdalena barely raised an eyebrow when the sleeping arrangements were announced.

'We're going to run a piece in the magazine about the disappearance of Pablo Errazuriz,' she told Fresia, turning the volume of the music down. 'We won't name Espinoza, just mention the presence of an ex-member of the Comando Conjunto in the bar. It's just to give him a bit of a jolt, make sure he realises we're on his case.'

'I think he might have realised that already,' Joe said, 'given your presence outside his house and his office.'

'You should be careful, Magda,' Vasily said seriously. 'That guy is a snake.'

Fresia told Magdalena about the mysterious phone call.

'Do you want to come with me if I meet this guy?' Fresia asked Magdalena. 'I would like to have somebody else with me. We can say that you're a friend of mine.'

'Well that's what I am, isn't it?' Magdalena looked at Fresia and smiled.

That night, Joe heard shuffling and whispering from downstairs, then silence, then some creaking, some giggling and then near-silence again. He grinned in the darkness. Fresia, who had been asleep when he got into his bed, murmured and sighed. Joe curled into his sleeping-bag and traced the sandy grooves in the wooden wall with his finger.

The next morning after breakfast, they made the short walk to Neruda's house at Isla Negra.

'Sleep well?' Joe asked Magdalena affably.

She glanced at him. 'Yes, thank you. Did you?'

'Not too bad. I was a little worried that somebody might have broken in though. I kept hearing the strangest noises.'

She looked away and then gave him a mock sweet smile.

'Mind your own business.'

'Vasily showing you his hard drive, was he?'

She laughed and walked ahead of him to catch up with Fresia and Vasily.

They wandered around the house separately. Joe passed through the bar where Neruda had written the names of his old friends and drinking companions as they died. In truth, he found something a

181

little disconcerting about the house-turned-into-museum, all the collections which no longer meant very much, the shells and bottles and toys, the fence with trite graffiti where some Athena-inspired tourist had written *Live your dreams and love your memories* in English. Joe wandered out to sit by a large wooden star structure hanging with bells, gazing out to where the long ocean waves boiled up on Isla Negra's rocky shore. He thought that a house by the ocean was possibly the greatest gift anybody could give to themself, to sit here like this just watching the waves foam against the rocks, the sea birds over the spray, the dim horizon.

'Hey,' Fresia came out and sat beside him. She had bought a poster from the shop. It had a red slice of watermelon on a blue background and Neruda's 'Ode to the Watermelon' running around the side in curly writing.

'That's nice,' Joe said.

'My mum and dad came here,' she said, 'when Neruda was still alive.'

'Your parents knew Neruda?' Joe asked.

'Not very well but they did know him. They came up here a couple of times.'

It was strange to think of the house as still a house rather than a museum. A black-and-white era, couples dancing the *cueca* outside the palace after the victory of Popular Unity, thousands of people jumping up and down in the street, *jump if you're not a reactionary,* and then planes howling over the rain-swept frightened city, the burnt pages of an abandoned book fluttering about a headless corpse, a line of men face down in the street. Away from the city, Neruda grief-stricken for his country staring out at the grey September waves on the shore of Isla Negra, no lilacs or poppy-petalled metaphysics now.

A man bundled into the boot of a car, a woman holding up her hands through sweat and tears for her newborn baby.

It's a girl!

'Where's Magdalena and Vasily?' Fresia asked.

'Probably necking on the beach.'

She raised her eyebrows. 'Are they . . .'

'Judging from what I heard last night, yes.'

'Oh well . . .' Fresia said, 'I suppose she wasn't going to wait for you for ever.'

Joe glanced at her, about to say something, but at that point Magdalena and Vasily emerged laughing. Magdalena had picked an argument with somebody from the Pablo Neruda Foundation and they had been kicked out of the house.

'I'm starving,' Vasily said.

'We'd better get back in case Lalo's arrived,' Joe said.

'You can't play in the regional championship,' Lalo told Joe as they walked slowly along the beach after their barbecue.

'How come?'

'They get more bureaucratic at that level. You have to have a valid ID.'

'That's a shame. I'll come and watch though.'

'Of course. We just have the minor problem of finding some kit.'

So Joe told Lalo that he could give him the money to replace what had been stolen and tears of relief seemed to spring to Lalo's eyes. Then he said,

'It was Lucho.'

'What?'

'Lucho told them where the money was. You know that.'

'I suspected,' Joe admitted. 'What are you going to do?'

Lalo shrugged and stared out to sea.

'He's my son.'

'Why did he do it?'

'Because he's a drug addict and he owed them money. They're powerful people. Or rather *they're* not powerful as such but they're linked to people with power.'

'And they wanted to get the team that badly?'

'Of course they did. We stand for everything they're opposed to. If they could have controlled it, everything would have been OK, but we stopped them from doing that and this was their revenge.'

'So?'

'I don't know,' Lalo said. 'There was a time when we could have just threatened to blow up their houses. We did that once, you know . . .' he laughed. 'These lumpen criminals were being paid to disrupt meetings so we put a bomb under one of their houses and that stopped it.'

They stopped and sat down and watched the waves running in at the shore.

'Not any more,' Lalo said quietly.

'What will you do with Lucho?' Joe asked.

'He's going to stay with his grandparents for a while. They're living in Talca now.'

'He'll get very bored there.'

'At least he'll be alive.'

They wandered back towards the cabin and the beach where Fresia, Ximena and Magdalena were lying on towels and passing round a bottle of coke. Joe watched as Fresia tilted the bottle back and drank, the glass glinting in the sun, wiping her mouth afterwards and waving at the approaching figures.

'She's nice,' Lalo said.

'Yeah.'

'You really like her, don't you?'

'Yeah.'

'And?'

Joe turned away from him and started walking towards the sea, the wide waves rolling in on the beach.

'You can't always get what you want,' he said.

The sun burned Joe's face and shoulders as he floated in the sea. He could not hear the others now; he thought he could see Lalo playing with his children on the shore, the glint of a bottle in the sun like a faraway star. He put his feet down but he was too far out to touch the bottom. It was so agreeable, floating like this, drifting, nothing but water between him and New Zealand. He closed his eyes and thought: what if this were the end, what if I just drifted away from it all. No more turbulence, no more history, no more Patio 29, no more photographs, no more blood on the manuscript, no more yearning, sea-borne to oblivion, just an island for the gulls to alight on. Dolphins plunging around him, laughing sea-horses, sighing mermaids combing their hair, the narwhal nudging the strange flotsam with its tusk.

A wave broke over his head, making him splutter, and he realised that he was further out than he had thought.

He took a few strokes back towards the shore and was suddenly surprised by a powerful undertow. He took stronger strokes but he was weaker than the current. He tried to call out and swallowed a mouthful of sea water. His swimming became frantic but he was still not able to make any progress towards the shore.

No dolphins, no mermaids, no sea-horses, no narwhal. Just a big, hostile, cold and lonely ocean. And, on the beach, human beings lying in the warm sand, or playing with their children, a dog fetching a ball.

Joe trod water for a moment. In spite of his panic attacks, in a real crisis he was actually quite calm: imagined fears always more terrifying than real ones. He decided not to waste his strength fighting the current and tried to swim at an angle rather than towards the shore in the hope that he might find calmer waters and then be able to swim in. He was at least able to swim sideways but he was still being drawn further from the shore.

His arms and legs were sore, he was growing tired. A wave broke over his head and he swallowed water again. He kicked sideways but he was really very tired now and the current was taking him still further out. Yet another wave broke over his head. He made one last choking effort, kicking sideways, and seemed to have dragged himself into calmer waters. He trod water again, trying to preserve his strength for a final attempt to swim back to the shore. Then he heard the sound of the outboard motor and saw the two men waving at him from the dinghy, holding up a life-belt.

'It was Vasily who saw you,' Magdalena said when Lalo and Ximena had left for Santiago and they were sitting out on the veranda that evening. 'He didn't know whether you were in trouble or not but he ran to get the lifeguard.'

'I couldn't swim out myself,' Vasily said. 'I'm not such a good swimmer, I wouldn't have been much help.'

'It would have made no difference,' Joe said. 'I'm a strong swimmer and I was having difficulties. I did manage to get out of the current and I was about to try to swim back when the boat came. But I'm glad it did.'

'Chilean beaches are dangerous like that,' Magdalena said. 'The lifeguards were saying that only a few years ago a couple of school-kids got swept away here.'

'They should have signs warning people,' Fresia said.

They all nodded, unable to think of much more to say about it. It was like stepping into a road and a car missing you by centimetres. A fraction of a second separating life from annihilation. If Vasily had not seen him, then Joe might have drowned. But this hadn't happened, he was just sunburned, they were sitting around getting drunk and telling jokes, laughing more at attempts to translate punch-lines than at the gag itself. Joe told his favourite joke about the ambassador of Nigeria presenting Pinochet with a monkey which responds to a slap on the head by giving the General a blow-job. After several enjoyable sessions whacking the monkey on the head and receiving oral satisfaction, Pinochet demonstrates his new toy to Admiral Merino, the stupidest member of the junta. 'Incredible,' says Merino. And because Pinochet is in a good and generous mood after so many blow-jobs he tells Merino that it is his turn. 'All right then, *mi general*,' Merino answers nervously. 'But please don't hit me so hard.'

That night, Joe lay in bed listening to the distant sound of the waves on the shore. Fresia came upstairs from brushing her teeth. She was wearing a blue T-shirt as a nightie. Joe turned his burned face away and placed the palm of his hand against the wooden boards of the cabin.

'Are you asleep?' she said, getting into her bed.

'No.'

'Are you OK?'

'Yeah,' he sighed.

What could he say? He felt a sudden misery at his knowledge that he could never tell Fresia how he felt about her. Maybe she suspected it but while it was unspoken it was OK, he had not changed everything, he had not lost his dignity. When she had suggested that they both sleep upstairs he had felt a childish excitement – *something might happen*. But now he knew that nothing was going to happen and, if it had not happened here, then it never would. He did not even know what he would say to her, what he might tell her. He knew himself that part of what he wanted in Fresia was unattainable. It was almost an envy of her, it was that easy grace that she seemed to have and that he didn't. Was he in love with her or was it that he wanted to be close to her, to watch her, perhaps even to be her? It was still painful, almost agonising at times, that quick smile she had, the smile he had seen her give to Roberto on their first meeting in the restaurant while Joe was trying to attract the attention of the waiter for another bottle of wine.

'What are you thinking about?'

'About my granddad,' Joe said. 'He used to tell me stories at night. I went to stay with my grandparents once. My mum and dad were having a terrible time, fighting and everything. My dad was an alcoholic. My mum took me up there to get me out of the way.'

'Where is he now, your dad?'

'Fuck knows. And I don't care. He saw my brother Mikey on a couple of his birthdays, maybe still does.'

'What about your granddad?'

'He died about ten years ago. Lots of people came to his funeral.'

There was silence for a moment and then Joe heard Fresia turn over so that her face was turned towards him. 'Joe?'

'Yes?'

'I'll really miss you when you go back to Britain.'

He didn't say anything. Now, now was the time. If he was ever going to say anything, it was now.

'Yeah, well, there's a little time left,' he said and closed his eyes. Fresia turned round again; he heard her breathing change almost immediately into sleep. He felt the soft warmth of his sleeping-bag, heard the sound of drunken laughter coming up from the beach. *Putas, Manolo huevón oh!* Downstairs, there were empty wine bottles, a half-full packet of spaghetti, washing-up that would have to be done in the morning. There was a holdall with a hooded sweatshirt hanging out, toothbrushes in the bathroom, sandy footprints on the stairs. And out there beyond the beach, the dark, cold, shifting waters of the ocean, the murderous currents that had so nearly swept him away.

Kama Sutra

Fresia walked down a busy Morandé Street, past the Moneda Palace, on her way to the Plaza de Armas where she was meeting Magdalena. Bright starry tricolours fluttered in the square behind the palace, people sat on benches with ice-creams and the sky was almost as blue as the colour on the flags.

Magdalena was already there when she arrived and they ordered espressos and mineral water. The man had called again and told them where to meet and Fresia had told him that she would be wearing a red vest and have a copy of *El Mercurio* on the table.

'I've been arrested in this square a few times,' Magdalena said, looking around her as she took a magazine from her bag and pushed it across to Fresia. Staring out from the page was the by now familiar face of Roberto's nephew.

The case of Pablo Errazuriz: the shadow of the dictatorship
Disappearance is a phenomenon with which we Chileans are sadly familiar. It is a form of ongoing torture for those left behind to imagine the fate of their loved ones.

Society has been shaken, however, by the case of Pablo Errazuriz. How can it be that a young, healthy boy from a privileged background just disappears without anybody knowing how or why it happened?

It is a sign of our insecurities as citizens, a testimony to the general lack of faith in our legal institutions, that so many rumours have circulated about those responsible for this crime. Some have even suggested the involvement of agents from the previous military dictatorship.

Why this is the case we may never know.

It is not the business of this magazine to tell detectives how to do their job but in the spirit of co-operation with the forces of law and order, we suggest they take a closer look at those ex-agents of repression – either from the DINA or the Comando Conjunto –

who might even have been in the Drunken Parrot bar on the night that the young man disappeared.

If it is found that such men were in the bar, then they would surely be able to provide useful information.

The current government – backed by the conservative hierarchy of the Catholic Church – is engaged in a desperate operation to placate the armed forces and halt the avalanche of human rights cases appearing before the courts. If there are some unpleasant truths about Pablo Errazuriz, then doubtless they would like to sweep these under the carpet as well.

But perhaps they might consider the case of Pablo Errazuriz sufficiently 'emblematic' to put pressure on the police to improve the lamentable investigation currently taking place. The case is emblematic because it demonstrates the vulnerability of our citizens, where doubt and fear still operate, and where the hand of the dictatorship can still be seen in the shadows in spite of the fact that we are now in our second decade of so-called democracy.

'The Sniper'

'That's our opening shot,' Magdalena said.

'And you're "The Sniper"?'

'Yes,' Magdalena said proudly.

A young man paused by their table.

'Fresia Castillo?'

'Yes?' For a moment Fresia thought that she must have met him somewhere before.

'My name is Raúl.'

He was a young man of such astonishing good looks that both Magdalena and Fresia were mesmerised by him for a few seconds.

'This is Magdalena,' said Fresia. 'She's a friend of mine.'

Raúl nodded, glanced at the magazine and raised a disapproving eyebrow. Then he sat down and ordered a coffee.

'I apologise for the drama,' he said solemnly. 'I had to take certain precautions.'

'How did you get my number?' Fresia asked.

'It was given to me by somebody,' Raúl said.

'Who?'

'You'll find out later. There is somebody who wants to meet you. We have to go somewhere else.'

Fresia glanced at Magdalena. Raúl said as if to reassure her,

'I live in a seminary. I'm training for the priesthood.'

'A priest? That's too bad,' Magdalena said.

Fresia tried not to laugh, stared at the bubbles in her mineral water.

'Why's it too bad?' Raúl asked.

'Oh . . .' Magdalena said. 'They might send you to somewhere really remote in Africa to spread the Gospel.'

'But that's exactly what I want,' Raúl said. 'To go and work in the Third World.'

Magdalena looked at him sharply as if she were about to say something but then she just smiled sweetly.

'So shall we go?' He finished his coffee.

'As long as all the priests are as . . . friendly as you,' Magdalena said.

Fresia coughed and Raúl smiled vaguely.

'Oh, yes they're very friendly. Some more so than others . . .' he trailed off.

Magdalena pulled a 'Help-we're-in-the-company-of-a-complete-moron' face at Fresia behind his back.

They took a taxi to the seminary which was out to the east of the city, almost in the foothills of the mountains.

'Could you wait here for a moment?' Raúl asked, leaving them under a lemon tree in the patio. It was a peaceful place and Fresia could understand why people embraced religion in order to experience this serenity and quiet sanctuary of soft footsteps and low murmuring voices. It offered the security and routine of the sanatorium – you might never want to leave. Another priest brought them a tray of plastic cups and a bottle of fizzy drink that tasted a little like Tizer. Finally, Raúl returned accompanied by a girl who Fresia did not recognise at first because Claudia Sepúlveda had decided to come without her fringe. She looked pale and tired, her hair was drawn back in a pony-tail.

'I'm sorry to have been so secretive,' Raúl said. 'But we can't take anything for granted.'

'How are you, Claudia?' Fresia asked.

The girl pulled a face and shrugged.

'So,' Raúl said, pouring them both a drink. 'My sister has some things she would like to add.'

'Your sister?'

'Yes. There are aspects of her behaviour which do not reflect well on her and which I do not condone . . .'

He coughed and glanced at Claudia who looked down at her hands. Magdalena rolled her eyes at Fresia.

'. . . but she is my sister and she has confessed to me in absolute confidence and asked for my advice. I have told her that she is to make her own mind up but to think of what God would wish her to do. So she wants to tell you the whole truth about what happened that night. Or at least what she knows. For reasons which will become apparent to you, this is not a story that she can tell to the police. She just needs to tell the truth to somebody. For some reason, *you* . . .' he smiled at Fresia '. . . made an impression on my sister and she wants to tell you about it.'

They all looked at Claudia who blushed and coughed and looked at her brother. He nodded calmly.

'We were in a bar,' Claudia said, looking at Fresia. 'The Drunken Parrot. When we arrived there were some men there. They made comments to me as we passed. *Mi'jita rica* and stuff like that. I pulled Pablo on because I thought he might say something and even though they were wearing suits they looked quite mean.'

'How many were there?' Magdalena asked.

'Four. They were pretty drunk and I think they were doing cocaine as well. They were hassling the waitress. Dropping things and asking her to pick them up so that they could look down her shirt. She went and spoke to the manager but he seemed to know the men and he made a sign at her, like to cool it? He took them over a bottle of whisky and sat with them for a while and we kind of forgot about them.'

'Was that the first time you had been out with Pablo? Was he your boyfriend?'

Claudia glanced nervously at her brother.

'You must tell the truth,' he said.

'At the time, I was really seeing this guy Jordan. I couldn't make my mind up which of them I really wanted. The Sunday before, Pablo invited me to his house for lunch. I got on well with his mum. She laughed a lot and told jokes and I wished my mum could be a bit more like that . . .'

Raúl Sepúlveda frowned and shook his head sorrowfully at this reference to their mother. Fresia, however, had seen Mrs Sepúlveda in action and could tell that she was a real bitch and that the holy, humourless Raúl had become the benchmark by which all the Sepúlvedas were judged. And Claudia – who was clearly unlike her heroine Britney Spears in matters relating to her sexuality – was probably not her mother's favourite.

'Pablo is very close to his mum,' Claudia continued, giving her brother a look of momentary defiance. 'She was painting a picture when we arrived – I don't know much about art so I can't say whether it was any good. It was of a horse. Anyway, like I say she was really nice to me. Pablo's younger brother and sister were there and I got on really well with them also. The house was much more relaxed than my house, and we had lunch together and then Pablo showed me around. There were miles and miles of vines and we went under them. Pablo had to bend down a little but I could almost stand up straight and we walked down the vines and then Pablo kissed me for the first time. It was sooooo nice.'

At this point, Claudia glanced slightly mischievously at her brother. Fresia laughed inwardly and thought suddenly of the first time that Roberto had kissed her by the pool.

'And after that I really wanted to see him again. I liked Jordan but it was kind of exciting hanging out with Pablo as well. That's why we went to that bar because none of my gang would be about. They would definitely tell Jordan if they saw me with Pablo.'

'So, in the bar?' Magdalena prompted.

'Pablo was buying me a Fanschop and some music came on in the bar and one of the men came over and asked me to dance. I could see the other men watching and laughing and I said "no thank you" quite politely but he kept asking and in the end Pablo came back and told him to get lost.'

'And that started an argument?'

Claudia nodded. 'The man starts telling Pablo to come outside with him and another man gets up and comes over. He tells the other man to come and sit down but the first man tries to grab Pablo and Pablo jumps up and knocks over my drink and it's a big glass and it spills all over the second man, the man who was telling the first man to come and sit down.'

'Hold on,' Fresia said. 'First Man is the one who was hassling you?'

'Yes. And Second Man is the one who tried to get him to sit down.'

'But Second Man got the beer over him?'

'Yes.'

'What were Third and Fourth Man doing?'

'Nothing. Laughing. Second Man looks really mad but he still pulls First Man away. He's looking at Pablo like he wants to kill him. The bar owner comes over and he calms the men down and gives them more whisky but the man with the beer over him is still looking at us in a really bad way. Cold and hard. It was scary. So we left.'

'You left together?'

'Yes.'

'So it wasn't true about him going to a disco?'

The girl shook her head.

'What happened then?'

Claudia glanced at her brother who made a vague gesture of renunciation.

'Pablo wanted to go to a motel.'

'And?'

'I wanted to as well. So we drove up on to the Pan American Highway and I was driving and I noticed that the car behind was up close and dazzling me with its lights. I thought it was just kids messing about and anyway we got to the motel which was called the Kama Sutra. The car also turned into the motel and we got out and Pablo was going to go and say something but I told him not to because we'd already had enough trouble and anyway I wanted to get to our room. I thought it was strange though because the people in the car didn't get out and it was an expensive car like a Mercedes and it was like they were watching from inside the car.'

'Were they the men from the bar?'

'I couldn't see them. I didn't think so at the time. I just thought it was other kids messing about.'

'What do you think now?'

'I think it must have been them.'

'So, what happened next?'

'We book a couple of hours and we're given our room number and we find our room and order some drinks. Then we get a phone call for Pablo to go back to reception. He goes off and he's joking about how I shouldn't go away. But then he doesn't come back. After about ten minutes I start to get really annoyed. What can be taking so long? Suddenly there's a banging on the door. It's a woman who says she is from the motel staff. "Get your things and go," she says. "What are you talking about?" I say. "Where's Pablo?" She's really nervous and keeps pulling my arm. She says something about him being arrested which I don't understand and she keeps looking out of the door. In the end, she shouts at me, "You don't understand. They'll come back for you. You're in danger." So I say to her, "Why would they want to arrest me?" And she drags me out by the arm and she says, "That's not what they're coming after you for." '

Magdalena raised her eyebrows at Fresia.

'Go on.'

'I want to cry as she takes me to my car. I can tell that she is nervous and that makes me nervous and she stands there watching me as I drive away. I look for where the Mercedes was parked but it is not there any more. I start thinking that maybe we were followed by detectives and they have arrested Pablo for drugs or something. Pablo doesn't seem like the type. Then I start to get angry with Pablo. If he was mixed up in something like that then he shouldn't have got me involved. Maybe he was even carrying drugs in my car.'

'Do you think he was?'

She shook her head.

'Not now. Sure, he smoked a little *pito* like everybody does . . .'

Raúl coughed.

'I don't, of course . . .' Claudia said hastily. 'I don't need drugs to enjoy life.'

'Lucky you,' Magdalena said drily. 'So you went home?'

'Yes. When I get home, I go to bed but I can't sleep. I feel angry with Pablo and worried about him. I phone his house in the morning and his mum answers. "Where's Pablo?" she asks me straight away. "Is he with you?" I say that we went for a drink and then he went to a disco. I can tell that she is really worried. She keeps repeating, "He always calls, why hasn't he called?"'

'Why didn't you tell her the truth? If you thought he had been arrested,' Fresia asked.

'I didn't know what to say,' Claudia said. 'I thought he might just go home later.'

'And because then she would have had to admit that she had been in a motel,' Raúl said. 'Nobody in this country tells the truth about that.'

'Yes, OK . . .' Fresia was still puzzled. 'But since then. It wouldn't be the end of the world to admit what really happened, even if it got you into a bit of bother. I mean a boy you really liked is probably dead. You're telling me that you're not going to give information because you're worried about your reputation or what your parents might say?'

'That's not the only reason,' Claudia said. 'A day or two later there is a knock on the door. It's a man who says that he is a detective and that they are investigating the disappearance of Pablo Errazuriz and that he needs to speak to me alone. I ask him if Pablo has been arrested and he says that he was never arrested. He asks me what I have told

194

anybody about Saturday night and when I say nothing he tells me to keep it that way. He tells me that they can prosecute me for obstruction of justice, hold me without bail, anything they want. Especially if I change my story. He tells me to stick to the story I have already told and everything will be OK. He tells me that they have a good idea where Pablo is and that he'll be home soon. So once I've told that story I have to stick to it and I'm scared as well because when I open the door to see him out, there's another detective in the car.'

'And?'

'It's the man from the bar. The man who was trying to make me dance with him.'

'First Man?'

'Yes. And he's smiling, sticking his tongue out, pointing at himself and pointing at me, making gestures. And after they've gone, I start to cry and I don't know what's happening any more and I switch on the TV and I see Pablo's mother and she is crying as well.'

'So First Man is a cop,' Magdalena said.

'That's what the guy in Valdivia said,' Fresia murmured. 'The one who was burned and then got stabbed. He said that Espinoza was there with two detectives.'

'Who's Espinoza?' Claudia asked.

'Nobody.' Magdalena took an envelope out of her bag. 'Is this . . .' she removed a photograph from the envelope '. . . one of the men in the bar?'

Claudia picked it up and looked at the man walking an Alsatian.

'I think that's the man who Pablo spilled the beer over. I'm not a hundred per cent sure but it looks like him. He was the oldest one out of them.'

'You mean, Second Man?'

'I'm not sure. I think so.'

Magdalena nodded and put the photograph back in the envelope.

Fresia remembered Fernando Araya on the outcrop overlooking the ocean.

Let's say there was some kind of an argument in a bar . . . maybe they only wanted to give him a beating to teach him some manners.

Four drunken, violent, dangerous men in a Mercedes following a pair of teenagers to a motel, luring the boy out of his room and beating him to death to teach him some manners. A girl only saved from a terrible fate by the intervention of one of the motel staff who knew what was going to happen, who had enough compassion, enough reserves of empathy to take pity on the girl and bustle her away.

And in spite of the peace of the seminary, Fresia suddenly felt another wave of revulsion for the country of her birth: the fake devotion, the dumb moral certainties, the sexual hypocrisy, the latent violence beneath the veneer of respectability.

'So what are you doing here now?' Magdalena asked. 'What made you suddenly want to tell somebody about this?'

Claudia sighed. 'Do you think it was easy? Do you think I didn't want to tell the truth? Once it came out that I was with Pablo that night, the pressure didn't stop. Police, journalists and one evening his mother phoning to shout at me, telling me to stop covering things up. And I had to watch the search parties on the TV, the bodies pulled out of lakes or dug up from the woods. I watched the investigating magistrate, all the crazy stories. People wouldn't speak to me at college. Jordan had a lot of friends and they would whisper things to me in the corridors. Especially after Jordan was interrogated. There was graffiti about me. I stopped eating. Then recently . . .'

Tears began to drop on to her clasped hands.

'What happened?' Fresia asked gently. The girl rubbed her eyes.

'One day I was walking back from college and a car pulled alongside me. It was the man from the bar, the man who wanted me to dance with him, the man who started it all.'

'First Man? The one we think might be a detective?'

Claudia nodded. 'I told him to go away and leave me alone. He just laughed and started saying the most terrible and disgusting things. He said that I should have had a dance with him and I started running away and he shouted, "Be seeing you. We'll have that dance, sweetheart. You can be sure of that." And that's when I knew I had to get away from there for good.'

Fresia looked at the young girl in front of her and felt a terrible sympathy for her, a wave of anger for those who had brought her to this position. She had just wanted to go to a motel with a boy she liked. Now she was surrounded by people who would tell her that such behaviour was sinful and that part of what had happened was the result of this surrender to bodily desire. And, in spite of her brief moments of resistance, Claudia was a fairly weak flame and it was possible that she would come to believe this herself.

'That's a horrible story,' Fresia said quietly.

Claudia bowed her head to hide her tears.

'That's enough now,' Raúl Sepúlveda said. 'You know where to find us.'

They stood up.

'Please will you tell his mum,' Claudia said, 'that I'm really sorry.'

'This is what happens when people confuse liberty with libertine behaviour,' Raúl suddenly said sternly to his sister. 'Freedom is all very well but with freedom comes responsibility.'

Any more fucking clichés? Fresia wanted to ask. Leave the poor girl alone.

Claudia's head dropped even further, like a broken sunflower.

A sudden summer storm broke over the Maípo valley. The tops of the mountains were invisible, hard rain drilled the plastic toys floating forlornly on the pool and thumped down on the wooden veranda. Fresia stood looking out of the window drinking a cup of tea and watching the dissolving scenery.

'I will go to Chillán tomorrow,' Roberto said. 'And tell Gilda.'

He had received the news wearily and had shaken his head when Fresia had suggested that it might lead to some kind of charges against Espinoza.

'Not a hope in hell. She can't say anything for sure, not even whether the man was definitely Gonzalo Espinoza. She didn't see whether the men in the car were the men from the bar. And anyway she's not going to say anything to the police.'

'At least the magistrate should interview Espinoza, maybe the waitress from the bar, the staff at the motel.'

Roberto shrugged. 'And what will they say, even assuming they can be found? They did interview all the staff from the bar anyway. They said that Pablo had been in the bar with a girl and that they both left without anything abnormal happening. They will never say that those detectives were in there, it would be more than their lives are worth.'

He had brought back a paper that day in which an anonymous student from Chillán had claimed that Pablo was well known on his university campus for being a user as well as a supplier of cocaine and marijuana. It was another of the stories that clouded and obscured everything and filtered into everyday conversations, *Ah but they also say that he was mixed up in drugs*, until everybody grew bored with the speculation and various theories and consigned it to yesterday's news.

The rain falls even harder, banging against the glass, churning up the path by the veranda, battering the hollyhocks. It thumps down on the valley, filling the river which flows out of the mountains. It turns the unpaved streets of the shantytowns into fast-flowing torrents, loosens the mud which might suddenly slide down and engulf the houses at the foothills of the Andes. And down in a seminary in the city a lonely girl also stares from her window at the hard rain which encourages melancholy. Her bag is packed, she is going away again.

The rain reminds her of the south of Chile where she is from, the sound of it on corrugated roofs. What else does she remember? A hot day under the vines, the thrill of a clandestine meeting. She remembers the flashing blue and red of a motel sign, neon bubbles rising from a champagne glass, the row of pine trees preventing jealous spouses identifying vehicle number plates from the road. She remembers the door to room 29 shutting, her swirl of anticipation as his hands began to move over her breasts, she remembers the ringing of the telephone, her car stalling in the entrance to the motel, fumbling for the key again.

The rain is so fierce now that she imagines the whole landscape shifting, unstable, evanescent. She imagines the layers of the earth being stripped away, the rain crashing through the canopy of a remote forest, some dense faraway hillside of overcrowded pines. She imagines the rain hitting the ground, dissolving it, washing mud and leaves from his bruised face. She turns her own sorrowful face to the Christ hanging from his cross on the wall, considers praying but cannot think of what to pray for.

She thinks instead of *sopaipillas*, the fried pumpkin bread that mothers in Chile make for their children when it rains.

There was a time when everything seemed normal, everything was safe.

Articulation Theory

The first game of the regional championship for which Villa Caupolicán had qualified was to be held in the countryside near to Melipilla. Joe went down to pick up the bus with Fresia and Magdalena. Fresia had her camera with her and took some photos of a few kids with the team banner.

'Did you know, Fresia . . .' Magdalena glanced maliciously at Joe '. . . that Melipilla was where Manuel Rodríguez . . .'

'. . . surprised the Spanish garrison with a tiny band of guerrillas?' Fresia said. 'No, I've never heard that. Did you know that I have an aunt called Inés . . .'

'. . . which is an amazing coincidence when you think that Pedro de Valdivia's lover was called Inés as well!'

They both cackled with laughter.

'I hear a buzzing noise,' Joe picked up the fly-swatter and patted them both gently on the head. 'What's this team like, Lalo?'

'They've got a lot of money,' said Lalo. 'And they're very good. In fact, I have a nasty feeling about this game.'

Fresia, Joe and Magdalena bought coffee and sandwiches and went to sit in the stand of the neat little stadium which was ringed with cypress trees. Cigarette smoke drifted on the warm air, kids chased each other around the edge of the pitch. Fresia told them that she was going to leave Guillermo's flat and find her own place to live. Magdalena offered to help her out, joking that she would need somewhere to stay in town when Joe had gone. At the mention of his departure, Joe felt a horrible pang, especially on this mild evening out in the countryside. London – and everything that went with it – seemed so far away now.

The team from Melipilla came out and started warming up. Although Caupolicán had been able to buy some new kit with Roberto's donation, it still looked cheap compared with that of Melipilla whose white shirts and black shorts bore the name of their sponsors.

'Oh dear,' Joe said.

A couple of the Caupolicán team did some stretches but most sat around smoking and ridiculing their opponents' warm-up exercises, group hug and chant. One of the players had to go back to get changed again because he had forgotten his ID card and was not allowed to play. Lalo paced up and down on the touch-line. At one moment he looked behind him at Joe and just for a second his face tensed with anguish. Then he waved and smiled at them.

When the game kicked off, it was painfully obvious that Caupolicán were going to get beaten. The team from Melipilla were not interested in humiliating them or showing off, they just proceeded to demolish them with cool efficiency. They did not even celebrate their goals with any great jubilation. Joe watched Lalo on the touch-line. He stopped shouting and put his hands in his pockets because he knew that there was nothing he could do, that this was a simple case of one team being crushed by another which was infinitely more powerful. Caupolicán had been a good team in the league they had won but here they were utterly outclassed. They actually made quite a brave show of it – in midfield Marcos played well – and the defence resisted desperately until Chelo was sent off for a pointless two-footed tackle that left his opponent writhing in genuine agony. A player who remonstrated with Chelo was pushed angrily away. Chelo retreated to sit under a tree where he began to drink a carton of red wine and cast angry glances at nobody in particular.

The game finished 3–0 and there was an argument in the dressing room afterwards when somebody overheard the opposition coach trying to tap up Marcos to go and play for them. Lalo and the opposition coach started pushing each other and the referee told them that he would be reporting them both. There was none of the usual banter as they wandered disconsolately to the bus which would take them back to Santiago.

'What now?' Joe asked Lalo, who was cradling America on his lap as usual.

Lalo shrugged. 'We try and win our league again.'

When they got off the bus in Villa Caupolicán, Joe noticed that the woman and man who had been hanging around on the night of the robbery were standing watching and smirking. He heard the man say, 'I like pisco,' the harsh laughter of the woman. And suddenly Lalo had turned on his heel and was crossing the road towards them.

'What did you say, *conchatumadre*?'

The man sneered at him. 'You know better than to mess with me, Lalito.'

Ximena appeared by his side. 'Leave it, Lalo.'

'Yes,' the woman said. 'Leave it. You were somebody once, but now you're just a nobody. Go back to your house.'

Lalo stared at them, his fists clenched. The man laughed contemptuously.

'You fucking traitor,' Lalo said, but there was impotent rage in his eyes.

Ximena took his arm and they turned away to mocking laughter.

But suddenly another figure had broken away from the group of watching players. The advancing Chelo dropped an empty wine carton from one hand and raised a gun with the other.

'That's our coach,' Chelo said. 'He's built this team from nothing.'

'So?' the man said insolently. 'It still is nothing.'

Chelo cupped his ear. 'Sorry? I didn't quite catch that . . .'

'You're mad,' the man said. 'I know people . . .'

Blood sprayed from his nose as Chelo smacked the pistol across his face.

'Shut the fuck up. Do not *ever* threaten me.'

The man held his bleeding nose and for the first time looked frightened.

'Get down on your knees,' Chelo said.

'Chelo . . .' Lalo started but Chelo waved him angrily away.

'Stay out of this, Lalo, you can't deal with it any more. Both of you. Get down on your knees.'

They stared at him and he released the safety-catch on the gun.

Reluctantly, they got down on to their knees in the dusty street. Everybody watched, appalled, as Chelo walked around and pulled the woman's head back roughly by the hair and put the gun at the base of her neck. He looked up at them and his gaze fell on Joe.

'OK, you're a clever guy,' he said. 'What's your theory, Doctor? Why are we so fucked up?'

'I don't have a theory.'

'No theory? You can't explain why everything we try and build up gets taken away from us? They even wanted to take Marcos today. OK, let's try something easier. What shall I do with these two?'

'Let them go,' Joe said quietly.

Chelo laughed. 'Wrong answer. Maybe you're not so clever after all. I guess you can't be that clever if you want to hang out down here. Still, you can always go back to Providencia I suppose. Maybe I should shoot you as well. What do you think, Wilson? The gringo took your place. Shall I shoot him too?'

'You're crazy,' Wilson said.

'Am I? Well, if I'm crazy maybe I'll shoot you for being so fucking useless. At least the gringo can play.'

Blood dropped into the dust from the face of the man that Chelo had struck. He tried to wipe his face but Chelo kicked his arm away.

'You see,' Chelo addressed them over the heads of the two kneeling figures. 'Look at it from my point of view. Lalo and his group have decided to abandon the armed struggle. Yes or no, Lalo . . .'

'Yes,' Lalo said.

'But I'm not interested in politics really. I'm just a *pato malo*, a criminal, a robber for whom a gun is sometimes necessary. And I like playing football and I admire you, Lalo, because you think this is all about building up social organisations and stopping kids from turning out like me and keeping the flame of struggle going and all that stuff. That's good even if it is a dream. And you're an honest guy, we all know you didn't take that fucking money. And we all know who did.'

He kicked them both in the back. Hard. The woman cried out and Joe – in spite of his loathing for her – felt pity for the kneeling figure, winced at her pain.

'Shut up, *puta*, the bullet is going to hurt you much more.'

'My children . . .' the woman muttered vaguely.

'Are going to be orphans in about five seconds' time. Now . . .' Chelo addressed his audience again, '. . . Lalo still believes you can change the world. He still thinks that one day the great avenues will open through which free men will pass to build a better society. Wrong. Sorry, *compañero*, but the world is full of envious lumpen motherfuckers. They have always existed and they always will. So I'm going to shoot just a couple of them. I know it won't do any good and before you tell me, Doctor, I know that they aren't the ones with the real power. But do you know what? I don't care. I'll do this just because it makes me feel good. Ladies first . . .'

He cocked the pistol. Joe heard Fresia half-whimper beside him and her grip on his hand tightened. It was quite obvious that Chelo's rage was growing and that his threat was not an idle one. He remembered Nacho telling him once that when Chelo lost the plot, it was better to keep right out of his way. He remembered the story about the last people who had crossed him and how they ended up floating in the Maípo river.

'Do you think I won't kill you? You think I'll change my mind. You're wrong because I don't give a fuck any more. Where would you like me to leave you afterwards? You can have the municipal dump or the Cajon del Maípo. That's more scenic I suppose . . .'

'Please,' the woman said. The dust beneath her was turning wet.

'That's enough,' Nacho, the goalkeeper and Chelo's best friend, stepped forward.

'Enough?' Chelo's eyes were glistening. 'This is just a start.'

'You're drunk. We lost a game of football. Stop it now. I don't want to see you locked up again because of these two.'

'Maybe I'll shoot you, you fat fuck. That would be bad, wouldn't it. Shooting my best friend.'

Gently, Nacho reached out and moved the gun from the nape of the woman's neck.

'You're not going to shoot anybody today,' he said.

For a second, both Nacho and Chelo held the gun and then Nacho said softly, 'Marcelo . . .'

And it was as if the use of his full name was some kind of code as Chelo lowered the gun and seemed suddenly to deflate like a balloon.

Nacho turned to the two kneeling figures.

'Get up . . .' and then more harshly, 'Come on, stand up, *huevones*.'

They stood up. There was a wet patch on the woman's jeans.

'Now,' Nacho said, 'we don't care who you know but if you mess about with us again you know what will happen. Do you understand that?'

'You'd better understand it,' Chelo said. 'Because if fatty here hadn't intervened, your brains would be all over the street now. You should put a fucking shrine in your house to him. San *Guatón* de La Pintana.'

A small crowd had gathered in the street to watch the scene. People were standing in their doorways. Even hosing the street – a more or less permanent activity in Villa Caupolicán – seemed to have come to a halt.

'You can do what you have to do here,' Nacho said. 'That doesn't concern us. But if you mess about with our club again *I'll* fucking shoot you. And remember that we know people as well. Do you understand?'

They both nodded.

'Good. Now go and wash yourself.'

They all watched the couple as they walked away, the man still leaving a trail of blood from his nose. Then Chelo suddenly swung the gun around towards his own players.

'Marcos?'

Everybody froze. The young men all looked at their star player. He frowned and blinked at Chelo.

'What?'

'Are you thinking of going to play for Melipilla?'

'No.'

'Good. Otherwise I would have had to shoot you.'

There was silence for a moment and then they started to laugh. All the players were laughing and Lalo was laughing. Even Ximena and the women who had protested to the mayor were laughing. Joe and Fresia looked at each other and Joe raised his eyebrows. People turned away from the street and the marks of blood and urine. Nacho put his arm around his friend's shoulders and took the gun from him and the team walked away together chatting, pushing each other and still laughing as if the whole thing had simply been an enormous joke.

Luxuries

'I really thought he was going to shoot them.'

Fresia and Joe were on a bus entering the little town of Pomaire which lay about an hour and a half away from Santiago. It was famous for its traditional ceramics and Joe wanted to buy some bowls to take back to Britain. Fresia was alarmed at Joe's imminent departure: they had arrived together, she felt as if her escort on a dangerous mission had just announced that this was as far as they could go together. At the same time, she was both pleased and disturbed by the fact that she did not envy his return or wish that she was going with him.

'So did I,' Joe said, peering from the window. 'It was touch and go.'

They got off the bus and wandered through the streets, inspecting the earthenware goods. Finally, they came to a little shop called Ceramica Galo where Joe selected some goblets and six earthenware bowls with handles.

'You can have a dinner party when you get back and make *pastel de choclo* in the bowls and drink pisco sour and think of me freezing here in winter. At least it will nearly be summer over there.'

'I like Chilean winter,' Joe said unhappily.

Fresia said. 'Here, let me buy them for you as a going-away present.'

'You don't have to.'

'Well, I know I don't *have* to, Mr Gracious, but I would like to.'

'OK, I'll buy lunch.'

'Don't be so Scottish. It's a gift, you don't have to repay me.'

She took his arm and steered him to a small restaurant where they ordered a *parillada* and a bottle of expensive red wine. Steaks, chops and chicken as well as some unrecognisable cuts arrived on a little charcoal brazier.

'We'll never be able to eat all of this,' Fresia said.

'Yeah, we will, we'll just take our time.'

'What is *that*?' She pointed to some small pieces of meat.

'I don't know. Some kind of offal, I suspect. The pituitary gland? Barbecued bladder? Do you want it?'

'No thanks. Just give me some chicken, please. And one of those sausage things. And some wine.'

'I thought you didn't drink during the day.'

She shrugged. 'Today is an exception.'

He poured her a glass of red wine.

'How's your flat-hunting going?'

'I'm going to see a flat with Magdalena next week.'

'Just the person you want to carry out delicate negotiations with a future landlord.'

Fresia laughed and sipped her wine.

'Yeah but she won't be fobbed off with easy answers. Plus Chileans are piss-takers and I'll just get embarrassed and agree to things I shouldn't.'

'You've got a point. What does Roberto think?'

'Oh, he'd be no good at all at flat-hunting.'

'No, I mean what does he think of you getting a flat on your own?'

'We haven't really discussed it.'

'He doesn't want you to move up there with him?'

'He might do but I wouldn't.'

'Why not?'

Fresia frowned. 'Because it's not what I want – it wouldn't work. What would I do for a start? I'm twenty-nine years old, I'm not going into retirement yet.'

'Do you think you're going to stay here?'

'In Chile? Definitely for the time being. I'm beginning to sort things out. I'm beginning to . . . it's very difficult to explain. Perhaps it is just the novelty of living in a different city.'

'Perhaps it's the weather,' Joe said.

Fresia thought of the day when she had stood looking out at the rain pouring down on the Maípo valley, how it had reminded her of Britain's green aqueous landscape, coastal towns in autumn.

'I sometimes miss the British weather,' she said.

'You're insane,' Joe said. 'But perhaps the only solution is to have both. I once heard a rather wealthy Chilean say that he intended to do a *seis y seis*.'

'What's that?'

'Six months in Chile and six in Britain.'

'Sounds good but you'd have to be rich.'

'Yeah,' Joe agreed. 'Money is definitely an important factor in life's aesthetic feel.'

'True, but then there are days like this when you can just wander about and drink wine in the day and everything seems right. This is better than any luxury.'

Joe speared another piece of meat from the little brazier.

'Ah well . . .' he said, '. . . the definition of luxury is something which depends very much on your place and angle of view.'

The following Sunday, Roberto was having his usual Sunday barbecue. Joe had excused himself to take Lalo, Ximena and their kids to the pool on the top of the San Cristóbal hill. 'Bring them here,' Fresia said but Joe said that he had promised the kids it would be San Cristóbal.

Fresia was sitting by the pool when Valentina came and sat beside her, handed her a glass of juice.

'Thanks.'

'Roberto tells me that you're looking for a flat in Santiago.'

Fresia glanced at her. 'Oh yes?'

'Is everything OK?'

'How do you mean?'

'I think it worried Roberto a little.'

Fresia frowned. 'Why should it worry him?'

'Oh, nothing to do with you getting a flat. But maybe he thinks you're tired of him. He really cares a lot about you.'

'Did he ask you to come and talk to me about this?'

'No.'

Fresia looked up at the mountain and bit her lip.

'I really don't have to explain myself,' she said finally.

'Of course not.'

'Especially to you.'

Valentina slid into the pool, bobbed up and rested a hand lightly on Fresia's knee.

'You don't have to explain yourself to anybody. I really didn't mean to annoy you,' she said. 'You and I have more in common than you think.'

'Oh yes?' Fresia looked at her coldly. 'Are you implying that I'm some kind of younger model of you?'

Valentina laughed and shook her head. 'Certainly not,' she said. 'In that respect we couldn't be more different.'

And she disappeared under the water, swimming a fast breast-stroke, her hair streaming behind her.

That night, Fresia sat on the veranda while Roberto escorted people down to the river. It was growing dark and she was listening to Billie Holiday singing 'Loverman' through the open window of the living room. She shivered slightly, thought about going inside where there were lights and soft chairs and old wooden salad bowls impregnated with years of oil and vinegar and garlic piled up by the sink. Roberto reappeared, rubbing his eyes. He looked tired.

'Are you OK?' he asked.

'I'm fine.'

'You seem a little . . . distant.'

She turned to him. 'Roberto, I'm not interested in what goes on between you and Valentina but be careful about the way you discuss me.'

'We haven't discussed you.'

'Yes you have. I'm not interested in the nature of your relationship with her – either now or in the past – but if I feel that you are making me into some kind of project then I'll stop coming here and you'll never see me again.'

Roberto blinked. 'I'm sorry,' he said. 'I don't know what you think . . .'

'I don't think anything. I don't want to have to think anything. That's the whole point. Do what you want but keep it away from me.'

'OK, I understand that. But you might think something that is not in fact the case and I wouldn't want that.'

'I know enough,' Fresia said. 'I know that Ariel is Valentina's son.'

Silence. Then Roberto said, 'Yes he is.'

'Well I don't want to interfere with that. It's between you and her. But I won't play the naïve young girlfriend as she wants me to.'

'How do you know that's what she wants?'

'She just has this irritating habit of implying that she *knows* me. What my next step will be. And she doesn't.'

'I'm not sure that she thinks that really,' Roberto said. 'Who knows what your next step will be? I certainly don't.'

'Nor do I,' Fresia said.

'I want you to be happy,' Roberto said.

'Well, I want a little more than happiness . . .' Fresia replied. 'But I am happy when I'm here with you.'

'It's always here for you.'

There was a long pause while they listened to the sound of cicadas.

'I'm reading a book at the moment where the author talks about the sound of cicadas,' Roberto said. 'He says it sounds as if they are having a competition among themselves to see who can be the loudest.'

Fresia laughed. 'It does sound like that.'

They both listened to the competing cicadas for a few minutes. Then she looked at him properly and took his hand.

'Would you really never come here again?' Roberto said.

'It would be hard for me,' Fresia admitted. 'I would miss it here with you. But I would do it.'

'I think you would,' Roberto said. 'And that would quite ruin my image.'

'What image?'

'The ageing intellectual hiding from life in the mountains,' he mocked himself. 'Dispensing largesse and sleeping with beautiful women half his age.'

'It's a tough job but somebody has to do it,' she said. 'Anyway, I don't think you're hiding from life.'

'Oh perhaps I am,' Roberto rubbed his eyes.

Later, in the bedroom, they lay in the half-light together on the clean white sheets of his bed and she looked up into his face and put her arms around his neck while outside the cicadas kept up their nocturnal competition.

The next morning, Fresia went down to the city to meet Magdalena for some flat-hunting.

'My God,' Magdalena was still laughing as she and Fresia sat down in a café and ordered some coffees. 'Can you imagine having her as a landlady?'

'She was completely insane.'

They had just visited a flat in the middle of town. The building had been noisy, in a poor state of repair, and the landlady had lived on her own in a flat downstairs. They had gone into her flat first and Magdalena had nudged Fresia and motioned to the wall where there were pictures of Franco, Pinochet and the Pope. They had then been treated to a long lecture on the evils of abortion and on the fact that with so many girls walking around in short skirts they could hardly complain if men groped them on the metro or even raped them. The landlady had dwelt at great length and with almost loving detail on how she envisaged this taking place until at last Magdalena had glanced at Fresia and burst out laughing and they had run out.

The waiter brought them coffees, mineral waters and a pack of cigarettes for Magdalena, who took out the new edition of her magazine and pushed it across to Fresia.

Pablo Errazuriz – the wall of silence

It is nearly ten months now since the disappearance of the young university student from Chillán. In spite of the many theories circulating about his disappearance no more has been heard of him. In their investigations, the police have faced an incomprehensible lack of co-operation from certain witnesses. Particularly culpable in this regard is the young girl Claudia Sepúlveda who was the last person to see Pablo Errazuriz and whose account of his sudden disappearance 'to a disco' is far from convincing.

What are these people scared of? Who are they protecting?

Could it be that the Drunken Parrot bar was not the last place that Pablo Errazuriz was seen? Could it be that there are witnesses who might testify to seeing Pablo Errazuriz much later in the evening but who are too scared to do so? These are questions for the investigating magistrate but we have received anonymous information which suggests that Pablo Errazuriz did not just go 'to a disco' but was last seen in a motel on the Pan American Highway. As yet, we do not know whether this information is correct but it is certainly worth investigation on the part of the magistrate assigned to the case. We can think of one motel in particular whose owner has repeatedly been investigated for his links to organised crime.

Or could it be that the fear which surrounds this case also extends to the authorities investigating it? Could it be that they would prefer to investigate the more ludicrous theories surrounding the disappearance of the young student so as not to reveal the complex links between organised crime, ex-agents of the dictatorship and the justice system in this country? Could it be that the police themselves have a vested interest in not uncovering the truth?

There are as many unanswered questions here as there are positions in the Kama Sutra.

'The Sniper'

'That's great,' Fresia said. 'And accusing Claudia of still hiding evidence is a good tactic.'

'Do you think so?' Magdalena put the magazine back into her bag. 'You know she's not in the seminary any more.'

'How do you know?'

'I went back there to ask her a couple more questions. That humourless idiot of a brother was there and he said she'd gone away and he wouldn't tell me where. I wouldn't have minded if *he* had pushed me up against the wall and ripped my clothes off.'

'Unlikely I think,' Fresia said and they laughed both at the memory of the mad landlady and at Claudia's handsome priggish brother.

'Claudia would be a hopeless witness anyway. Roberto thinks they're about to close the case.'

Magdalena nodded. 'They will. Even the media are bored of it now.'

'I don't think Pablo will ever be found.'

'No. They'll have got rid of him properly and nobody will talk. The case is dead. But we're still chasing that bastard. Vasily has written a program or something so that we send an e-mail with a picture of Espinoza saying *This Man Is a Torturer* to the companies he works for. Not only that, but the e-mail will then send itself to everybody on the address book of that company.'

'Like those viruses?'

'Yes, but it doesn't actually do anything destructive. It just means that every employee and client of, say, the forestry company will receive it. I think that they're already getting sick of the bad publicity which Espinoza brings them. And if there's one thing that Espinoza cares about it's his business interests.'

'And he'll get pretty angry with anybody who interferes with them.'

She suddenly remembered the testimonies she had read about all the people who had had the misfortune to fall into Espinoza's hands. She remembered Fernando Araya's words as they sat overlooking the sea.

If you ask too many questions about Espinoza then you'll find out his true character. And believe me, you don't want to see that.

As if she knew what Fresia was thinking, Magdalena told her that she had been receiving an increased volume of threats and that she thought they were linked to Espinoza.

'They upset my mum,' she said.

'They must upset you as well,' Fresia said.

'I'm used to them,' Magdalena said. 'Lots of people get them, not just me.'

Joe had been to the market that morning to buy fish for dinner so Fresia and Magdalena bought some wine and headed for Providencia. They sat around in the kitchen drinking white wine and watching him as he sprinkled coriander and squeezed lemon over the fish.

'I love thinking how much this would have cost in Britain,' he said as he put the fish in the fridge and began to shell some prawns. Fresia watched his brisk, certain hand movements. She loved people who prepared food with authority in that way, bossing it about and making it do what they wanted.

They sat out to eat on the balcony, watching the people hurrying along on the street far below. The evening was soft and mild with just the suggestion of autumn. Joe was tidying things away – Fresia had become melancholy when she noticed the boxes filling up with books and papers. Apart from his academic stuff, there was a huge Chilean cookbook that Magdalena's mum had given him, a book of Violeta Parra lyrics, a framed poster of Allende with the text of his last speech, his *I ♡ Chile* oven glove, the bowls and goblets that they had bought in Pomaire.

'How will you get all of that on the plane?' she asked.

'I'm sending most of it by air. It's really expensive.'

'What will you do if they get lost?'

'Slash my wrists . . .' he stopped quickly. She saw his discomfort and smiled at him, shaking her head.

'Let's hope they don't get lost then.'

They went inside and Joe turned on the TV for the news. After bulletins about the under-17 football team, a new blood-weeping Virgin who had turned up in Iquique, and a round-up of bikini-clad bottoms from Chile's more exclusive beaches, there was a report that foreign extremists were expected to arrive for a forthcoming national protest against Globalisation and Impunity. The Minister of the Interior announced that the protesters were supporting a spurious cause and must expect a swift response from the forces of law and order if there were any disturbances on the march. It was the same Minister who had once dismissed the Allende government as a bourgeois distraction and called for an armed uprising.

'At least now I'm leaving it won't matter so much if there's a riot and I get deported,' Joe said.

212

'They're talking about real activists,' Magdalena said. 'Not some academic whose main obsession is with Pedro de Valdivia and Manuel Rodríguez.'

'Thanks,' Joe said. 'Not even on the deportation A-list.'

Magdalena turned to Fresia. 'Make sure you get your camera ready. It's going to be great. Like old times. The smell of tear gas in Santiago is the first sign that summer is over.'

A Certain Age

Green, red and blue, Joe watched the bright neon legs going round and round outside the window of Valentina's flat.

'You're going soon,' she said.

'Yes.'

'Everybody will miss you.'

'Thank you.'

Valentina went to the kitchen and came back with two bottles of beer. She handed him one.

'Especially Fresia. She'll miss you a lot.'

'For a while maybe.'

'Oh for longer than that. You're her best friend here.'

'Great,' Joe said.

Valentina studied him.

'Don't underestimate it,' she said. 'And don't misunderstand Roberto. I know you see him as some kind of collector.'

'No, I know he's not like that now. Although he has very good taste for a non-collector. In women that is, not in literature . . .'

'What's wrong with his taste in literature?'

'He thinks *Love in the Time of Cholera* is the best book ever written.'

'Does he?' Valentina frowned. 'That's funny, he's never said that to me.'

Joe stood up and wandered over to the shelf where he picked up the photo of the young man.

'Why do you have a photo of Roberto's son?'

Valentina did not answer for a second. Then she studied him calmly.

'Because he is my son as well.'

Joe nodded. 'Fresia knows that.'

A strange expression flickered across Valentina's face.

'Did Roberto tell her?'

'I think she worked it out for herself.'

'Has she said anything else?'

214

'No. Just that she had guessed that you were the mother of Roberto's son.'

Valentina drew her finger nervously in circles around the top of her beer bottle as if trying to make it hum.

'I want to tell you something,' she said. 'Something that nobody else knows and can never know.'

'OK.'

'You must not tell Fresia. Promise me that. She may find out one day but that would have to come from Roberto and not from me. I trust you, Joe, and I really like you. You are one of the few people who might understand, which is surprising for a foreigner. Promise me you won't tell Fresia.'

'I promise.'

She got up and went to her room and came back with an old cigarette box.

'I wanted to show you this when you were talking about your work earlier.'

'I thought you were worried about how much I smoked.'

She did not laugh, but opened the packet and took out a scrap of paper covered in tiny writing and handed it to him.

'Please be very careful with it. It is the most precious thing I have.'

It was a poem addressed to Valentina, both tender and sad. It ended with the words:

Never forget me, my little comrade in pain.

It was signed *Rosalía* and dated February 1975.

Joe turned it round in his hand and then looked up at Valentina.

'Her name was Rosalía Maldonado. I met her when I was eighteen years old . . . I met her in Londres 38 and in Villa Grimaldi.'

Joe frowned at the names from the constellation of DINA torture centres established in Santiago during the 1970s.

'You were . . .'

'I was eighteen years old when they took me. I was denounced by a woman who they had tortured and turned into an informer. She arranged a meeting with me and when I turned up they were waiting for me and took me away. In Londres 38, I met Rosalía and she became my best friend. She was twenty-one years old, a primary-school teacher. She had been the girlfriend of a man they were searching for quite intensely. So obviously they treated her terribly, beyond belief. But even after they had finished with her, she would always try to comfort me, to reassure me. After Londres 38, they took us both to Villa Grimaldi where she wrote that for me, hid it inside a cigarette box. She was always terrified they would come back for her and one day they did. That was the only time I really saw her break in front of me, when she knew they were taking her away. And I never saw her again, nobody ever did. I met her family and they gave me this photograph of her.'

A cheerful, smiling, good-natured face. The right kind of face for somebody teaching children to read. A very Chilean face, a face passed every day in the street. Although it was black and white, the photo looked as if it had only been taken recently.

'I used to hate it when they called out her name,' Valentina said. 'Sometimes I was more scared for her than I was for myself.'

Joe looked at the photo again and then handed it back with the poem to Valentina.

'I shouldn't have escaped either. But my brother Joel knew Roberto – they were great friends. And while nobody had any influence really over the whole process, sometimes a word from somebody higher up could help.'

'And Roberto knew people higher up?'

'His family are well-connected. That would have counted for nothing if I had been important but I wasn't. Roberto got me out and took me up to the Cajon del Maípo. I was a wreck, a total mess . . .'

Valentina bowed her head suddenly.

'. . . and I was also six months' pregnant.'

'Pregnant? But I don't understand. You knew Roberto before . . .'

Joe stopped for a moment as he tried to understand. Then he felt a stab of horror as her words from the night he had stayed at her flat flashed into his consciousness.

Maybe if you had been speaking in English . . . I can't . . . I don't like being commented on.

Valentina looked steadily at him.

'Roberto cared for me. If he hadn't, I might not be here now. Nothing can ever change that. And one time, after Ariel was born, they came looking for me again at Roberto's house and Roberto, who is a terrible coward like most intellectuals, he was even more terrified than I was. But he stood in front of the door barring the way and he shouted at them and told them to leave me alone and that he had contacts and everything and he grabbed the phone and pretended to be speaking to General God-knows-who. It was really funny actually – well not at the time obviously – and in the end I think they just decided he was mad and went away.'

'And he brought up Ariel.'

'He *is* Ariel's father. Just not the . . . not the other one.'

'Do you know . . . ?'

She shook her head and raised a finger.

. . . In the hour of shipwreck and darkness, somebody will save you . . .

They sat for a while in silence as the neon legs revolved outside the window, listening to the sound of children playing in the courtyard below. There were so many questions spinning in Joe's mind. How could you love . . . could you love . . . how much could you forget . . . what if . . . how could you not resent . . . ?

As if she were reading his mind, Valentina said, 'Nobody is born bad. We have to believe that. Otherwise what was it all for?'

'Does he know?' Joe asked.

She shook her head again.

'For a time it seemed like Roberto and I discussed nothing else. How can I tell him? Does he have a right to know the truth? What good will it do him?'

'He knows nothing?'

'He thinks that I am his godmother.'

And suddenly Valentina began to weep, brushing the tears from her eyes with mechanical gestures as if she were not really aware that she was crying. Joe felt ridiculously awkward and redundant. He was reluctuant to touch her – not out of any kind of change produced by her story – but because to do so made him feel culpable. So he slid from his seat and across the floor to her and took her hand, which she allowed him to hold, while in the other she held the cigarette box with its fragment of hidden poetry.

'Why did you leave?' he asked.

'I had to try and have a life as well. I was very young.'

Joe studied her. She might have been dead. There was no Rosalía Maldonado now but there was a Valentina. She sat here in her flat with the neon legs revolving in the night sky, her guitar, the photos on the wall, the bowl of oranges on the table, her terrible secret. These were all of the things that made up Valentina, and the slight downturn of her mouth, the tiny crow's-feet around her eyes were a gift, a testimony to her survival, the marks of life that prevented her from being the smiling face in the photograph, a piece of paper in a cigarette box.

Never forget me, my little comrade in pain.

'Do you want to stay tonight?' she asked. 'To say goodbye?'

And he nodded.

Joe's head was hurting and he pinched his nose just under his eyes. He had been staring at the computer all morning, stopping only briefly to look out across the city to the mountains in the distance.

The ferocity of the coup was followed by a systematic campaign against political organisations. As the stadiums emptied, new detention centres were set up in places such as Londres 38, the 'Venda Sexy', and the infamous Villa Grimaldi. The far-left MIR was the first to be targeted by the actions of the DINA, which was made up of agents such as Miguel Krasnoff Marchenko, Marcelo Moren Brito and the grotesque sexual deviant Osvaldo Romo. The coup allowed these individuals unrestrained access to torment their political opponents . . .

Was their fury simply political or was it something else? They did it, after all, in secret and tried to conceal the evidence afterwards. What kind of something else? Nobody is born bad (Joe was uneasy about this) but some threw away their guns, some conscripts wept and vomited in private, some generals even offered their resignations. Why didn't Romo or Moren Brito or Krasnoff Marchenko? Why did they kill their victims with such terrible malice, such perverted energy? It really was like staring at the stars and trying to make sense of it and after all you just couldn't, you had to accept that you just didn't know why.

After the destruction of the MIR, the regime's attention turned to the Communist Party where the Comando Conjunto joined and competed with the DINA in its repressive activities . . .

There was a book he had read about the Gunpowder Plot and the unfortunate Guido Fawkes. The book contained two examples of Fawkes' signature. One of them was a fairly neat if wobbly script but the other – following his torture on the rack – was like a great scream of pain, utterly unlike the first, with large distorted spiky letters and his surname tailing off into nothingness.

The buzzer rang and Joe went to answer it. It was Fresia who had arrived to pick him up. They were going to Magdalena's house for a barbecue. He left the front door open and returned to his laptop.

'Hey, Joe,' Fresia said as she came in. 'You working?'

'I'm just finishing up.'

'Good. Put your historical playmates away now, it's time to go out.'

She came over and stood behind him, resting one hand on his shoulder, reading what he had written and then glancing at the pile of books, documents and newspaper clippings.

He saved his file, logged off, closed his laptop and stood up. He was suddenly assailed by dizziness and nausea, his head banging. He sat down again heavily.

'Joe?' Fresia was alarmed. 'Are you OK?'

'I'm . . . yes . . . I'm sorry . . . I haven't taken a break today.'

She went and got him a glass of water, watched him while he drank it.

'You have to take breaks from it,' she said.

Magdalena's mother had cooked an enormous feast to mark Joe's imminent departure. Potato salad, beetroot salad, tomato salad, avocado salad, cabbage and coriander salad, meat and seafood and cheese *empanadas*, chorizos, pork ribs, chicken drumsticks, steaks, bottles of red and white wine, litres of beer, a couple of bottles of Alto del Carmen pisco.

'The only thing you must do is go and get some ice-cream later on because Liliana has eaten it all again,' Amanda said.

'You think we'll manage ice-cream after all this lot?'

Fresia showed them the photographs which she had taken in the south.

'Who's this?' Magdalena picked up a photograph of an old man staring out to sea.

'Oh,' Fresia said, 'he was an old blind man that I met there.'

There were more photos of Chiloé – a boat full of pink life-jacketed tourists watching penguins gathered on a rock, a chunky man laughing and toasting the photographer with a bottle of beer, a small dark-skinned kid dancing for the camera and swinging a blurry object which Fresia informed them was a dead rat, a couple of shots of some islands taken from high on a cliff somewhere, a dusty path winding back down to the beach. Everybody laughed when a photo of Joe suddenly appeared, sitting on Guillermo's roof terrace with a beer. It was the day he had called on Guillermo and found Fresia sitting up there with her sprained ankle, drinking beer and eating crisps.

The telephone rang and Señora Amanda answered it. Her normally cheerful face immediately went pale, with a mixture of anger and fear. Magdalena walked over, took the receiver out of her hand and replaced it.

'I've told you not to listen,' she said.

'What's going on?' Joe asked.

Magdalena shook her head slightly at him as if to say, 'Later.'

'How can people talk like that?' Magdalena's mother was still distressed.

'Because they're fascists,' Magdalena said calmly as she put a chorizo into a roll and handed it to Joe.

Liliana appeared with her boyfriend Iván. They were discussing the forthcoming battle with the police at the demonstration against Globalisation and Impunity, for which they had already been practising outside their college in the Avenida Grecia by hurling stones and Molotovs at the police.

'You shouldn't throw things at the police,' Amanda said. 'That's not right. They're human beings just like you and me.'

She was growing anxious and tetchy with her daughters.

'No they're not,' Iván said. 'If you don't hate the police and want to throw things at them then you're not a normal human being.'

Joe thought that this was one of Iván's saner pronouncements but it cut no ice with Amanda.

'You're a long way from being normal, young man,' she said tartly. 'And I hope you'll wash your hands before you touch the food. And how many times do I have to ask you, Magda, go and get some ice-cream.'

'We don't need ice-cream.'

'Yes we do and we need some more lemons.'

'I'll come with you,' Joe said. 'I need some cigarettes.'

'Buy some Coca-Cola.'

'Pass me my bag, Liliana.'

'Get it yourself.'

They walked down the quiet suburban street towards the small corner shop where they bought ice-cream, lemons, cigarettes, Coca-Cola. Some kids were out skate-boarding, dogs prowled their patios. They walked back towards the house down the middle of the quiet road and when Joe heard a car behind them, he moved over to let it pass but it stayed crawling behind them.

'Go on then, what's the matter with you?'

Magdalena grabbed his hand and guided him on to the pavement.

'What . . .'

'Quickly.'

They turned around and stared at the car, which had stopped about thirty yards behind them. Joe could not see the occupants because he was facing into the sun.

The car remained just behind them as if it was playing a game of Grandmother's Footsteps. A woman with a hose watering her front lawn noticed it and shaded her eyes with her hand until it suddenly did a three-point turn and screeched away, disappearing around a corner.

'What was that all about?' Joe asked.

'Just some idiots trying to frighten us. Don't mention it to my mum.'

'But . . .'

'Please, Joe. Don't say anything to her. It's bad enough with the phone calls.'

'Was that linked to the phone calls?'

'Oh I don't know. Maybe it was just some local morons. Come on, we're here now, don't say anything about it.'

Amanda was cheerful and slightly tipsy when they returned so, rather than what had just happened with the car, Joe told her the joke about Pinochet and the monkey and Amanda went red in the face with laughter even though Magdalena told him, when he was leaving, that she had heard the joke several times before.

Joe and Fresia got off the bus from La Florida in the Plaza Italia and Fresia said that she wanted to go for a walk as she was still feeling so swollen from the quantity of food they had eaten. So they wandered through the Forestal Park beside the Mapocho river, chatting about the two signatures of Guido Fawkes and the superiority of parks in London. Then they crossed over the river and walked back towards Bellavista, passing the closed restaurant where they had first gone together with Roberto Walker – pink-lipped razor clams, an earth tremor, a fork falling to the ground. They reached the small road where they had seen the mugger being beaten by the police, headed back over the river and walked quietly under the San Cristóbal hill with its white statue holding its arms out to the city. They paused again at Fresia's turning.

She put her hands on his shoulders and kissed him lightly on the cheek.

'Don't do any more work tonight,' she said and he watched her make her way through the gate, towards the entrance to her flat and the little room by the roof terrace that she would soon be leaving.

When Joe got home, he made himself a drink and stared from the window. He remembered how he had stood here with a drink one night soon after his arrival. That was before he had called Guillermo Castillo to ask for help and the man had generously invited him to a party, before he turned round in the shop where he was trying to buy cigarettes and saw the girl whose hand he had held on the plane. It should have been set up for them from there, such a coincidence should have led to things happening. He tried to think of how it might all have been different but couldn't; it had all come to nothing. It was a common syndrome really, otherwise there would not be so many songs and poems about it, so many people trembling and nauseous with the pain of it, so many laments at ungrateful, unresponsive and treacherous hearts. And now things were coming to an end; now he was leaving and he might not even see her again.

. . . Blue violets for my sorrow, red carnations for my passion . . .

That night, Joe dreamed that he was a child again and that his mother was taking him to see the deer in the park, that his hands were burned and that he was holding them out for the deer to touch with soft tongues.

Spurious Causes

'A professional,' Señora Cruz glowed when Fresia went for an informal interview about a flat. Señora Cruz lived in a gigantic mock-Georgian house in Vitacura and had the high-pitched singsong voice that certain Chilean women adopt as a badge of respectability and femininity.

'And, of course, you were brought up in Europe. We used to travel to Britain every year. Until all that nonsense with the arrest.' She shook her head sorrowfully. 'London, Bath, Edinburgh, Stonehenge,' she listed. 'Did your father go over there to work?'

'Yes,' Fresia said. 'He was a professor. At the University of Oxford.'

Señora Cruz almost squealed with joy at this information. She called in the maid.

'We'll have some tea now, Rosita . . . I don't know what I would do without Rosita. People say the Peruvians are untrustworthy but Rosita is an absolute treasure . . . now where were we? Ah yes, your father. So when did he leave Chile?'

'In the early nineteen-seventies,' Fresia said.

Her host nodded understandingly. 'It was a very . . . complicated period then. The food shortages, the land occupations . . .' She shook her head. 'My sister Marilú wanted us to leave like your father but my husband said we had to stay and fight the Communists. He was confident that we would be able to sort things out and *gracias a dios* we did and everything went back to normal. I suppose by then your family had settled down in Europe?'

Fresia smiled vaguely.

'Well, what are we doing sitting talking about politics?' Señora Cruz said. 'Tell me about your *novio*. A lovely girl like like you must have a boyfriend or fiancé? Don't worry,' she winked conspiratorially, 'I'm not conservative about these things like some Chileans. I'm very *European* in my outlook if you're worried about your boyfriend staying with you.'

'Edward is with the Foreign Office,' Fresia said. 'At the moment he's on a posting in Washington DC. I miss him terribly.'

Señora Cruz took the keys, pressed them firmly into Fresia's hand and told her not to worry about the deposit.

'There's just one thing that concerns me,' she said. 'You be careful down there in the centre. Marilú was telling me that she saw a *delincuente* just rip a woman's necklace off on the bus. And that was in Providencia!' Her smile vanished and she almost snarled, 'They are losing all respect for us again! *Mano dura, por favor, Señor Presidente!*' Then her face rearranged itself once more. 'Will Edward be coming out here to join you?'

'Probably,' Fresia said.

'*Regio.* Well, when he does I'm sure you'll move to a more . . . suitable area. Just make sure you give me a month's notice.'

The flat was in a quiet little cul-de-sac just off the Avenida Vicuña Mackenna next to a Chinese restaurant, a couple of blocks down from the Baquedano metro station. It was easy for Fresia to take the Line 5 Metro down to La Florida where she could pick up the *collectivo* to Puente Alto and then out to the Cajon del Maípo. It was also convenient for Magdalena to drop by on her way home. Fresia knew that she would see no more of Señora Cruz as her landlady was more likely to leap into a river full of crocodiles than set foot over the boundary of the Plaza Italia.

Although Fresia did not have many possessions, Guillermo gave her some kitchen stuff and a paraffin heater for the coming winter. Magdalena promised her some sheets from her mum and Joe brought round a large wooden salad bowl as a housewarming gift. She went shopping in town with Roberto and he got her a little TV set. With some of the money she had left from her father's will, she also purchased a laptop computer and Vasily sorted her out an Internet connection so that she could communicate with her mother. She framed some of the photographs she had taken in the south and put up the watermelon poster from Isla Negra. Then she held a small house-warming party where everybody danced in the living room.

One Saturday, Fresia was having breakfast on the veranda of Roberto's house before returning to Santiago to meet up with Joe and Magdalena for the march against Globalisation, Poverty and Impunity.

'Sure you don't want to come?' Fresia asked Roberto mischievously, who laughed and put his hands in front of him in mock supplication.

The night before, he had been anxious about telling her that he didn't want to go on the march but had said he would do so if she really wanted it.

'It's not that I don't support the cause or anything . . .' he had said carefully. 'And I'm not going to make any excuses either. I just don't want to go, and my belief in the cause is not enough to outweigh that. I hate crowds and I'm frightened of the police and I want to do some writing.'

'It's OK,' Fresia had said. 'You can accompany me to catch the *collectivo* though.'

They walked together across the bridge and up the road to the corner where the *collectivo*s stopped.

'By the way,' Roberto said as they waited in the sun by the roadside, 'it might sound strange, but have you ever heard me say that *Love in the Time of Cholera* is the best novel ever written?'

'No,' Fresia was puzzled. 'You don't think that, do you?'

'No, of course not.'

'Why do you ask then?'

'Oh, it was just something somebody said to me the other day.' He laughed and shook his head. 'Don't worry about it. I think that might be your taxi coming.'

He kissed her goodbye and held on to her hand.

'Be careful with the *pacos*,' he said. 'They can behave like real thugs on these marches.'

'I'd be more worried about this driver,' Fresia said as her taxi came racing towards them at breakneck speed.

The banners of different groups fluttered in the autumn breeze – members of various political parties, indigenous organisations, relatives of the disappeared and executed, the Funa commission for outing torturers, the movement for the recognition of sexual diversity, different environmental groups. Old people carried photographs of their missing children, kids rode on their parents' shoulders and waved little Chilean flags.

The march turned into Morandé Street alongside La Moneda and paused for a moment as somebody laid flowers at the spot where there had once been a door to the palace, the point from which the body of a dead president had been removed wrapped in a blanket and men in suits had been dragged out and forced to lie in the gutter beneath a tank.

'Take a photo,' Magdalena ordered.

Fresia was growing slightly irritated with the way that Magdalena had appointed herself director of photography but bit back her retort as Vasily grinned and raised his eyebrows at her behind Magdalena's back. Fresia moved past a couple of people so that she could get a decent shot and was about to take the photograph when she heard a cry and saw the person with the flowers turn to look back down the march. Then all she could feel was people pushing at her, scrabbling, trying to get past. She nearly fell under the pressure of bodies, not understanding what was happening until suddenly she began to choke, her throat swelling, her head pounding, unable to breathe. 'Please!' she screamed uselessly. 'Joe!' Somebody tore at the strap of her camera and it fell to the ground but she was not interested, she just had to get out of the narrow street. She stumbled and nearly fell, knew that if she did so she would be crushed, supported herself on the back of the person in front of her. Behind her, she could feel hands pushing and clawing desperately at her. She had to get away but the problem was that everybody had the same idea and although some people were screaming for calm, most were just caught up with the imperative of flight and the desperate need to escape from the effects of the tear gas. She herself was tearing and pushing at the people in front of her, saw a child topple from his father's shoulders, heard somebody screaming about being pregnant. She didn't care, all she cared about was survival.

Finally, Fresia was expelled from the street into the square behind the palace where she collapsed to the ground and vomited. She was weeping with fear and anger and the effects of the choking, stinging, unbearable gas. Other people were shouting for their friends and relatives, some were cursing the criminal stupidity of the police at releasing so much gas into a crowded street of entirely peaceful protesters. One girl was so enraged that she was trying to pull up one of the benches to hurl at the police, who began to move among the distressed crowd picking people out to arrest or beat.

'You fucking fascists!' Fresia stood up and screamed furiously in English through a mouthful of hair. 'You haven't changed at all, you bastards.'

'Fresia?' The apple-faced woman trying to uproot the bench had turned and was staring at her. For a moment, Fresia did not recognise her.

'Fresia, it's Fabiola.'

It was Fabiola Aguilera. She had been an exile in Sheffield and they had discovered that they shared a similar sense of humour at a conference of Chilean youth when they were about sixteen. Later, Fresia had gone to stay with Fabiola and her large, unruly family but they had lost contact when Fresia had moved to London and cut off most of her links with the Chilean community.

'Are you on your own?' Fabiola asked.

'I was with my friends. Joe, Vasily and Magdalena. I can't see them now.'

'Maybe we'll find them later. Here, take this tissue, your face is a mess.'

A group of demonstrators with masks over their faces suddenly appeared and began hurling stones at a police van parked on the corner of the street. Almost immediately, an ominous black-and-white vehicle with a turret and cannon already dripping water appeared around the corner. It was accompanied by a second, smaller vehicle which was emitting little puffs of gas. People ran back towards the Alameda where shopkeepers were beginning to pull down shutters and where a few of the waiters in a bar helped some people in and locked their doors.

'Come on!' Fabiola grabbed her. 'The Metro station!' They began to run back down the Alameda.

'Not that way!' somebody screamed. 'There's cops all over the place.'

They turned and ran in the other direction down the Alameda towards the Santa Lucía hill, pursued by a water cannon which turned and blasted any person out on the street, driving them into shop entrances where the special forces followed up swinging their batons into the groups trying to take shelter. A couple of kids threw some stones at the vehicle which bounced harmlessly off it. Fresia and Fabiola crouched with a small group behind the entrance to the Santa Lucía Metro station and the water cannon stopped. For about ten minutes, figures darted out as if taunting the vehicle, which would advance and then retreat again. Fresia could still smell the sickening, choking gas as suddenly a Molotov cocktail arced out of a sidestreet behind them and spattered its flame across the road in front of the water cannon. Then another one.

'Shit,' Fabiola said. 'We've got to get out of here. Come on.'

'Do you think Fresia and Vasily will turn up here?' Joe asked as he and Magdalena sat eating ice-creams and swinging their feet on an old family vault in the General Cemetery.

'Sure,' Magdalena said. 'They knew that's where we were heading. Look, people are still making their way here. They'll get here somehow.'

'What if Fresia's not with Vasily?'

'She's not stupid. All she has to do is follow the crowd.'

Joe stood up on the vault and looked out over the crowd which was straggling into the cemetery. He couldn't see Fresia so he sat back down again.

'The kid we bought the ice-cream from said there was some fighting in the centre,' he said.

'Probably.' Magdalena cupped her hand under her rapidly melting ice-cream. 'People were pretty angry about them firing gas into the crowd like that. There was a helicopter overhead as well so they knew exactly what they were doing . . . Shit, I wanted *chirimoya* and he's given me pineapple.'

'We'll swap then.' Joe handed her his ice-cream.

When the gas had hit the crowd, Magdalena had grabbed Joe's hand fiercely and ducked down, weaving fairly quickly out of the street and into the square. They had headed northwards away from the palace, just making it across a line of police which had split the march into two halves. But Fresia had moved away from them to take a photograph and they had lost her. Joe was not sure if she would have been able to make it across the square before the police sealed it off.

'What if Fresia's caught up in it?'

'I doubt it,' Magdalena said. 'I think the best thing we can do is just wait for her here for a bit.'

'What will we do if she doesn't turn up here?'

'We'll go back to my house and wait for her there. She was supposed to be coming round tonight to pick up the sheets from my mum, remember? My mum's got her some other stuff as well, you know how she fusses. She's even got her a hot-water bottle and a frying pan.'

They sat for a bit longer inspecting the names on the gigantic mausoleum – different generations of the Pinto family buried beneath them.

'The whole of Chile's segregation is reflected in this cemetery,' Magdalena said. 'This is the *barrio alto*, the high-class area, then further over there . . .' she pointed with her ice-cream stick '. . . are the middle-classes and then the poor and then the people with no names.'

The speeches were beginning at the monument to the disappeared and Magdalena hopped down from the vault.

'Do you want to go and listen?' she asked Joe and he shook his head.

'Come on then, let's go,' she said. 'If they are still fighting in town, then we might just catch the last of it.'

By the time they arrived back in the centre of the city, however, there was only the lingering smell of tear gas, shops with broken windows and black patches on the street where petrol bombs had exploded.

'*Putas,*' Magdalena murmured. 'They really went to town here. I hope Fresia got some good photos of all of this.'

They walked towards the Plaza Italia to catch a bus, passing vanloads of waiting cops. When they reached the Plaza, they saw Iván, Liliana's boyfriend, who was sitting smoking with a couple of punks.

'We let off a smoke-bomb in McDonalds,' he told them proudly. 'But the cops went crazy and shot a girl outside the Santa Lucía Metro station. They say that she's dead.'

'It's true,' one of the punks said sadly. 'The *mina* got hit bang in the chest with a plastic bullet from point-blank range. She's more dead than Elvis, man.'

'Where's Liliana?' Magdalena asked Iván.

'Gone home. We had an argument. The cops went fucking crazy. There's lots of people hurt, arrested. I saw them get this guy and they had him down on the ground and they were beating him so bad I reckon he'll be lucky to be alive as well. What happened to you guys?'

'We went to the cemetery,' Magdalena said. 'Come on, Joe, we'll check to see if Fresia's back at her flat. If not, the best thing we can do is go home.'

Joe felt sick. He knew that it was unlikely to be Fresia who had been shot but he felt certain that something bad had happened to ·her.

They wandered down Vicuña Mackenna to Fresia's flat but there was nobody there so they took the bus to La Florida to wait for her call.

'She hasn't called,' Amanda said when they arrived at the house. 'There are three people dead, they say.'

'One of them was a girl?' Joe asked.

'Yes, apparently the crowd started attacking La Moneda. I hope you weren't involved in that, Magda.'

Magdalena snorted contemptuously and pulled out the white linen bread bag.

'Come on, Joe,' she said. 'Let's go and get some bread.'

They were walking down to the shop past some skateboarding kids when Magdalena froze.

'What's up?' Joe asked.

'I thought I saw that car again, the one that followed us before.'

Joe peered down the road but could see nothing. He shook his head and they went into the shop where Magdalena bought twelve fresh *maraqueta* rolls, some cheese and pâté.

'We'd better get some ice-cream as well,' Joe said. 'Or we'll just get sent back.'

'I lost my camera,' Fresia said sorrowfully as she sat with Fabiola in a small bar just off the Avenida Vicuña Mackenna. They had ordered *completo* hot dogs and were chatting happily about the people they had known among the exile community of their early teenage years, the *rotos* and *cahuineros* and *viejos verdes*; the arguments and splits and scandals; homages and anniversaries and conferences; singing 'La hierba de los caminos' on a minibus to London; fly-posting and marching and picketing the Embassy on the 11th of September. They became helpless with laughter as they remembered Antonio Vargas who had famously been demoted from his post as General Secretary of the exiled Communist Party for getting drunk on an outing to Hastings and showing his arse out of the back window of the bus.

'We were special,' Fabiola said. 'In spite of everything, there hasn't been anybody like us since. How's your brother by the way? He was so serious and clever but I really fancied him.'

And Fresia told her about Alex and mild-mannered Lucy and about how she had gone into photography and about deciding to come back to Chile and about meeting Joe on the plane and about Roberto and the trip to the south to look for his missing nephew. They exchanged addresses and promised to meet up again.

'You will call, won't you?' Fresia said.

'Of course. I need a friend like you . . . somebody who understands a little.'

Fresia was about to walk away when Fabiola suddenly took her hands.

'We were sorry to hear about your dad.'

'Even *your* dad?' Fresia asked because Fabiola's dad had always denounced Ricardo Castillo as a Trotskyist, an anarchist, the Trojan horse of imperialism, while her dad had teased Oscar Aguilera for being an unrepentant old Stalinist who put his umbrella up when it rained in Moscow.

'He cried,' Fabiola said simply.

The kids on the skateboards watch the couple walking down the street with their bread. They know her, she lives around here, she has a horrible sister and a nice mum who sometimes gives them sweets. The man is one of her friends, a foreigner, an Englishman. One of the kids, Juanito, says that it rains every day in England and that the English always drink tea at four o'clock. The others ask how he knows and he says his mum told him. The man and the woman are pretending to have an argument, she is swinging her bread bag at him. At the end of the road, there is a squeal of tyres as a car suddenly accelerates and the kids turn their heads. The couple walking down the road don't notice; the girl swings her bag again at the man, aims some mock slaps. They are concentrating on their play-fight so that by the time they notice and turn around, the car is nearly upon them. The girl screams and the man grabs her and throws her away from the car. She skids across the road with her bag as the man just manages to fling her out of the way. Things fall out of her bag, objects scattering everywhere. The man is left to face the oncoming car. He puts his hands out as if he might stop it like Superman. The car hits him, lifts him on to the bonnet and then drops him on to the street again. The car stops and a man gets out. He ignores the figure lying in the road and walks fast towards the girl who is cowering by a tree. She puts up her hands to protect herself. He brushes her arms aside, pulls her glasses off and drops them to the ground where he grinds them under his heel. Then he hits her in the face several times very hard. Blood pours from her nose, he is shouting as he hits her. He holds her up by the hair with one hand and punches down with the other. Again and again. Her hands are raised but they are useless to prevent the blows. The man hits her one last time and then he spits down at her and makes as if to walk away but suddenly spins in a kind of karate movement and kicks the girl in the head. It is almost as if he wanted to practise the move. He spits again on to the sidewalk, rubs his knuckles, and then he gets into the car, the door slams and they drive away.

231

One of the boys, with his mouth open, drops his skateboard. It clatters to the ground.

They run over to the girl. She is still, her face covered in blood, moaning very quietly. Her broken glasses are beside her, she is surrounded by *maraquetas* from her bread bag. They pick up the girl's handbag and some of the stuff that has spilled out of it: her purse, some keys, a book, cigarettes, a lighter in a leather holder with a little man climbing up it, and a funny metal thing with a handle. When one of them turns the handle, it plays a tune. They put all the stuff back into the bag. One of the boys skateboards frantically off to the girl's house. The others go to where the man is still lying in the road. He is not moving either. The man is English and might not understand them.

'*Caballero*?' they say, timidly. 'Hey, can you hear us?'

'He's dead.'

'Look at his leg!'

Part of the bone in the man's leg is sticking out through his skin. His face is turned to the road and he does not make a sound. The silence is broken suddenly by a scream, a gate slamming and a woman crying out her daughter's name as she runs down the street.

The Great Avenues

Hush now, don't be frightened and I'll tell you about a place that's so far away that it is right at the end of the world.

There are voices that are near and voices that are far away.

I take one step out of the darkness.

There are people all around me and the sun is warm. The air smells of cinnamon and butterflies flutter like scarlet confetti.

Sitting on a chair, Violeta Parra is playing the guitar and singing. Beside her chair is a revolver. She looks up at me and winks through her hair.

'Any requests?' she says. 'I don't do "Gracias a la vida" before you ask.'

'Could you sing "La Jardiniera", please.'

She nods. 'An excellent choice but I would have expected no less from you.'

I look at her to see if she is mocking me like somebody I know but cannot quite remember. Her hand strums downward on the guitar and she begins my favourite song about tending her garden to recover from her unrequited love – blue violets for sorrow, red carnations for passion, white camomile for uncertainty – all the colours of love, all the colours of the nation.

She loves me, she loves me not.

'Do you know where you are?'

A figure steps towards me.

I shake my head.

'You are at the point between dreaming and waking,' he says. He has coke-bottle glasses and terrible scars on his wrists and throat.

'I am looking for my grandfather,' I say.

'You won't find him here,' he smiles at me. 'This isn't the place for him.'

'Where shall I go?' I ask and he points towards an avenue lined with orange trees.

'Please tell my daughter that I love her very much.'

'I can't,' I say. 'We never talk about love.'

'Perhaps you will some day.'

Look, there is a tear on his cheek. Can you hear me? Can you hear me?

And then I see him. Not my grandfather, another man, the man from his stories, the man who brought me here. He is wearing a turtle-neck jumper as he walks towards me down the tree-lined avenue. He lifts a hand and waves just as I have seen him wave from so many photographs, in old black-and-white newsreels. My eyes fill with tears as he turns to me.

'Come back,' I call to him. 'Please come back.'

'Don't worry . . .' he calls to me. 'You will continue to hear me, I will always be beside you. Remember . . . the great avenues . . . the great avenues will open and free men will pass through them . . . remember . . .'

But out over the ocean the currents of air are beginning to swirl.

. . . I will always be beside you . . . or at least my memory . . .

The harsh wind gathers his words and scatters them like butterflies and I am not in the garden any longer, black crows wheel in an icy sky, and I am very frightened, things are getting bumpy now, the turbulence has returned and they all flash past me: Caupolicán writhing on the stake; Galvarino shaking bloody stumps at the sky; Manuel Rodríguez smiling on the way to Til-Til; Bernardo O'Higgins staggering about his ranch; Rosalía Maldonado cowering in Villa Grimaldi; Pablo Errazuriz dragged from the motel. There is a hole in Violeta Parra's head, there is a splattering of brains in the *salon* of the presidential palace, there is blood on the manuscript, the river is high.

. . . Close your eyes, sleep, dream a little.

A cool hand on my forehead, somebody is whispering to me, somebody is telling me not to be frightened, somebody is telling me stories again. It is not my grandfather's voice, it is another voice calling me back.

But the voice also fades and now I am falling, I am tumbling towards the ocean and I plunge in and drop like a stone scattering sea-horses and starfish, startling the narwhal. It is cold and dark at the bottom of the ocean, there are no sailors singing love-songs, just strange and grotesque creatures drifting detached from the light, staring through empty pitiless eyes, and I am fighting and kicking to return to the surface, to the humans in the warm sand, to the laughter and the voices.

Up, up, up through the deep salt waters, through black, navy and indigo, up towards the light, bursting like a cork on to the surface of the ocean. Fortunately there are no dark currents to drag me away and on the beach, sitting in the soft foam, a mermaid is combing her jet hair, singing softly to herself. She looks away from the shore, out to sea, out to the blue horizon where instead of crows there are flying-fish hurling themselves from the waves, sea-horses and star-fish, a narwhal's tusk in the foam. She does not see me but I am content just to sit and watch her. I will wait for a while to deliver the message with which I have been entrusted. And so I lie, once again safe upon the shore, blinking at the figure in the coral light as she stretches, yawns, gathers up her black hair and gazes out towards the plentitude, towards never-again.

Blue Violets

'And Caupolicán Juniors are doing really well in their league and we've retired your shirt in honour of you . . .'

Lalo turned and smiled at Fresia as she entered Joe's room. He got up and offered her his chair.

'I have to go now anyway.'

It was nearly two weeks since she had turned to see Joe's eyes open and the strange little movements that he was making with his arms as if he were trying to swim in his bed. They had really thought he might die, it had seemed as if he would never open his eyes again. She had sat by the bed talking to him, she had told him about her school in Oxford, about a day spent in London with her father, about meeting a girl called Fabiola on the day of the march that he could remember nothing about. His eyelids had occasionally fluttered but his eyes had not opened and she had laid her hand on his forehead and carried on telling him stories as there was nothing else to do. When she had turned her head from the window to see him blinking at her, he was muttering incoherently about the wind over the ocean. His memory was still patchy but he joked that this should qualify him for honorary Chilean citizenship.

Lalo held on to Joe's hand.

'Don't leave it for a long time before you come back. We've made you an honorary member of the club and we want to be able to bring your shirt out of retirement again.'

Joe nodded, glanced down at his leg in its cast.

Lalo squeezed his hand and departed. Fresia sat down in the chair which he had vacated.

'So,' she said.

'So,' Joe echoed.

Joe's departure for England would be taking place any day now. He was insured by his university and they would be flying him home.

'Ready?'

'As I'll ever be.'

'Did Guillermo talk to you?'

Guillermo had offered Joe a post at the research institute.

'Yes.'

'And?'

'I'll have to think about it in England.'

'Everyone would be very happy if you came back.'

'I want to finish the book first anyway.'

And Fresia suddenly remembered how they had met on the plane and the cocky, cheerful way in which he had announced that he was writing it. She remembered watching him as he gazed over the top of his laptop, she remembered ganging up on him with Magdalena, asking him questions about Chilean history which he would always start to answer before he realised they were teasing him. They would make deliberate mistakes about the dates of famous battles and then snigger together when he corrected them.

'Magdalena's going to try and come and see you today,' she said.

Magdalena had recovered more quickly than Joe, released from hospital after a week. After a few days at home with her mother, Fresia had suggested that she stay for a while in the Cajon del Maípo and, although Amanda was reluctant to lose sight of her daughter, she had agreed that it might be for the best. Magdalena sat in the garden writing new denunciations of Gonzalo Espinoza and his links with detectives in the south. Fresia found it interesting to watch Roberto and Magdalena together because, in spite of their many and obvious differences, they had a shared knowledge and language which still made her feel – not uncomfortably – like the outsider.

'How's Roberto?' Joe asked.

'He's fine.'

Joe nodded and then he turned to her.

'He's a good person.'

Before Fresia could answer, they saw Valentina's head pop round the door of the room. She was carrying a bag with some books and CDs for Joe. When she saw Fresia she said, 'I can come back later.'

'It's OK,' Fresia said.

'Are you going back to the Cajon del Maípo afterwards? I can give you a lift.'

'Sure,' Fresia smiled at her.

The two women sat on either side of the bed and from time to time Joe drifted in and out of sleep, murmuring as he did so. When the time came to leave, he was half asleep and Fresia got up and stroked his head and kissed him gently on the forehead. 'See you in London,' she whispered. Joe held on to her hand and mumbled something in his sleep about going home to tend his garden.

'What do you think he meant by that?' Fresia asked Valentina as they drove into the valley, every turn and landmark of which was now intensely familiar to her.

'I don't know,' Valentina said.

But Magdalena knew. Fresia told her about it later as they sat by the pool drinking a bottle of pisco and she laughed.

'It's his favourite song,' she said. '"La Jardiniera".' She glanced at Fresia over her wineglass and sang,

'To try and forget you, I will cultivate my garden . . .'

That's all I remember but Joe knows all the verses. You know what a show-off he is about these things.'

And Fresia stared at the empty branches of the cherry trees and realised that it would soon be too cold to sit out in the garden.

PART FOUR

Turbulence

Subject: Nuptial Bliss
To: FresTam@hotmail.com

Hello my favourite daughter,

As this is going to be more of a letter than an e-mail, I am typing it out and then pasting it on to the e-mail. I may also send it as an attachment. I may do that both in Word and in Rich Text Format to be sure you can open it. So don't mock me any more about my tech-nological prowess because I know about these things now.

I hope that the freezing winter you have complained so bitterly about is now at an end. It has been a rather typical British summer here, with lots of rainy days, a semi-permanent grey overhang and then the odd wonderful day when you think 'if only it could be like this always then this might be quite a civilised country'. Now we have clear, sunny autumn days mixed up with . . . grey overhang.

Proceedings for the wedding continue. I have to have occasional meetings with Lucy's parents who are very very very English. There was great excitement recently because her father managed to get on to one of those daytime quiz programmes. I can't remember whether it was '15 to 1' or 'Going for Gold' but anyway he did terribly, much to Lucy's shame, especially when by sheer coincidence they asked him which South American country had a capital called Santiago and he blurted out 'Honduras'. He is mortified by that now of course. The mother looks like a frightened rabbit (like Lucy in fact), laughs too loudly and says 'Indeed' nervously to everything I say. Anyway, they are very pleased that you have said that you will do the photographs.

Your friend Joe finally came to see me as he was in Oxford for some Latin American conference or other that Alex was also attending. They came back here for dinner and we had a really nice evening. He is quite recovered although he says that he won't be playing football for some time. He was very charming and funny although I felt obliged to tell him that chain-smoking is neither a) good for your health b) attractive or c) pleasant for non-smokers in the room and then he looked terribly sheepish and uncomfortable. He managed to combine being incredibly self-assured and confident with this odd nerviness. Anyway, his book sounds interesting and I lent him some old stuff of Ricardo's which he got very excited by.

And how is your love-life? Joe told me that Roberto thinks that 'Love in the Time of Cholera' is the best book ever written which I have to admit makes me question his judgement somewhat. I was sorry to hear, though, that they have given up looking for his nephew and closed the case. I cannot imagine anything worse for his mother, it is too unbearable to contemplate.

Anyway . . . I must stop now. But first, a lecture. Fresia Tamara Castillo Morganstein, you have been in Chile for over a year now and you still have not been to see your Aunt Sara. It would not hurt you to do this small thing for me, she knows you are there and it is very embarrassing for me that you refuse to visit her. What if she were to get so angry that she never speaks to me again?!?!

A thousand besos for you, mi querida hija. Please take care of yourself and bring yourself over to see me again. I am counting the hours until you arrive.

Fresia smiled as she imagined Joe smoking nervously with her mum and brother in their house in Oxford. It was five months now since he had left but he had e-mailed her a manuscript of his book which she had spent a frustrating afternoon of flashing lights and paper jams printing off at the research institute and was saving to read on the plane back to Britain. Joe had also written to Guillermo politely turning down his offer of a post at the institute.

Fresia wandered to the kitchen where she poured more red wine into the sauce she was making for some spaghetti. It was still a little chilly but nowhere near as bad as it had been during the winter, when she had sometimes wanted to weep because the flat was so cold. And the one thing that to her mind made Chile very definitely still part of the Third World was that there was no central heating so she had to wheel the heater from room to room. After taking a shower, she would run from the bathroom to her bed and dive under the covers.

She checked her watch and went to the window, looking out towards the road behind the flat, busy with people and buses, the neon dragon of the Chinese restaurant blowing flames through its nostrils. When she was little, Chile had been a faraway and mysterious country that people grieved and longed for, while Chileans themselves had been a special minority who served wine and *empanadas* in solidarity events organised together with well-meaning British people called Diana and Jeremy. Chileans might also arrive suddenly late at night, sitting up drinking with her parents and causing much resentment to her and Alex when they were unceremoniously kicked out of their bedrooms. But, as a child, Fresia principally understood the condition of being Chilean as somebody who did not live in Chile; it was as if it were their defining national characteristic. Now here she was staring out at a street where *everybody* was Chilean – the man in the newspaper kiosk, the old nosy woman from the flat downstairs who complained when she had people round late, the gaggle of schoolkids smoking and flirting on the corner.

And out of the crowd, walking slowly towards her, came another Chilean. Fresia waved at Magdalena who would be looking after the flat while she was away. She opened the window to drop the key to the downstairs door.

'You know that Joe has dedicated his book to you?' Fresia said to Magdalena after they had finished the spaghetti.

'Yes, but I won't be able to understand it.'

'Maybe when it's translated.'

Magdalena shrugged and stared out of the window.

'You'll be able to see him,' she said. 'When you're over there.'

'Yeah, I'm really looking forward to it. It will be strange though – seeing him in Britain.'

Magdalena nodded. 'It's easier for you two. You can decide when you see people. I only see Joe when he phones me and tells me that he is coming or even that he has arrived. I could never do that . . .'

'You could go to Britain though.'

'Once, maybe, if I saved for long enough. But it's not the same. I couldn't just do what you do, moving back and forth more or less when you want to.'

She looked even further out of the window as if straining to see somebody in the street below and Fresia suddenly realised that she was weeping silently.

'I'm sorry,' she said helplessly.

Magdalena sniffed and took her glasses off. She suddenly looked so delicate and bird-like that it was impossible to imagine that anybody was capable of such a vicious attack upon her.

The doorbell rang and Fresia went to the window. It was Fabiola. She made a drinking motion with her hand.

'Do you want to go for a drink?' Fresia asked Magdalena. 'Let's go to the Barrio Brazil.'

Magdalena laughed and wiped her eyes and nodded.

'You'll come back,' she said and it sounded more like a plea than a question.

Fresia looked out at the neon dragon, at Fabiola waiting for them in the street, at the early spring sun on the mountains. She thought back to a year ago when she had first arrived, sitting on Guillermo's roof terrace. Then she turned to Magdalena and smiled.

'Sure,' she said. 'I haven't put up with the winter to miss the return of the sun.'

Fresia's red rucksack sat in Roberto's living room. He had spent the day in Santiago at a writers' workshop and Fresia had prepared a meal for their last night before she went away. It was early evening and somewhere out in the valley she had heard, for the first time in months, the sound of a cello through an open window.

She checked her ticket and passport and then she poured herself a glass of wine and looked through Roberto's CDs until she found the one that she wanted. Violeta Parra had sung in the same city where Fresia would arrive in only thirty-six hours' time. The recording was made in EMI's London studios and Fresia smiled as she heard the clipped English accent of a technician announce, 'This is H' and then Violeta say, 'La Jardiniera'.

. . . To try and forget you, I will cultivate my garden . . .

All those years ago, those hands on the guitar when her father was still a young man before Fresia was even born. She imagined Violeta on a cold and wet day beside the Thames or visiting the British Museum, the woman who would later – in an empty tent – turn a revolver to her head.

Sing me an unforgettable song, wrote her brother after her death. *A song that never ends, just a song is all I ask . . .*

And Fresia sat listening to Violeta Parra sing about the flowers of solace and recovery, the healing flowers, while the smell of lemon verbena floated in on the spring breeze and the hollyhocks stuck

nosy heads through the window and Roberto came up the garden
path waving at her.

. . . In order to see you better I close my eyes . . .

The Air France jet paused for a second as it turned on to the runway
and Fresia gripped the sides of her aisle seat. She glanced up at the
overhead compartment in which she had the bag of presents –
bottles of pisco, fresh chilli sauce, some pottery from Pomaire, a
lapiz-lazuli bracelet as a wedding gift for Lucy. Sitting next to her
was a nun who – rather worryingly – was praying fervently. The
exhilarating, terrifying thrust of power began and the plane roared
down the runway, watched – she knew – from the safety of the
terminal by Roberto.

The plane soared into the bright spring air and, beneath her, the
jets on the tarmac grew smaller, the fields arranged themselves into
neat patterns. They banked and headed across the mountains which
hemmed in the strange, narrow strip of country, isolating it from the
rest of the world. She looked down as if she might see Roberto's
house, the pool around which she had sat so many times, the plastic
dolphin bobbing on the surface.

They stopped in Buenos Aires and Fresia remembered how terrible she had felt the last time she had been in this departure lounge
after sixteen hours of travel. She remembered Joe sitting smoking
and looking at his feet and how she had deliberately avoided him,
the sheer coincidence of meeting him again. Then they were called to
re-board the plane and Fresia listened to music and watched the
little red jet on the video monitor as they crossed southern Brazil and
headed out over the Atlantic Ocean.

*Was it the sound a bird made (Chi-le, Chi-le) or the name of a legendary
gold-abundant valley, a name which the Spanish extended to the entire
province, from the desert to the glaciers?*

*An archipelago of tribes lived in the thin strip of land between the
mountains and the sea, long before the Niña, the Pinta and the Santa
María set sail from Andalusia.*

Fresia smiled as she placed her fingers on the clean white manuscript of Joe's book and read the first page. Then she stared out of the
window into the blackness. Down below, she thought she could see
a bright glow as if from the lighthouse of a tiny island right out in
the middle of the ocean. She closed her eyes and drifted into the

fragmented sleep and jumbled dreams of plane travel, her hand resting on Joe's book. In one dream her father appeared before her carrying his own bloodstained manuscript; in another, she was on a train to Lucy and Alex's wedding but had left her bag behind and had to go back and get it. She dreamed that she was up in the mountains with Roberto, that his nephew Pablo Errazuriz had been found, that they were all sitting together with cold drinks around the pool and that his mother Gilda was painting a picture of them.

She was woken from this dream by a violent shuddering and the *Fasten-your-seatbelt* sign flicking on overhead. They were right out in the middle of nowhere, beneath them the vast, deep ocean, not even the lights of an island in sight. Fresia felt panic rising. Next to her was the nun whose hand she could never hold.

The last page from the manuscript fell to the floor and Fresia picked it up.

The case of Pablo Errazuriz will never be resolved, the body never found, the guilty never punished. It is a lesson in the far-reaching consequences of impunity, a sign of the insecurity and fear that lie not far beneath the apparently calm surface of economic progress and institutional stability. In this sense of course, and in spite of the obvious notoriety of the Pinochet years, Chile is not exceptional. And yet, just as there are torturers so there are those who throw flowers on to the sea in memory of their victims. Just as people disappear, so people search for them . . .

The plane jolted violently again. 'I hope Juanito's pisco will be OK,' she heard somebody whisper anxiously behind her. 'I'm sure I can smell it.'

It was true. The fragrant smell of pisco, with all its rich nostalgia of drunken nights, was filling the cabin.

'*Pucha*, Manuel, can't you check it's OK?' the woman hissed at her husband. Fresia put her hand over her mouth and tried not to giggle. All around her, people were beginning to grin and sniff the air ostentatiously. Then they smiled at their neighbours and began to laugh, crack jokes and pretend to be drunk on the fumes. The woman who had bought the bottle for Juanito put her hands to her face and pretended to be embarrassed but soon she was laughing too. An air hostess wagged her finger in mock admonishment and laughed. Even the nun stopped her speed-praying and turned around and smiled. Soon it seemed as if the whole plane was joined in laughter by this rather trivial occurrence of a leaking bottle and had forgotten the jolting and buffeting of their fragile craft.

Fresia hugged herself and stared ahead of her at the little red jet on the monitor which showed them where they were – almost exactly halfway on the journey from Chile to Britain, out over the dark freezing ocean. She thought about how her mother would wait for her at Oxford station and meet her from the train, she thought of going to the pub in London with Joe. The jolting of the plane became less violent, the laughter subsided, things became calm again and the *Fasten-your-seatbelt* sign went off. And Fresia sat with one hand on Joe's manuscript, the smell of pisco still sneaking like a mischievous spirit around the cabin, tickling the nostrils of the passengers and making them smile and mumble with recognition as they drifted into sleep.

Everything became very quiet and still as Fresia looked around the crowded plane; you could barely even hear the plane engines or sense any movement. Even the air hostesses' heads were drooping, the children resting in the protection of their parents' arms, couples clinging to each other in this astonishing moment of silence and stasis. Only Fresia was awake now; she imagined that even the pilots were snoring gently at their controls. And as she looked around her at all the slumbering passengers she knew that she was safe and so she too put her head back, drifted into sleep and began to dream a little again. And the plane lay hanging still and silent in the empty black space while, far away, the coral light flew over the horizon and rushed through the darkness towards them.